The

Sorrows

by
M. Earl Smith

AMink PUBLISHING

To Nisa:

I'm sorry that we failed. I know that we tried.

CHAPTER 1

In the best of conditions, the primitive rural road that Travis traveled was a hazard to man and beast alike. In the wintry conditions of the Himalaya Mountains, it was deadly. The road was a slow, yawning, curve-filled hazard, yet this was the norm in Bhutan, a country that barely registered a blip on the radar of Western tourists. Despite being named the Happiest Nation on Earth by several self-important publications, strict visa laws and the requirement of a return ticket to one's country of origin kept even the most dashing of globetrotters from making the trip.

Esther, Travis's estranged fiancée, had spent six months in Bhutan prior, using the country as a case study for her dissertation while she worked on her Doctorate in Humanities from San Francisco State. It was no small irony, at least in Travis's mind, why she had come to Bhutan. For someone that spent as much time studying happiness in the world, the thought that she would come to The Sorrows, Bhutan's solemn national forest, to end her life was humorous, in its own twisted way.

Silence enveloped Travis, save the occasional whine of the clutch of the old Jeep he had rented in Thimphu, the sprawling capital of Bhutan. The vehicle was a late 70's model, dirty, and rusted through in half a dozen places. If not for the mud and snow that caked the outside of the ancient vehicle, one would see that it had been green in its heyday. It was not the appearance that Travis considered when renting this sad little wagon; he had given far more consideration to the four-wheel drive and the undeniable power of the ancient inline six-cylinder motor. The odometer registered close to three hundred thousand miles (as opposed to the standard

1

kilometers for the region; apparently someone had imported the vehicle many years ago), but seeing as it rarely budged, Travis could only assume the mileage was twice that.

The serpentine road stretched out before him, the s-curves laid out like an omen of hopelessness. It was a pity, given how the danger detracted from the beautiful, white, crystalline beauty provided courtesy of the harsh winter snows of the tiny landlocked nation and the highest mountains in the world. It was depressing, really, given the reason for the trip, that Travis could not enjoy the natural beauty that enveloped his world. Of course, then again, not many trips were made that would result, at best, in finding someone, only to have them committed, and at worst, in recovering the body of the one person you loved.

Travis and Esther met in 2004, while he was a junior and she a freshman at San Francisco State. There was nothing remarkable about Travis. In fact, if he was notable for anything, it was how average he was. Sandy blond hair, worn in whatever fashion one of the nameless chain barbers felt was in style. Warm brown eyes, that gave little away, and at the same time conveying that he had few secrets. Travis was of average height, weight, and physique. He was an average student, majoring in English, although he had no aspirations of teaching. It seemed like a good idea at the time, although there were vague notions of being published somewhere down the line. Anglo-Saxon heritage, normal brow, jaw line—one of the many nameless faces in a crowd, for all intents and purposes. The fact that he had paired with Esther was, in itself, all the more astonishing.

The clutch whined, and Travis slowly downshifted, compensating for the lack of grip with a lower gear as he neared the end of the trail. The memory of the day he had gained the gumption to ask Esther for a date was fresh in his mind, and he could not help a chuckle as he let his thoughts drift back. Given his mission, he was prone to allow himself one last good memory...

"You've walked past her half a dozen times, you fool," Travis muttered to himself, ignoring the odd glances as he paced slowly towards the common area, staring at his feet. Not a leader by any means, it was still odd for him to be as shy as he was. However, when it came to Esther, as he had learned her name was, there was no rationale behind his actions. Being as pragmatic as he was, thoughts of romantic love and such were not ones that crossed his mind. Sure, he had his fair share of dates, and given that he had called California, and the liberal Bay Area, his home his entire life, he was by no means inexperienced as it came to the fairer sex. However, Esther stirred a depth of feeling within him that he was quite uncomfortable with, yet smitten with, all at the same time.

How could he not be? Esther was striking. She stood close to six feet tall, with a thinness that had started whispers of anorexia among the jealous types on campus. Paying witness to her boundless energy, however, had quickly quelled such talk, and had left the nastier of the campus tarts to stew in anger and envy. Her hair was fair enough to appear white, a pale waterfall that cascaded down past her shoulders, almost to the small of her back. Her eyes were ice blue, depths that Travis had caught himself daydreaming of losing himself in for hours. She sported high cheekbones—a gift, along with the other Nordic features, that her father had bestowed upon her before he was deported back to Norway. Her father's heritage would have bled through perfectly if not for the undeniable mocha of her skin, the slight upwards curve of her eyes, and the small, pouty lips, all blending in perfectly with the petite, rounded nose. These were gifts from her mother, the Thai heritage bleeding through proudly, finding a way to harmonize, as opposed to quarrel, with what her father had bestowed upon her.

Travis was convinced he had no chance with Esther.

It would not be the last time that Esther proved him wrong.

"Hi, Esther," Travis muttered as he walked past. He'd greeted her before, yet until this moment, she'd never bothered to respond. Travis was convinced it was because she was ignoring him. Truth of the matter was, the words were uttered at such an inaudible level that Esther had never heard them, until now. Be it fate, destiny, or simply a shift of the breezes off the Bay that carried his words to her ears, she heard him.

A small smile formed at the corners of her lips. Pink lipstick, Travis had noted. Never red, as Esther's mother had told her that only whores wore red lipstick. It was one of the kindest things her mother said to her over the course of her then 19 years. "Good day," Esther said softly. Not "hello" or "hi." Always prim and proper, a trait Esther had instilled in herself. "Have we met before?"

Travis's eyes shot up from a point on the ground, somewhere above his worn tennis shoes, and straight to her. His initial thought was that she was addressing someone else, perhaps a more handsome fellow from the male crowd at San Francisco State, of which there were plenty. Perhaps it was a female friend or professor that was enjoying the beauty of the mild, breezy Bay day. But then again, why would she ask someone she knew if they had met before? Travis stared at her, eyes meeting hers for what would be the first of many times. Esther looked away, shyly, and laughed.

"Given that you're an English major, I assumed you would be better with words than this, Travis," Esther said lightly, teasing him.

Travis was shocked. "How did you know I was majoring in English?" he stammered, muddling his way through words that failed to mask his astonishment. In his

4

confusion, Travis had missed the more obvious question, that being how she knew who he was.

"Most English majors take Literature 101, although why you're just now taking it as a junior is beyond me." The look of befuddlement on his face must have grown, and Esther laughed lightly. "I have it on the same date and time. We're classmates. Although, seeing how Lit is one of the larger classes here, I'm not surprised you missed me." Another shy smile was offered. "To be frank, I'd be lying if I said I hadn't stolen a glance, on occasion."

Today was a day destined to leave Travis befuddled. He'd barely bothered to dream, once he gained the courage to approach her, that she would actually have found him attractive. After all, he was so...average! "Hah! Now I know you're just being kind. What reason would you have to steal a glance at me?"

Esther smiled. "Well, why not? It seems everyone here is still clinging to their high school days, grasping at a clique or a cliché that would not even begin to suit them in the real world. Trust me, I've seen every stereotype played out in every sordid way you can imagine. But from what I see, that just does not apply to you, does it?" Esther offered a wry, knowing smile. "Besides, college guys are so...forward. What happened to asking a girl out, taking her to the movies or to dinner, as opposed to walking straight up to a perfect stranger and suggesting fornication in some of the more perverse ways known to humanity? At least you had the decency to say hi. Although if your next words are something akin to what you plan to do to me in front of some fraternity..." Esther giggled, and Travis would remember how the sound was akin to the sounding of bells, forever etched in his memory...

Bells. Instruments that were very simple in their setup, yet extremely difficult to master. Travis let the sound of her laughter echo in his memory for a few more breaths, allowing a memory that was so close to his heart warm him, almost taking the edge from the cold Bhutanese winter. The song on his MP3 player changed, and Travis was jolted back to the here and now. As the power chords and angry vocals of some self-righteous heavy metal act strained through his earbuds, Travis couldn't help but to allow a little anger to rise in his chest. After all, if she had only sought help when she needed it...

In Travis's view, what Esther had done was incredibly selfish. He had decided, long ago, that the depression and paralyzing mood swings that seized Esther were an illness, a disease that, if properly treated, could be regulated and even cured, in a sense. Perhaps he was too pragmatic, too analytical, in his thinking. He couldn't come to terms with what there was no rationale for. Moreover, that was what frustrated him beyond end. It's not that he didn't care! Travis loved Esther on a level deeper than anyone could ascertain. He had stood by her through the tumultuous years of their college experience, which seemed to be a huge growing pain for her. Nuances, human nature, and the filtering of social cues had been lost on her. For someone as breathtakingly beautiful as she, social interaction was awkward, and at times, almost forced. It had taken Travis almost all of the first year of his courtship to fully drag her out of the protective shell she had forged—one woven of circumstance, fear, and apprehension.

While he had tried, showing patience with someone who had little experience with this type of interaction slowly eroded his patience. A sigh escaped his lips as he drove. He was still upset with himself for getting short with her. How does one make rationale of a disease, a sickness that has no rationale? Esther could no more control what she was going to do than she could control the air she breathed. It didn't make Travis's life any easier that his harsh words and personal confusion had been what had led them both to Bhutan.

It was one of the few times that her needs and whims had frustrated him to the point of wanting to end it. Travis had refused to let what bothered him weaken him, at least in her eyes. He had internalized and dealt with his sorrow, his rage, and the simple hopelessness that he could not make the one he loved better. When it had gone too far, he snapped, changing himself, gradually, as a sand wall erodes at high tide.

He was short, conflicting with her, even as he knew inside that she was simply reaching to him for help in the only way she knew how. He stopped seeing her as much, stopped spending hours with her as he had before. Any lie, any excuse gave him the rationale to stay away from the apartment they cohabited. When that didn't break the bond, he went into a form of arrogance, becoming very un-Travis like, hyping up his own greatness in his own field as it pertained to his contributions to their relationship. Despite how she loathed such arrogance, she stuck with him.

When that didn't work, Travis became cruel. He hurled countless insults at her, often in the heat of the moment with no regard for what damage they would cause. When insults didn't work, Travis went further, trying to kill the relationship because he simply did not feel he could hold the responsibility of the relationship by himself. There were moments of reprieve, such as a trip to the Cascades, a small cottage, and three days of soul bearing and lovemaking that seemed to put things back on track. Once they returned home, the arrogance came back and Travis set plans into place. He announced to her that he no longer wished to be together, and asked her how soon she could leave. He tossed her out, like the broken, confused lesser form of filth he saw her as. He started dating another woman, but after a few short weeks, his resolve wore away, and Travis knew how wrong he had been.

He had climbed behind the wheel of his broken down Hyundai (a college car that, despite his comfortable and consistent salary as a teacher, he could not bring himself to part with), disgusted with himself. "What have I done?" he moaned over and over again, as he flew across the Bay Bridge, the popular spot for suicide jumpers, an ominous sign of what was to come.

It was a miracle that he managed to avoid a ticket, or worse still, wasn't hauled into jail for the reckless manner in which he wove through the San Francisco streets to get to the small apartment she had taken up in since he had unceremoniously ejected her less than six weeks before. He knocked on her door once, twice, a hundred times. No response. He tried to ring her cell phone, and on the third try, he finally heard the faint ringing, coming from somewhere within the apartment.

He was suddenly filled with dread. Esther was religious about carrying her phone, and about answering it; she took great pride in being ready for any situation, emergency or not, with a plan, a backup plan, and a backup to the backup plan. For her to not answer her phone meant she was physically unable to, or that she did not have it. Travis began to panic as it rang away, the solemn ringtone set to the strains of one of the numerous instrumental rock acts that had become vogue. The song gave the macabre scene its own sense of morbid foreboding. It was more than Travis could stand.

He rammed his shoulder into the heavy oaken door. It did not budge. Again, and again, Travis tried, but the door held true, and Travis cursed his own average build and his lack of physical training. A funny story came to his mind--about how Jack Nicholson had been so powerful that during the filming of *The Shining*, the infamous "Here's Johnny" scene had to be reshot with an actual door because the stunt door that was in place fell with a single blow. Come to find out, Nicholson had worked as a volunteer firefighter, and slicing through a stunt door was an easy task for him. Travis shook his head and tried to return to rational thought, the same thing he had accused her of being unable to do, accusations filled with vile invective that would make the most sanctified of people question if they were able to forgive.

Pragmatism returned, and Travis, panting heavily, used his head and quietly lifted the mat in front of the door. Esther was prepared, as she always was. There was a key, allowing him access to her apartment. Shaking hands twisted the key in the lock, the tumblers falling and clicking into place with a finality that slammed home into Travis's very being. He gently pushed the door open, dreading what he might find within.

The door offered little resistance, and beyond it lay an almost-barren room. Boxes containing all of Esther's possessions lined the walls on either side; a single chair, along with a note, Travis's passport, his visa to Bhutan, her cell phone, and a small photo of Esther lay on the coffee table. Travis was aghast at the cleanliness, the sanitary state of the room. It had the air of an abandoned museum, and the very appearance of the room made him uneasy. The note was sealed in a white standard print envelope, and Travis set it aside, terrified of what it held. He looked at his plane tickets, passport, and visa with both nervousness and wonderment. They were round trip tickets, as was required by Bhutanese law. First class, and that little perk surprised him. In the loathing he knew she must feel for him, she had cared enough, and had become so used to seeing to his every need, that she knew, on instinct, to provide only the best for him. A sense of guilt swelled in his chest, and he again cursed his own stupidity. What followed was a sense of endearment, pride, and love. Travis knew that, despite her claims that their love had been killed off by his foolishness, she was still very much in love with him despite all the hurt, anger, and rejection of being carelessly discarded like a child's plaything that he had left behind.

Travis picked up her cell phone and scrolled through the missed calls. Most were from him, starting four days ago, and he kicked himself for not knowing then that something was amiss. "Hindsight is ever perfect," he muttered to himself, reciting what had been one of her favorite sayings. His attention and eyes finally returned to the letter, a ticking time bomb, and, as he would soon find out, a letter hurtling him down a road in the dark, with no end in sight. He pressed it to his lips, the hope within that some essence of her would still attach itself to him. He slowly opened the letter, careful to preserve the seal, wishing to keep it as intact as possible. His hands shaking, Travis began to read the handwritten letter.

CHAPTER 2

Travis,

I always knew, within my heart of hearts, that it would be you that came across this letter. After all, as cruel, mean, and unforgivable as your words were, I was loath to think that you had stopped loving me.

Sure, you crushed how I felt for you, destroyed it, pushed it away, and I can only assume because you no longer love me. I mean, how does one that professes to be a man allow himself to
take the foundation of what we've built together over seven years and rip it asunder as you have our relationship?

I gave you my heart, my soul, my body, and my being, Travis, and you tore it all apart for a few cheap thrills and a desire to chase a greatness that was simply not there. You're an English teacher, Travis, not Muhammad Ali, and the sad part is, all I needed was an English teacher. I didn't need all the self-righteous proclamations of greatness, promises, and threats of what you were going to do, what you could do, and who you would be.

All I needed was Travis, my lover and partner. Travis, who always had me arrange time for us together when I knew our schedules would not conflict. Travis, who brought me flowers for no reason other than it made me smile, if only for a brief instant. Travis, who worked hard in his line of work and did what was expected of him and then some, but never let what was going on at his job get in the way of the life we were building together. Travis, who told silly jokes and came up with silly gimmicks to make me laugh, but never took any of his nonsense seriously, until there at the end. Travis, the man who I thought would be my first, last, and only true love.

I know that, at times, I was a difficult person to live with. There were times I was downright anal-retentive! I know my sickness was not something that was easy to bear, and at times, the quiet determination and

11

courage you showed when dealing with my oddities and frustrating obsessive-compulsive behavior, my mood swings, and the like was something I always found so endearing about what you did. I felt, for the only time in my life, that I had someone to fight with me for what I was instead of destroying me for who I am.

Just like everyone else in my life, you changed. You gave up. Once times got rough and the ocean was too dark to sail, you started looking for a way out, and I knew, as I always did. It hurt so, knowing it was you that would be the next one to hurt me, but as I always do, I prepared. I got myself ready for making it on my own, for life after Travis, for striking out and showing the world that, once again, Esther Sansui would be able to adapt and overcome, and against all odds, survive and thrive.

Sansui. I rarely think of my last name, the name of my mother's ancestors, graced unto me because my father did not stay around long enough to grant me the "honor" of carrying his name. I've done research on my people, as I have most of the races of Southeast Asia, as you well know. The topic has always fascinated me, how a group of people behave, and those of Southeast Asia are no exception.

Their habits as far as honorable death and suicide are far different from those we were taught at San Francisco State, Travis, as you well know. Theirs is almost a romantic, honorable view of taking of one's life, as opposed to the stigma and shame we as Americans take towards the subject. I am prone to find comfort within the romanticism of death.

As evil as you were, Travis, my descent into madness and death is not your fault, not entirely. I should have sought help when I wasn't strong enough to carry the burden, as you told me many times. Perhaps I should have succumbed to the myriad of drugs, therapists, and treatments offered to me over the years. Sure, it would have negated me to a mindless, walking zombie, but as long as beautiful little Esther was quiet and did what the world expected of her and kept her petty problems to herself, then what did it matter if she was physically incapable of caring for her wants, her needs, and her whims? I refuse. Death before dishonor, Travis, and I'll break before I bend on these principles, and I'll do so with a grace and honor that you never possessed.

Have you ever suffered from depression, Travis? Of course not! If you had, you would understand. I lost the ability to think straight, the multitude of things on my mind so overbearing that it felt as a weight was crushing my chest constantly. Everyone kept asking me what was wrong, why I could not just snap out of it, why I could not be normal. God above and the lowest circle of the nine hells below, I wanted the normalcy that everyone told me was so easy to grasp. If it was so damned easy, then why in the name of God could I not find it?

I realized that the problems I faced weren't of my making, Travis—it was of their doing, and you became one of them. You abandoned me; you sold me out to save your soul. Save your shame, Travis, I don't want to listen to you spout it off. You're just the same as the rest of them. If you still care, I wish to never know.

That being said...

There is still a small part of me that does not want to die, that wishes to rage against the dying of the light, as Dylan Thomas once said. For as much as I'm predestined to walk the long walk into death, part of me, albeit a small part, wishes to scratch and claw back against that lonely road, to find a way to make it work as opposed to the desperate, final end I know that Death shadows me always. You see Travis, unlike you, Death is a gentle and patient lover that is willing to take me as I am, flawed little porcelain dead doll that I am. He courts me in my dreams and offers me love that you ripped away and discarded, all on a whim that I will never understand.

That part of me is what placed this letter here, for you to find. It's my guess that it's been three to five days since I boarded an Air India Flight to Delhi, and from there a flight on Druk Airways to Paro, Bhutan. You know the rest: taxi to Thimphu and then to check in with the

Consulate. Given my relationship with the country from my previous studies, they give me leeway when I am there, and I'm not required to have a tour guide. I included you on my forms as my assistant, hence the Indian and Bhutanese visas that await you here. I hope you don't mind, and I hope you don't find reason to mock my sanity again for doing this.

The time you spent with me a year ago here in Bhutan was the best time of my life, Travis. Bhutan is what every nation should strive to be, one where the focus of the happiness of the people overshadows the whims and desires of a bunch of rich, arrogant, corporate schmucks. It is a nation where those that rule it make sure none goes hungry, none is asked to provide outside their means, and a nation where most are, for the most part, happy. They've managed to resist the harsh brutality of Chinese communism and the lax, overbearing chaos of the growing Indian capitalism to form a niche for themselves in Southeast Asia and the Indian subcontinent. Unlike the America we hold so dearly, the people there are...happy.

Happiness is all I ever wanted, Travis.

Happiness is what we all deserve, frankly. We deserve to be happy, healthy, and truly free. Free of mental illness that cripples us and brings us to our knees while the rest of the world stares and wonders what is wrong with us. Free of physical ailments that make us cry out in the night, that make us ache and hurt, and make us wonder if we can bear one more singular instance of pain. Free from worries of how we'll pay to cure these ailments, and if the cures being forced upon us by a group of rich men in suits that watch the bottom line closer than the cures themselves. These are not truly cures, but a treatment of symptoms that line the pockets of those who make the treatments, all the while delaying the implementation of science that could bring us a true cure.

Happiness does not exist in the United States, where we are fed fairy tale endings to overcompensate for the grim reality we all face. We are a wretched, arrogant people that have no idea what it is we bring unto ourselves...or what it is we shortchange ourselves of. We spend so much time chasing the American Dream of prosperity that we forget that, somewhere in the equation, we're supposed to be happy.

I know you've heard of the suicide forest in Japan. Aokigahara, they call it. I was quite obsessed with it for a while, and you showed a great measure of patience with me as I fed that obsession. A tranquil plot of land that sits at the base of Mt. Fuji, and, in essence, one of the most tranquil places for one to travel to in order to end their life. Such a death seems too clichéd for me and besides, the Bhutanese visa process was a much simpler one for me to undertake in my deteriorating state.

So, I guess, in essence, this letter is my last gasp, my last hope that somewhere beneath the shell of evil that you became, my Travis still exists. Yesterday was a million years ago. Now that you've found this letter, it's almost too late. It may be too late, as I may have lost my resolve and ended my misery in the quaint happiness of Bhutan before you arrived. I hope not. I am hoping against hope that you can see past your own arrogance, your own flaws, and find the love that existed for me one more time, to make what was wrong in my world right again.

I'm sorry, Travis. I'm so incredibly sorry for what I'm asking you to do here, but even as you abandoned me, I knew you were still the only one in my life that gave a damn. I love you, despite your flaws, and I hope this becomes an important side note in our story as opposed to the final, sordid chapter.

As the boxes on your left and right let on, I packed lightly for this trip. I have taken a few articles of clothing, mostly the silks and robes of the local Buddhist monks, along with some of the favorites that brought you to devour me, if only with your eyes. I have also brought some of my writings. There is also, smuggled upon the folds of my favorite robe, a capsule of Cyanide. At least that way, if you find me dead, you can look upon the one you claimed to have loved without disfigurement.

If something doesn't change, Bhutan will be where I die. I'm sorry to leave you this cryptic entry, but there will be more. My flaws are open season now, and you will see how truly into the madness I have descended before this comes to a roaring conclusion. Maybe, just maybe, this shimmer of hope I have is a good thing, and you'll be able to pull me back from the brink.

Hotel Riverview, Room 16A is reserved in your name for the next month. You'll find my next letter there.

Please, Travis. Don't let one good turn, my love for you, be what earns me my death.

-Esther.

CHAPTER 3

Travis blinked into the sunlight, unsure of how long he had sat in one spot. The sun had blasted through, and then vanished from the single window in her humble little apartment, so it must have been hours, Travis reasoned. The letter was clutched in his hand, wrinkles becoming permanent along the edges of the three pages it was written on. Slowly coming back to reality, Travis folded the letter and set it aside so that he could peruse the rest of the contents of the envelope. There was a digital printout, the reservation for room 16A at Hotel Riverview in Thimphu. A month! Would it take him that long to find her? Another sobering thought: it was August, and class was soon to start. How was he going to travel eight thousand miles when he had the responsibility of a job?

His first response was to be incensed. She was selfish, so incredibly selfish! The help she needed had been at her fingertips for years! He had begged and pleaded with her for years to seek the medicines and the therapy she so railed against in the letter he had just set aside. For her to pull this was completely self-centered and arrogant, almost as if she knew he would come for her, that she knew she held more sway over his conscience than anyone on Earth. In that moment, for a brief second, as a warring of emotions raged through his being, he hated her, all over again.

Then guilt hit home like a leaden weight, and his heart quickly sank to the vicinity of his feet. Bile rose in the back of his throat, and, for what seemed like the millionth time in the last few weeks, Travis realized what he had allowed himself to become. He saw himself as a cocky, brash go-getter who could find all the answers within. The truth was he was a selfish, inconsiderate failure that had thrown away something that should have remained dear to him. The resolve to make this right hit him like a lead weight in the gut.

There was irony in this moment. For someone as pragmatic as Travis, the irrational, manic thoughts that rushed forward were akin to standing full face in the path of an avalanche. As the snow of his own emotions hit him full force, the walls of common sense and self-

preservation fell like those in biblical Jericho, except that it hadn't taken 24 hours of daylight to do the deed. All it had taken was a guilt, along with a large helping of adrenaline and a coarse disregard for the rest of his humanity.

He brought his attention back to the letter, brought it softly to his lips, pressed gently in a dry kiss that he hoped he'd be able to grace his love with one more time, hopefully while she was still on the mortal coil they currently shared. He folded it, taking great care not to wrinkle it any more than his careless hands had done before. If he made it back, this would be a story for him to tell, in all of its sound and fury. If not, the letter would still be on his person, and with any luck, someone else would be able to deliver the dark details of the last days of Esther Sansui and Travis Saint Croix.

There were calls to make, and plans to arrange. He'd need a leave of absence from the suburban middle school he taught at, and if the district would not grant it, well, they could fire him. Teachers were needed everywhere, and he'd find another job. Bills needed to be prepaid, funds withdrawn from the bank, credit cards frozen (as American credit cards, by governmental design, were worthless in Bhutan), mail and emails and calls forwarded and held...his thoughts soon drifted away from these mundane tasks. For reasons unknown, his mind wandered to their first date, the first dinner he'd had with Esther, and the sly little memories that were wrapped within...

Chinese!

Of all the food clichés that she could have requested, the thought that she wanted Chinese was not one that Travis expected. He had spent countless hours, preparing...no, preparing wasn't the right word. He had been preening in front of the mirror, like a vain little peacock, getting himself ready for this date. Every fold of his Oxford button down had been smoothed over again and again, the soft blue color being what he thought was a wonderful companion to her ice blue eyes, not to mention the hope that such a vibrant color would take focus away from all his features that were, well, average. A pinstriped vest fit handsomely on his frame, the black and thin white stripes complementing nicely to the deep blue. Black slacks and black dress shoes complemented the outfit, as did the black socks and belt. It was remarkable how the black made him look a little more daring, as well as a little older. The ensemble was topped with a black pinstriped derby, a style that caused gentle eye rolls from the hipsters at San Francisco State, but one that, nonetheless, Travis liked.

He spent several hours in front of the mirror, rehearsing lines, topics of conversation, ideas that he hoped would keep her intrigued and smitten with his charm and grace. Charm and grace he knew he was lacking, sure, but if one can fake it, time was there later for the true side to be known, gently, and without pause. He reminded himself beforehand that certain topics were off limits, primarily his family. They were rednecks from the hill country of North Mississippi. How a group of such racist hicks had made it to the super liberal paradise of the Bay area was beyond Travis's understanding. Oh, he knew the reason they had relocated was due to his father being transferred from his electrician's job for promises of greater pay with a larger company. The transfer had been encouraged by a trade union that had stopped serving the purposes of representing its members and had become a clearinghouse for the big energy companies that were working in silent concert to wrangle the best talent in America. It was plain to see a monopoly was coming, but, like most things with Congress, at least as it pertained to the now nonexistent middle class, this was ignored, cast aside for the needs of great men with even greater egos.

The dream scenario had not lasted long. Travis was convinced his father was lying, but nonetheless, less than a year after the transfer, his father was diagnosed with fibromyalgia. While Travis was no doctor, he had done his research, and it was with no small irony that he noted that many people were slapped with the fibromyalgia label when there was no idea in hell what was wrong with them. For someone that was in constant pain, it was a marvel at the things Edward Saint Croix was able to do. Given his name, there was a claim of being 1/16th Crow Indian, somewhere in the family's indistinguishable past. Grant money was thrown at the family, and thanks to some correspondence classes from an undetermined university in Stockholm, his father now boasted a law degree with a minor in physics. Physics, without having ever taken algebra! It was a wonder the man was an electrician, but now a lawyer/physicist? Travis laughed long and hard at the news, his suspicions confirmed when his father tried, and failed, eighteen times to pass the bar exam in California. This was followed by an ill-fated jaunt into Oregon to take it using a distant cousin's address, a stunt that almost landed him in jail and pretty much killed any dreams he had of practicing law.

His old man's shenanigans had never bothered Travis, not really. Up until September 11, when Travis had been a sophomore in high school, his dad was just a quirk, an oddity in a life that had been a truly average one up until that point. Travis had been on campus the day the first plane hit the towers. He had just finished some pre-school weight training for football and had barely a chance to shower and start preparing for classes in a couple of hours when his cell phone rang incessantly. Scowling at the name on the Caller ID, Travis had been half tempted to toss the cursed thing aside, but, instead, he answered to his father's hysteria filled voice, calling him home and cursing those "damned Arabs" without letting Travis get a word in.

He hurried home, and walked in just as the second plane hit the second tower. He watched with the rest of the free world as America was attacked on her own soil for the first time since the 1940's. He kept an eye on his father, who always claimed to be a red-blooded patriot, but in truth would have hidden behind his mother's skirts if he'd ever been called to war. The old man cried, ranted, and raved at the television screen. As most Americans, Travis was shaking, but his father's actions and words that were soon to follow would jolt him into a harsh reality that he was not prepared for.

His father was soon screaming hysterically. "Those assholes! Assholes! We'll show them what for! We'll show them how Americans fight! Get in the truck, son, I'm taking you down to the recruiting station, and in the name of the honor of this family, you'll enlist right now!" He was shouting at the top of his lungs now, all the while carrying on a futile search for his keys.

Travis was stunned. His old man had a few screws loose, sure, but Travis had always viewed them in an endearing sort of way, sort of like watching a puppy chase its tail, and knowing its clumsy efforts would never come to fruition. Nevertheless, this? Going to war against an unknown enemy in a land far away over the actions of some zealots who warped religion to suit their needs? Travis would have rather jumped in the Bay with a weight tied to his foot. His next words changed the course of his teenage years, and his adulthood...

Travis shook, his head, jolting the memory from his thoughts. Somewhere in the background, a guttural punk metal ballad kicked on, straining the speakers of his ancient boom box, and Travis allowed the distant memory to fade into nothingness. Indeed, any talk of his family was off limits.

Anything else was pretty much on the table, and Travis wondered what he would speak of with her as he walked at a languid pace to his then almost new Hyundai, taking care not to wrinkle any of his outfit.

Upon arriving at the restaurant, a small, family-owned affair that seemed to fit every stereotype of a typical Chinese restaurant, from the tapestries depicting great battles on the wall, to the all-Asian wait staff, Travis quickly spotted Esther. As striking a figure as she was, her appearance was, at this rendezvous, breathtaking. She was clad in a crimson silken dress, one that tightly hugged her form, starting with a raised collar that, if not for the fact that she always carried her chin slightly raised, would be touching it. Golden butterflies were embedded into the deep red fabric, and it was bound at her thin waist by a piece of black silk, close to an inch thick. The dress fell to her ankles, and a pair of black heels adorned her feet. Closed toe, but with a strap pattern at the top that repeated itself thrice and clung tightly to her skin. Her whitish locks were wound in a bun to the back of her head with a pair of chopsticks, with a few strands falling to the base of her neck. She was the striking image of royalty and beauty and a geisha, all at once, and Travis hid behind a decorative fountain for a moment simply to buy himself more time to stare.

"Don't mess this up," he muttered quietly to himself.

One of the wait staff eyed him suspiciously and offered a loud "How many?" that seemed to jar him back to the here and now.

Travis offered a meek smile to the short, nondescript woman and nodded in Esther's general direction. "I'm meeting her," he said softly.

The woman offered a puzzled look before breaking into a broad grin. "Oh, okay. You on a date with her?"

The woman's nosy question startled Travis, insomuch that he didn't think before he answered, "Uh, yeah," suddenly eager to bail from the conversation.

The waitress smirked, grabbing a couple of menus and hustling in an exaggerated stride that betrayed her petite stature. "This way," she said, rolling her eyes slightly as she motioned for Travis to follow her to the table.

The walk to the table seemed to take ages, as the nervous apprehension that had sunk into the pit of his stomach was replaced by a fluttery excitement and anticipation for the scenario he had daydreamed about for what seemed to be ages.

As he eased himself into the booth, Esther looked up from the placemat she had been idly reading and offered him a shy smile. "You're punctual, Travis, even if the time you took to gawk from behind the water fountain almost made you late. I like that in a man. It's important to be on time, yes?"

Esther smiled again and returned her eyes to the placemat as the waitress plopped two plastic and leather menus in front of the pair. "You want drinks?" she said, in a flurry of words that she had repeated quite often, yet showed no regard for proper syntax or, for that matter, pronunciation.

Travis gave an absent mutter about a glass of water; Esther offered a raised brow and a grin, but said nothing to him. Instead, she turned to the waitress and said softly: "Plum wine—
Takara, if you have it. If not, the house brand will suffice. And bring the bottle. We plan on being here awhile."

It was Travis's turn to offer a raised brow of his own, to which Esther replied, with a smirk: "The first date is like a job interview for me, Travis. I have an issue with the pretentious habit that Americans partake in of auditioning several potential suitors before making a knee jerk decision to settle with one. Why do you think divorce is as rampant as it is in this day and age? People get married for all the wrong reasons, whereas if they sat back and looked at a potential suitor from all angles, people would be a lot happier and a lot less likely to run though several people before finding someone they were compatible with. The wine just makes the process a little less tedious, and a lot more fun."

The impromptu diatribe offered up by Esther did more than catch Travis a little off guard; it would suffice to say it astonished him. Being a child of divorce, and of one that was a rather long and nasty mess, Travis could understand exactly where she was coming from, yet to spill so much of one's personal philosophy in a first date setting was not something he was expecting when he sat down. Strangely, it did not bother him; in fact, it was something he found quite refreshing. It was a unique twist on dating: knowing where someone stood on certain matters from the onset. It made it less likely that something would be done out of haste, or pressure, or lust. Travis offered a grin of his own, seeing that the spur of the moment speech had left Esther flustered. A strand of her pale hair had found its way into her face, and Travis gently reached over and brushed it from her view, tucking it behind her ear before quickly withdrawing his hand and returning to his menu.

Esther flinched, allowing him to do as he intended as she looked away, her eyes flashing anger before regaining their serenity, focusing on a point just above his head. "As much as I have daydreamed of that touch, Travis, let me speak frankly: I am overly cautious when it comes to physical interaction between myself and another. Too many false implications can be laid onto the table, too much can be left unsaid without proper qualification of one's actions. That is one of my core rules: always be sincere in your actions and be sure that you're not implying something with your hands that your mind is not ready to back up." She smiled again, and laid her hand on his, albeit for an instant, before retreating it to her side of the table. "It's not that I question your intentions, Travis. I just feel that a relationship should be planted on the roots of honor, trust, and respect, as opposed to a physical desire that can be brought on by touch."

Travis nodded, slowly. Pragmatic as always, Travis knew at his core that some childhood trauma had brought her to be so closed in, so skittish when it came to a man's actions towards her. He'd seen it enough; in fact, his response to such childhood trauma had been the fostered sense of pragmatism, the stone cold reality that he stared at every situation with. It was a blessing and a curse, although at this moment, Travis found a way to lighten the mood. "I see. It's like my father said: Don't let your mouth write checks your ass can't cash." As he delivered the punchline, he winced, realizing as he said it how lame the joke was. Brow furrowed, a weird half grin plastered to his face, Travis could barely look at Esther. He knew he had to, and it was with weary eyes that he waited to see her reaction to the crude and poorly timed joke.

She laughed. Of all the reactions he would have expected from her, laughter was not one of them. "Profanity aside, that is exactly what I was referring to, Travis Saint Croix." She grinned, a relaxed, genuine grin, the first of many she would have for Travis as the drinks were set in front of them. Eying his hat, she chuckled again, and offered a snide comment: "Maybe there is something to work with under that hideous hat."

Travis feigned offense, but he offered a broad grin of his own as he offered the first hint of the arrogance that bubbled below the surface. "Please," he said, smirking as he offered his retort. "Do you see anyone else on campus wearing one of these bad boys? It may be retro, and it may be 1930's gangster, but have no doubt, Esther Sansui: I make this look good."

A gentle roll of brilliant blue eyes was offered, and Esther decided to one up the game, her ice blue hues never leaving the warm brown of his. "Waitress, bring this arrogant fool a glass; I have a feeling he'll be partaking in some of this wine as well. After all, it seems that he may already be drunk!" She eyed the bucket the bottle had been brought in before pressing forth, looking to score a verbal knockout with a punchline of her own. "And do you have a larger ice bucket? I'm afraid we may need it. Fill it to the brim, if you could. The head on this one is starting to swell, and not only do we need to bring the swelling down, we need something larger than that hideous hat to adorn it with as well."

Travis laughed, at the joke itself and the fact that she had managed to one up him, confounding the humor. Being one upped in wordplay was not something Travis was used to, and he licked his lips as he stared at her for an instant. Anticipation of his response left the air pregnant with silence; other patrons shifted uncomfortably in their seats, and even the waitress stood, rocking back on her heels, unsure what to expect. Slowly, Travis unwrapped his silverware and set them aside. The napkin was raised slowly, and Travis grinned as he waved a white flag of surrender.

Scattered laughs echoed off the walls of the establishment, and one drunken old man even managed to clap and shout "Give 'em hell, girl!" before returning to his cheap import beer.

For her part, Esther stared straight at Travis, a smile playing again at the corners of her lips. "You learn quickly, Travis," she said, loudly enough for the patrons of the establishment to hear. She chuckled, leaning in slowly, motioning for him to do the same. "Let's just hope you're not as passive in all manners of the relationship," she whispered into his ear, before straightening in her seat and pouring each of them a glass of wine.

Travis took the offered wine. Eyes locked on her, he partook of the beverage for the first time in his life. It was sweet and slightly tart all at once, an experience he was a little startled to find from a beverage. He allowed the flavor to roll around the inside of his mouth and against his tongue before swallowing, storing the memory of the essence of the drink in his mind's eye, to be recalled as a sincere reminder of his first encounter with Esther. Perhaps it was the wine; perhaps it was a need to defend his masculinity in the aftermath of Esther's verbal knockout. It was his turn to motion, and Esther leaned in herself, trying to hide the fact that, indeed, she was eager to hear what he had to say.

"While our society has decided that we should be equal as sexes, sweet Esther, make no doubt: while in public eye, you are and will always be my equal, and rightfully so, once the door shuts home and we are in private for the first time, know that it will be I that will be in charge." It was a shot across the bow, a verbal retort that he was sure she would have no response for. Travis leaned back and sipped once again at the wine, still savoring the flavor as he eyed her with a mix of humor and apprehension.

Esther was startled, although she kept her expression schooled to one that had been trained for years not to allow a trace of surprise to show. Slowly, a grin played at her lips again as she took a sip of her own wine, careful not to stain the lip of her glass with the thin coat of pink lipstick she had applied before leaving home. Light, lithe fingers slowly twirled the stem of the glass in her hand, and if the lighting had been better, Travis might have noticed a slight blush.

"Beast," she said simply, teasingly, with a knowing grin before her attention returned to the menu.

The rest of the dinner was a blur. Food was ordered, as both managed to avoid the toxic plumes of the buffet. The entire buffet option made Travis nervous, as the food raised a thousand questions. How long had it been there? How many other people had touched a portion of what you were about to eat? How many different germs and how many parts of someone's DNA were you about to consume? These were questions that would drive most people paranoid if they stopped to worry over them. For Esther, the desire to order from the menu was a lot less sinister. She enjoyed the freshly cooked food, along with the selfish little thought that the cook had slaved over that particular meal just for her.

Mindless conversation followed, the normal questions about future plans (his to teach; hers to use her lessons from Humanities to run a nonprofit dedicated to ending hunger in Southeast Asia), the desires for family (oddly, him, yes; her, not so sure), taste in music (his was an eclectic mix of rock, jazz, rockabilly, and instrumental; hers was pop rock, with some heavier strains, as well as some blues and soul) favorite foods, vacation spots, books, and the like. Esther was correct in the fact she saw this as an interview process, although Travis could not help but notice there was a certain thirst for knowledge within as well. Esther had her own thoughts on the process. She gathered the unsettling sense that while Travis would know things about her, there was a chance that, in certain areas, he'd never know who she was. And she was oddly okay with this. There were certain dark parts of her past that Esther was prone to keep hidden, locked in a box in the corner, never to come out and hurt her or the few she was close to.

The bottle of plum wine was consumed, and then another, and the food was devoured with the standard sense that, with all Chinese food, they would be hungry again in a couple of hours. A joke about grabbing pizza later was lifted by Travis, and Esther laughed, now unable to take her eyes from him, the battle she discussed between the underdog lust and the favorite common sense raging, with the underdog looking to pull the upset. There was an attraction between the two that neither was able to explain, and both were loath to tamper with.

In a nod to the impromptu that they both feared, a walk along the Santa Cruz Beach Boardwalk was brought up. With a wicked smile and a light head, Travis asked the waitress to call for a cab. As they stood, Travis was quick to assist Esther with the light silken coat she had worn in with her ensemble, quietly noting two small butterfly tattoos, one with the wings enclosed, angular, tattooed at the base of her skull, barely visible through her silken strands of pale hair. The second was on the underside of her left wrist; another butterfly, this one purple and orange, newer, and full of vibrant color. Wings lay open, the sight was one to behold, standing out in stark contrast to the mocha of her skin. It was meant to draw attention.

The cab soon arrived, and then the pair was off to the beach, a few short hours spent wandering up and down the coast, the gentle waves lapping against the shoreline providing a cool, languid melody as they walked and conversed, from decided-on starting points and ending points, back and forth. There was no hurry to their walk, and there were long gaps of silence, which neither minded. They were more prone to be careful with their words than most; and in fact, at times, words were not needed. Once they had their fill of walking, Travis called for a cab, a lingering regret in doing so that he was puzzled by.

A bench was procured as they awaited their driver, both looking at the other and offering a laugh or grin, and both unsure why shyness had gripped them once again. In the late hours of the Bay evening, all was quiet, and given the circumstances of the day, it took a moment for both to gather their thoughts, and their emotions.

Without warning, Esther laid her head on Travis's shoulder. "You know, Travis, I like you. Kind of," she said, a smirk on her face as she stared straight ahead, wanting the comfort of touching another, even if it was as innocuous as the contact she offered now, without the commitment of eye contact—eye contact that would allow him to see the small embers of desire that he had managed to light within her.

Perhaps it was the wine, perhaps it was a high he was experiencing from the combination of the wine and the chemistry between the two of them, sent and received, throughout the night, but for whatever reason, Travis was emboldened more than he realized. As she rested, he reached down and took her hand in his, fingers quickly intertwining in hers, a smile playing at his lips. "I like you too, Esther. Kind of. I've daydreamed about this for a while, and here we are. My question is simple: can I see you again?"

She had no time to react to his boldness. At this point, the cab pulled up, the bright headlights blinding them. Travis quickly pulled his hand free to shield his eyes, while she turned her face to his shoulder, another instance of submissiveness that Travis had not expected. Esther was quick to recover, and as she stood, they walked to the cab, side by side.

Travis held the door open for her, but Esther shook her head. Giving a raised brow to the driver, she smirked. "I'd rather sit behind the driver. He's a heavyset fellow, and if there is an accident, I would not mind having the extra cushion between me and whatever fate of twisted metal awaited me on the other side."

Travis nodded, entering the cab while chuckling at the joke. As he stepped in, Esther slid a note into his pocket, unseen. As soon as Travis had settled behind the passenger seat, Esther shut the door and grinned. A second cab pulled in, and Travis rolled down the window with a sense of bewilderment. "Why don't we just share a cab, Esther?" Travis asked.

"Not so fast, lover boy." Esther said with a coy smile. "Check your right pocket when you get home." An overly exaggerated kiss was blown his way, and she offered a smirk one more time. "Goodnight Travis."

The cab ride was an hour long, and for about fifty minutes Travis waited with bated breath, until impatience finally wore him to being frazzled. He yanked the folded paper from his pocket. With eager anticipation, Travis hastily unfolded the note, and read it.

Travis: I had a wonderful time tonight, which, after all my daydreaming, is what I expected, although, truth be told, I did have a second note on me, in case things went south, the contents of which you will

29

never know. You've earned a second date, tiger. So while we're on clichés, meet me next Friday at the Cracker Barrel Deli in Fremont. The name lends more towards your side of the equation, but the fare may surprise you. Wind to your dreams, Travis.

Her name was signed underneath, in a beautiful script that betrayed how little time she had actually put into it. Travis stared at it for a long time, a thousand questions running through his mind. When did she write it? Did the second note even exist? Had she known the evening would go this way? And countless other questions, all of which, he knew, would go unanswered. Travis chuckled, paid the cabbie, and stepped from the cab, beginning the final few steps to his apartment.

CHAPTER 4

Airports. What an unmitigated disaster!

As far as those in their mid-twenties went, Travis and Esther had both been experienced fliers, insomuch that they shared a frequent flyer card through one of the Big Four credit card companies. The odd tone that the credit card agent had aside (based on the accent, Travis had deduced she was from somewhere in the deep South; the exaggerated "OH" he had received when informing the agent that the pair was from San Francisco seemed to confirm this belief), it was by sharing this account that they were able to travel as much as they did. Apparently, fornication is still a sin in the South, but if one says they are from California, it was suddenly explained, if not fully understood.

The reason the pair had taken up this particular card was the fact that they had partnered with one of the huge carriers, which in turn allowed them to transfer their points to regional, international, and minor air carriers, such as Air India and Druk. A quick call to the airline miles' hotline revealed that their miles' balance was precariously close to zero; in fact, Travis could

not recall it ever being this low. The phone menu allowed him to scroll through an audible menu, detailing the transaction history, and with a review of the last few transactions, Travis had his answer.

Esther had cashed in all of the pair's points, but, oddly enough, the only first class tickets purchased were for the "to" and "from" portions of Travis's trip on Air India. Part of this was easily explained; Druk was a small regional carrier, and the flight from India to Bhutan was to be on a regional plane, a small, sardine can of a plane that was airborne for all of a half an hour and offered little besides cramped seats, a small pack of peanuts, and a warm soda. As he scrolled back through the menu, however, the transactions revealed she herself had flown coach to India before embarking on the Druk portion of the flight.

Guilt slammed home again for Travis, and it was with a selfish pity he pondered if it was going to be a constant theme for this little excursion. She had placed his comfort above her own needs; in fact, in what could be construed as a mockery to his own arrogance, she had treated him as royalty and herself as a commoner. Stateside, the term would be middle class, but in the Indian caste system, it would amount to peasantry. The symbolism was not lost on Travis, and as he stepped up to security screening, a plan started to formulate in his mind about how he could right the wrong.

"Step through the scanner, please," the TSA agent said, half-bored and thankful that she had drawn this particular gate assignment for the day. Traffic to and from India was light this time of year, and despite the relatively large Indian population of the Bay area, it seemed that precious few were in a hurry to rush home. Travis set his small carry-on on the conveyor belt and stepped through the scanner. The alarm went off, as it always did, and the burly TSA agent on the other side eyed Travis with suspicion.

"Do you have anything on your person that could cause harm to another?" the agent asked, eying him even closer now that the alarm had confirmed that, indeed, this guy looked too average to be just another wayward soul traveling about.

Travis shook his head in the negative.

"Remove your shoes and step back through the scanner, sir," the agent said warily.

Travis removed his worn Nikes, and for good measure, his socks as well, with a small grimace at the fact that his feet would now be filthy on account of sharing a floor that had no doubt been used by millions before him. As he stepped through, the alarm went off again.

The agent was getting frustrated with having his daily routine thrown off. "Sir, are you wearing a belt with a metal buckle?"

Travis, in his state of distraction, had forgotten about the buckle. He said nothing, simply nodding in the affirmative.

"Remove it, please," said the guard, as his partner watched intently.

The belt removed, Travis stepped back through the scanner and gave a sigh of relief as the alarm remained silent. The agent handed him his shoes, socks and belt, and Travis quickly grabbed his carry-on and scooted over to the seating section at the gate.

As he sat, Travis rolled the first class ticket over in his hand several times. It seemed like it would be a light flight, as there were less than a dozen people in the concourse with him, seven of which were a large family preparing to travel to the homeland, some of them for the first time. Several children scurried about, and Travis could not help but smile as the exasperated parents glanced at one another warily while the kids kicked up a small storm of chaos. The few other passengers in the lobby were not disturbed, but nonetheless, Travis could not imagine having one child, much less the litter the couple possessed.

Glancing at the ticket again, Travis scanned the room, warmth in his brown eyes as he silently perused the other passengers sitting nearby, mostly in silence, waiting for the plane to pull up to the gate so they could board. A young couple, college kids no doubt, made a very public display of affection in a far corner, and Travis wondered why some people did not have any sense of decency when it came to the mating rituals that mankind was biologically driven to partake in. A couple of businessmen chatted quietly, and the cut of their well-tailored suits told Travis they were most likely his companions in first class. As he was about to give up on his plan, Travis finally caught sight of the one he sought.

The old man was eighty-one, but based on Travis's guess, he was probably in his late sixties. He had never been very keen on estimating age. The man sat alone, in a simple white button down Oxford and a pair of worn khakis. The outfit was pressed to perfection, pride taken in appearance, and what the clothes lacked in age and style, they made up for in care. His black dress shoes were buffed to a mirror shine. The man was apparently on his last legs of health, as a raspy cough shook his frail body at times, but he sat erect, proud, and seemed quite eager for the trip. Travis finished lacing up his shoes and stood slowly, absently snagging his carry-on as he headed to where the old man was sitting.

"Is this seat taken?" Travis asked softly.

The old man looked around the terminal, apparently taken aback at why a perfect stranger would ask to sit beside him with so many empty, welcoming seats available to use. However,

Sathya Bhatt had seen much stranger things in his eight decades, and this barely registered a blip on his radar. Maybe the kid was lonely. Maybe he needed money. Maybe he was gay and was attracted to much older men. Quite frankly, Sathya didn't care; however, it was not his custom to be rude.

With a thin smile, he nodded to the chair. "Have a seat. Name's Sathya. What brings you to make a trip to India, my lad?" The English was precise, Sathya having lived his formative years in India, during the last throes of the British Empire.

The question caught Travis off guard. How does one, exactly, explain to a perfect stranger that the meaning behind their trip was to try and rescue a loved one from trying to kill themselves, when the very reason suicide had become the solution was because of his own actions? Travis, ever pragmatic, decided to play cautious with his words. "My fiancée surprised me with an early wedding gift. We had been to India and Bhutan before as a part of her studies, and she wanted to surprise me with a trip back." Travis looked away, unable to bear the taste of the lie on his tongue, yet knowing he could not speak the truth. The ticket shuffled nervously in his hands.

Sathya smelled a rat, but he let it pass. Not many people knew of Bhutan; it was too neat a coincidence for the lad to just travel to the tiny nation on a whim, especially considering the visa process and the work it took for one to be able to visit the Hidden Empire. Something was amiss. He watched the lad roll the ticket over in his hand, and grinned. Sathya was a very patient man. He had left his wife in India for sixty years; waiting Travis out was child's play in comparison. "At least your reason for heading over is one of joy, lad," Sathya said softly, his voice monotonous, no trace of emotion. "I'm going to bury my wife of sixty years. I have the last of my savings here in this ticket." The old man smiled, and patted Travis on the shoulder. "Don't be so down, boy! You're going to celebrate a beginning, and I'm going to celebrate an ending, even if I have to fly coach to do it. We are granted but one life, child, and it should be a celebration, not an eighty-year bout with worry as you Americans tend to make it."

Sathya had a right to be mournful. He had managed to visit his wife twice a year, a week at a time, faithfully, for over sixty years. His job with the Department of the Interior and the meager pension that came with it were enough to provide for her and their children in India, but despite his governmental position, he was never able to pull the strings to bring them over to the States, his adopted country. Circumstance seemed to kill the hope of his family living the American dream. Her visa was killed in 1950 because of the birth of the Indian nation. Her application in April of 1961 was squashed because of Sathya's minor role in the Bay of Pigs fiasco. (Very minor, in fact, considering he had simply delivered the Interior's Department's view of the operation to the CIA a mere three days before the attack.) The next attempt, in 1979, had coincided with the Iran Hostage Crisis, and Sathya had withdrawn his family's application before it could be considered. The children made it over eventually on scholarly visas of their own, and all had resided with him at some point before spreading out globally, all becoming vital little cogs in the world's machine. His next attempt was launched in 1990, six weeks before the outbreak of Operation Desert Storm. It seemed to get lost in the shuffle, and Sathya almost gave up hope. His wife was diagnosed with cervical cancer in early 2001, and in a desperate Hail Mary, Sathya had filled out one more visa application for her, on hardship grounds, and delivered it to the Indian embassy on September 10th, 2001. About the time Travis was standing toe to toe with Edward, Sathya resigned himself to the fact that his wife would never make it to

the nation he so proudly called his home, and on September 16th, Sathya filed retirement papers, cashed out a portion of his pension, and spent the next six weeks in Delhi with his wife. It was then, away from the din of the rat race, he had realized how much he loved her, and was thankful they had remained loyal to one another, despite having half a world between them, for sixty years.

Upon arriving back in the States, Sathya, a loyal and hardworking retiree of the United States Department of the Interior, was arrested and held without cause, due to his village's proximity to the Pakistani border. He was ushered off to solitary confinement for almost four months; twenty-three hours in an eight-by-ten concrete cell was his reward for forty years of dedicated servitude to his adopted country. He was later released, never charged, but the experience had made him a bitter old cynic. He renounced his citizenship, and vowed to never spend a penny of the rest of his pension until the end. After having worked eight years as a gas station attendant,

Sathya got a call from India he had been dreading for years. At the ripe age of seventy-nine, his lovely wife had passed away peacefully in her sleep, leaving behind him and their six children, not to mention two dozen grandchildren and nine great grandchildren. She was the matriarch, the glue of the family, and most importantly, his first and only love.

Sathya told his story to Travis quietly, happy to share but with no desire for the overbearing attention that Americans seemed to heap on those who were going through a personal tribulation. As for Travis, he managed to turn his head away before the old man could see the tears well up in his eyes. The guilt had returned, along with a sudden finality of what would happen if Travis found Esther dead.

"So I spent the remainder of it on her funeral," Sathya was saying. "One hundred and eight thousand American dollars will buy quite a ceremony in India, and I intend to celebrate her life in a way that I feel is quite fitting to her. She always wanted blue orchids, yet could never find them in India. Quite a sum went to importing a hundred of the plants to the ceremony, after which they will be donated to the local Hindu monasteries, to allow the rest of our spiritual word to partake in their beauty." Sathya grinned. "If she means this much to you, treasure her, young man. Men do not court as they used to, nor do they hold up their commitment like my generation does. Treasure her."

Travis said nothing for a long instant before sighing as the pair watched the plane taxi next to the window. "For every breath I have left, I will, Sathya," Travis said, unable to control the sudden outburst of chivalry and resolve that sprang into his chest. For his part, the old man simply nodded and stood, preparing to head to the gate. Travis, seeing his chance slipping away, rushed forward and swapped the pair's tickets. Sathya went to protest, but Travis raised a hand. "Please. I insist. If you're going, you should go in style."

Perhaps the thought of flying in first class was too alluring for the old man, or perhaps he simply could not say no the insistent, pleading look in Travis's eyes. He closed his hand gently around the ticket and grinned. "Hmm! How often does one get to fly first class?"

Travis grinned again, and clasped the old timer on the shoulder. He had one final question. "Sathya, once the funeral is over, what will you do?"

Sathya regarded Travis with a knowing smile, and shrugged. "Who knows? I've lived eighty-one long years, and I've been blessed enough to have enjoyed almost every one of them. I won't return to the States. Too many regrets, too much hurt, and too many bad memories. Perhaps I will just join my wife in the afterlife. Besides, wasn't it once said that 'old legends never die, they just fade away?'" With that, Sathya grinned and boarded the plane, carryon in hand, and a smile reserved for the comely attendant at the gate.

Travis had to smile. He simply did not have the heart to tell the old man it was General Douglas MacArthur that had uttered the quote, and that it had been "Old soldiers never die, they just fade away." Shaking his head, Travis offered Sathya's wrinkled ticket to the attendant, and with a grin, stepped onto the plane, leaving the soil of his homeland one last time.

CHAPTER 5

As it is in most cases, the flight to Delhi from the Bay area was uneventful. In fact, between the storms of emotions on the issue itself, and the time spent preparing, Travis had not slept for forty-eight hours, a Herculean feat he owed to several cups of coffee combined with an impending sense of doom. Once he was on the flight, sleep came with ease, although how he had managed to sleep so soundly that he almost missed the connecting flight in Hong Kong was beyond him. Settling in, Travis was soon asleep again as the plane departed the tightly wound Chinese city, roaring into the darkness in the general direction of Delhi. Despite some turbulence, Travis stirred little as the plane touched down in the ancient Indian city. After awakening, Travis groggily made his way to the small connecting flight that would take him to Paro.

The Bhutanese airport was devoid of most tourists. This was the off-season for tourism, and combined with the fact that the Gross National Happiness policy severely limited the number of people who could enter the country at any point, it made customs far less crowded, which expedited the process. An airport employee brought his luggage to him, and Travis wandered the concourse idly, making his way to the governmental outpost within that would validate his visa and allow him to move on to Thimphu, and the Hotel Riverview, to prepare for whatever adventure Esther had planned for him. Travis grimaced as he sipped the lukewarm cup of instant coffee; the coffee craze that had swept the world had not apparently reached Bhutan yet, and he wondered with a sense of bemusement how the people here survived without something he considered as basic as gourmet coffee.

Travis strolled up to the office that handled the visa validation. It wasn't an office; really, it was a kiosk that stood against one of the barren walls that seemed to be the standard architecture in most of the larger cities of the country. The clerk stood at attention, his erect posture making Travis a slight bit nervous. The cold efficiency that such operations were carried about in other nations unnerved him; it was almost as if they were required to be as inhuman as possible in their posts, as if it would help with their productivity if they discarded any trace of personality. The upside of this, of course, was that the process normally went off without any hiccups, and the ever-pragmatic side of Travis could appreciate this.

"Travis Saint Croix," he muttered to the clerk, who offered a terse smile and a quick nod before reaching under the counter to produce a small file box, lightly setting it between the pair. It was labeled on the side in the Dzongkha language, the ancient tongue of the Bhutanese empire. The letters themselves were beautiful, a strange mix of Chinese and Russian influence that looked similar in many instances, yet if one was trained in the tongue, they could deduce the subtle differences. Travis watched as the clerk worried with several forms before finally pulling a manila folder with his name written across the top in block-lettered English. It was apparent that the scribe was someone to whom English was a second language, as they were trying to an extreme to perfect their penmanship. America's bastardization of the English language had perplexed the rest of the world, and Bhutan was no exception.

Travis opened the file to view the single-page visa acceptance form that was the norm for these types of trips, but as he signed, he noted a paper clip in the upper right hand corner. Perplexed, Travis turned the form over and was greeted by a single white envelope with his name printed in the same block style lettering. Flustered, fear and excitement jumped into his stomach. Was it another letter from Esther already? No, she said her next letter would be at the hotel, and given how Esther was prone to making sure her words were the exact truth, Travis knew, in his heart of hearts, that the letter was not from her. So who was it from?

Travis raised a brow at the clerk and spoke. "Excuse me, but what is this letter?" Travis held the envelope aloft, awaiting a response, not knowing the one he was to receive would raise more questions than answers.

The clerk eyed him for a moment, processing his words, and shrugged. "It was attached to the visa form when your sponsor sent it here." With that, the clerk offered another thin smile as he removed the box from the counter. A line had begun to form, and with a short nod, the clerk seemed to be dismissing Travis. "Next!" he said simply.

Travis walked away slowly, lugging his bags over to a small bench that, while out of place in the general architecture of the concourse, suited his needs perfectly. With a sigh, Travis sat down. The letter was set aside for a moment, and Travis let out another long sigh. He was used to structure in his every day; in fact, he craved the simple routine of doing the same task over and over on a regular basis. However, Esther had flipped the roles here, leaving her
submissive shell to lead him on a wild goose chase, and Travis knew in no uncertain terms that she would be the one that was choosing the course until this task reached its moment of finality, whatever conclusion that may be. He pinched the bridge of his nose and regarded the envelope as if it were laced with anthrax. He was unwilling to open it, but as much as the dread held him in his spot, a desire to end the madness, coupled with his love for Esther, brought a shaking hand to open the parcel.

Inside there was a simple piece of brown parchment, folded three times to bring it to its current size. A piece of parchment? It was not a material that was used very often, only reserved for documentation that was of vast importance, or by

41

those who were used to using the material, due to station or life experience. Travis pondered the note for a moment, a sudden realization dawning. Someone else had sponsored this trip. Universal Happiness, LLC, had been the group that had sponsored the first trip to Bhutan, a small, tight-knit group out of Washington, D.C. that was using graduate students from several different disciplines to try and incorporate some of the norms found in happier nations into American life. They had been pleased with Esther's work, but Travis knew they were privy to some of the best resources and technology on the planet, the group having benefited for years by a nonstop lobbying effort on the Beltway by its members and executives. Any correspondence from them would have come using the latest technology, directly to Travis, or more likely, to Esther, seeing as the research journey was her work, not his. This letter had come from somewhere else, and it was with a sense of puzzlement that Travis slowly opened the folds of the parchment.

In the upper right hand corner was a charcoal sketch of Taktsang Monastery, the birthplace of Buddhism in Bhutan and an iconic image known around the world. Perched on a cliff 900 meters above the city, it also carried the nickname "Tiger's Nest," because Guru Rimpoche was said to have flown on the back of a tigress in the 8th century to meditate in a cave where the monastery was later built. The cave and the monastery were said to be the origin of Buddhism in Bhutan. Travis and Esther had always made a note to visit the cradle of Buddhism, but, as with other things, circumstance had always tempered the desire. Apparently, Esther had fulfilled the desire, and Travis was surprised at the twinge of hurt he felt when he realized she had done so without him. Shaking his head, Travis began reading the letters below. It was in the same straight, all capitalized letter forms as his name was, and despite the dull headache that began to form at the front of his skull, he read on:

TRAVIS- GREETINGS AND SALUTATIONS. IF YOU ARE READING THIS, YOU HAVE ARRIVED IN BHUTAN, AND FOR THAT I AM MOST THANKFUL. MY NAME IS DAIMYO SINGH, AND I AM ONE OF SEVERAL MONKS HERE AT THE TAKTSANG MONASTERY IN PARO. YOUR BELOVED, ESTHER SANSUI, CAME TO ME IN THESE PAST FEW DAYS AND ASKED FOR MY ASSISTANCE, AND THE SPONSORSHIP OF THE TEMPLE, IN A SPIRITUAL JOURNEY SHE WISHED TO PARTAKE IN WHILE HERE IN BHUTAN. WHILE I WAS SET AT UNEASE BY HER REQUEST, IT IS NOT OF OUR TRADITION TO DISSUADE SOMEONE FROM WHAT THEY DESIRE TO DO, ESPECIALLY IF THEIR DESIRE IS SINCERE. SHE MENTIONED YOU WOULD BE ALONG, AND AGAIN, IF YOU ARE READING THIS, YOU HAVE MADE IT. PLEASE BRING YOURSELF TO THE TEMPLE BEFORE YOU CHECK IN TO YOUR HOTEL. I HAVE SEVERAL MATTERS I WISH TO DISCUSS WITH YOU. MAY YOU FIND PEACE ON YOUR WAY TO ENLIGHTENMENT.

The note was signed, the signature done by a small paintbrush in wonderful, broad strokes in a hand that had been steadied over many decades of doing such work. The lines were straight, without hesitation, and beautiful yet bold all at once. The skill would have made a studied artist weep. Travis allowed himself to marvel at both the writer and the note itself before folding the note along the same lines and placing it in his carry-on bag, with the note Esther had left him in San Francisco. A vague notion was forming in his mind, a wisp of a thought about the content of the letters and what they could become once this journey was over.

Travis looked at his luggage for a second and sighed. The best way to reach the temple was to hike, a several miles walk that also ascended 900 meters into the air, taking over two hours. He was in no mood for such a walk, jet lag kicking in despite the several hours of sleep he'd managed to get while airborne. Not in a mood to delay the inevitable, Travis sighed and walked to the other side of the concourse, storing all but his carry-on bag in a storage facility provided therein. The clerk smiled and handed him a ticket, to be presented when he sought to claim his luggage. Travis said nothing, only offering a small smile as he headed into the chilly Bhutanese morning.

For a country that was as hell bent on the true happiness of its citizenry as Bhutan claimed to be, the lack of green spaces in Paro was astounding. Grim concrete structures rose all around him, and in the chill of the morning air, it tended to give the city a sense of gloom, especially in the dark of the governmental and travel sections. Travis turned a corner and walked into the main business district of Paro. The streets were lined with vendors of all sorts. The smells of cooking food filled the air, the spicy scent of chilies dominant in the cold, frosty atmosphere. Travis was not a big fan of spicy food, and in fact, recalled a sliver of a memory of his first foray into Bhutanese cuisine, where upon he had spent several following hours dousing his mouth and throat with milk and yogurt. He smiled at the memory and his own silliness before walking on, taking in the sights of the clothing vendors and others, offering trinkets and hocking their wares. A small pack of street dogs, notorious in the country, ambled their way towards him, no doubt drawn by the strange scent of a foreigner. The dogs were docile, however, and after a few pats and a couple of gentle rebukes, they departed, leaving Travis to walk quickly into the general direction of the start of the ascent to the temple.

The trail started at the northwest base of the cliff land, one of three trails that offered a winding, relaxing walk through a stand of pine forest as the view was accented with colorful tapestries and ribbons along with several Buddhist prayer flags, accenting the deep green of the stand of ancient pines. The cliff stood high above the valley, but the walk was a languid, gentle one, and Travis found himself wondering several times if he was going uphill or downhill. About two-thirds of the way to the buildings, Travis stopped at the scenic overlook that was offered, taking in a quick view of the breathtaking scene. A twinge of loneliness hit home; this was something he was supposed to have seen with Esther, not something he was wandering upon in a mad attempt to save her from herself. He missed her, simply put. There was a cafeteria, and Travis grabbed a bottle of water and a ginger ale before striking back out onto the final path to

the temple, taking a moment to look at the wares offered by a small kiosk. Many were prayer related, and while Travis did not see the need to partake, he could certainly respect the deep reverence "…the Bhutanese people had in their Buddhist faith." He could see why Esther loved Bhutan so much, because it seemed that instead of forcing their views of happiness onto people, they lived it, and it made life much simpler.

Travis soon arrived at the entrance of the main temple, inhaling his breath slightly at the beautiful sight he beheld. Visible were several works of art, as well as a cave—the very cave in which it was said that Guru Rinpoche himself meditated for three months. The entrance of the cave had a barrier across the front, and Travis remembered reading somewhere that the cave was open to visitors once a year. He stared breathlessly as he walked toward the main entrance of the temple. Arriving there, he stepped onto a stone platform, removing his shoes and fedora, sliding a long robe over his frame as he prepared to enter. An offering bowl was next to the entrance, and Travis slid a few American coins in the bowl before entering, quietly so as to not disturb those who were in prayer or meditation. In nervous anticipation, Travis made his way to the balcony that was provided in each of the buildings of the monastery, stepping out and taking in the breathtaking view of the Paro Valley that lay below.

How long he stared, allowing his thoughts and emotions to ebb and flow as he stared into the nothingness of the valley below, he was not sure. The sight was breathtaking, as if one was truly standing on top of the world. His breathing was even, but internally Travis was a storm of emotions. The guilt in his actions, actions that had led him to the very edge of the world, warred with the sense of dignity he held in the fact that he had the decency to come to the edge of the world. Guilt won out, however, and as he stared over the breathtaking valley, a small tear

rolled down his cheek. He was alone, filled with sorrow, and utterly without hope. The valley below was his sanctuary, and he stared into the distance as he slid his headphones on. A slight breach of protocol and respect, sure, but this memory was to be his, and he wanted to savor it, come whatever may. With the volume on the lowest setting, he pushed play, and allowed the driving, mournful rhythm to catch his very soul up in the moment; the tears flowed freely, and Travis allowed the joy and sorrow of the moment to war with one another as he softly mouthed the lyrics to the song. He sang for a while, careful to keep what was coming from his mouth respectful, until the song sang of goodbyes and second chances. It was at that moment he was interrupted.

Apparently, Travis had not been singing as softly as he had intended. A heavy hand came to rest gently on his shoulder, and as the song ended, he heard a soft voice. "Yes, Travis, but sometimes goodbye is goodbye as well." The monk was younger, close to Travis's age, adorned in the robes that were the tradition of his walk of faith, and his journey into enlightenment. "Daimyo Paro is my name; Daimyo from my Japanese mother who was Shinto and showed great reverence to her country, and who thinks my walk into enlightenment is silly and unneeded. Paro, from the valley that is my home, and from my father, whose name and lineage stretch back in Bhutan for several centuries. You've come a long way, Travis, and I am sure you are weary. But if Esther's story is to play out as I fear, you still have a long way to go, and you may not like what you find." Daimyo smiled, and clasped his shoulder again. "Come, you should rest. Do you require food? Drink? Perhaps you wish a chance to bathe?"

All at once, Travis was hungry, parched, and suddenly aware of the fact that his skin crawled with the need for a bath. Travis quickly pulled the ear buds from his ears and nodded. "All three," he confessed softly.

With that, Daimyo smiled and nodded in the general direction of his quarters. "Come with me, then, and let us refresh your mind and body before you undertake this long journey." The words flowed, with a sense of eloquence reserved for those who dedicated their life to a singular cause, and were able to speak of other matters with a quiet indifference that failed to betray any scorn for said matters. Travis followed silently, the beauty of the inner sanctum of the monastery going unnoticed as a storm of emotions raged through him.

If Daimyo was able to tell the turmoil within Travis, he was quite adept at ignoring it. Nary was a word spoken until the pair stepped through the curtains that sectioned off Daimyo's quarters, and Travis allowed for a sharp intake of breath as they crossed the threshold. If simple and beautiful met at an abandoned intersection, the result would be the space that made up Daimyo's quarters. The walls were adorned in red and black, a few simple tapestries hanging securely within view. The bed was of a dark wood, rounded, rustic, and barely raised off of the floor. There were two small chests of the same small wood, no doubt holding the vestiges of his vocation and all of his worldly possessions. Travis had not seen anything like this. Another small entryway was visible at the back, and Daimyo smiled. "I hope my quarters are pleasing to your eye. Behind the second curtain is the bathing room. There is a large copper basin, one we use for bathing, and I have filled it with warm water. Take your time, and when you have finished, I will be here, waiting with food and drink, and then we can discuss." Daimyo stepped forward, and offered a quick hug before stepping back. "Well met, Travis Saint Croix, and know that despite your mistakes, I welcome you with an eager heart and an open mind." Daimyo smiled. "These tribulations you find yourself in with Esther can be worked out, through deeds and faith, if that is what is intended." With this, the monk stepped back, smiling one more time before settling on a mat on the floor to meditate.

Travis was taken aback at all of this. He had not known what to expect. How much had Esther shared with the monk? How much of Travis's filthy deeds had he been made privy to? Shaking his head, Travis stepped behind the curtain and stared at the copper basin. It was as if he had been thrust into the twelfth century. The basin was huge, twice the size of any bath tub Travis had ever used, and almost six feet deep. Travis wondered how he would use the thing. Sighing, he slowly removed his grimly clothes and used a step stool beside the tub to step up and look inside. The seating arrangements were settled quickly: one side held a ledge about two feet from the top, the other about four feet. The inside of the basin was white, a sharp contrast to the dark and bold quarters of the rest of the establishment. Soap, shampoo, and a washcloth awaited Travis on a perch built into the wall; from the high bench, it was easily accessible. Travis stepped over the ledge, and with a renewing sense of adventure, plunged feet first into the deep copper basin. The water was warm—hot enough to relax and allow for proper cleansing, yet tepid enough as to not scald him when he made his awkward entrance.

Travis proceeded to the low bench first, reaching for the bar of soap and the washcloth. He scrubbed with vigor, eager to remove three days of sweat, tears, and grime. Once the offending particles had been scrubbed from his skin, Travis moved to his hair, using the gel from the small glass vessel provided to remove the sweat and oil from his scalp. He plunged in, shaking his head below the surface with vigor, and then repeated the process a second time, not satisfied until he was sure all traces of filth had been washed away. Sighing contently, Travis made his way to the low podium, sitting heavily against it as he leaned back. Exhaustion took over, and soon, despite worries of drowning and his troubled mind, Travis was soon drifting off to sleep again…

How long he had dozed, he was not sure, but Travis was startled to find a single finger raising his chin away from the water's surface. Daimyo grinned, and shook his head slightly. "You have such a long way to go, Travis. I don't feel that drowning while relaxing in my bathing quarters will accomplish your missive." Travis smirked, and slowly came to alertness. With awareness back, Travis realized he was still in the tub, and still quite nude. The waters had dissipated the bubbles from his bathing; anyone that wanted to see what Travis had to offer simply had to glance into the tub. Travis flushed, contorting his body so that the most strategic areas were out of view from the monk. He flushed slightly, unable to bring his eyes back to Daimyo. The monk simply laughed. "A modest one, are we? Even before one who has taken vows to pass on life's more carnal pleasures. Very well, then." Daimyo smirked, and hopped down from the ladder, pointedly turning his back to Travis. "There's a towel and a set of robes there for you to use for the short time you are here. I have your key for the hotel room, also; there is a note here from your beloved. I have not read it; to do so would be an egregious breach of privacy." Daimyo spoke over his shoulder, making it a point to keep his eyes away from Travis. Travis quickly pulled himself from the basin, keeping the tub between him and the monk at all times. He dried quickly and slid into the robes, realizing with a wry grin that Esther had changed the rules of engagement on him once more. So there was no note at the hotel. Everything he needed was here, with Daimyo. Travis stepped from behind the basin and grinned, nodding once to the monk as they reentered his living quarters.

Daimyo knelt on the same pad, and motioned for Travis to do the same. Doing as instructed, Travis placed a hand, palm down, on each thigh and stared forward at the monk, filled with apprehension. If Esther had exposed the entire truth of his misdeeds, how would one as revered, as holy, as a Buddhist monk hold his sins? Did Daimyo secretly loathe Travis and was only meeting him for Esther's benefit? Would he lead Travis astray? Would he be subjected to some sort of harsh punishments for the sins against the one he loved? He dismissed the notions without a thought. The man was in the business of spirituality, of the soul, and of matters of the heart. It was not his place to judge, or to condemn; it was his place to simply counsel, as Travis was sure he had done with Esther.

The monk seemed to sense the uneasiness in the air and smiled. "Relax, Travis, there are no enemies here," he said simply. "Your Esther spoke to me quite candidly of your mistakes, and in spite of them, I hold no ill will towards you, nor does any one of my brethren here. We are simply vessels, not judges of men and of powers above and below." Daimyo smiled. "Besides, bitterness was not all that Esther held for you. She loved you, Travis, and despite your missteps, she still does. There is something to be said for love on such a level; indeed, it is the very basis of what we strive for. Although we are of different disciplines, I have read the works of the Dalai Lama quite often in my journey. He is quite enlightened, and I hold an admiration for what he faces in the light of oppression that is quite strong. It was he that said: 'All major religious traditions carry basically the same message, which is love, compassion, and forgiveness; the important thing is they should be part of our daily lives.' Esther is a sister of mine in the spiritual sense, Travis, and I cannot condone your actions against her. But, in the same spirit, and the same token, you are my brother, and I will provide you with whatever assistance you need." Daimyo smiled as a young boy came forth with a plate holding cheese, bread, and fresh fruit; a basin of water; and two earthen glasses. "Eat. Drink. You'll need your strength. For where Esther is will require every bit of your strength and resolve to toil through, and I will endeavor to ensure you are prepared physically, mentally, spiritually, and emotionally." Daimyo brought his eyes to Travis's and offered a knowing, mournful smile. "We cannot change the past, Travis, but it's what we do with the future, and how we make amends, not for our own selfish interests, but with a desire for the betterment of all involved, that defines who we are."

Travis bowed his head. "Sometimes, Daimyo, it's hell getting to heaven." Raising his eyes back to the monk, he tried to ignore the sting of his own tears, splashing hotly against his own cheeks before continuing. "If I had any idea it was going to hurt this bad, and that it would take such an effort as this, and that even at the end of my effort, I may not be able to fix what I had wronged, I would have never let her go in the first place." Travis paused, wiping his eyes with the sleeve of his borrowed robe before pressing on. "I had no experience in how to end things, especially considering how I allowed them to end. I was a fool, an idiot, and a charlatan, Daimyo, and I deserve every ounce of grief that my foolish decisions have circumstance to force upon me." Travis offered a sorrowful smile of his own. "I wish I could have turned my eyes inward, to look inside and see all of this before me. It's not my hurt I worry for anymore. What hurts is the fact that she is hurting a lot more than I am, and I am the reason for that hurt. I have to find her, and I have to do what is best for her. I have to do this, or I'm not me."

Daimyo nodded. "As I said before, my mother was Japanese. I know Esther spent a lot of time in the suicide forest in Japan a few years back. She recounted her memories and her emotions with it over the course of several letters. She seems quite proficient in the written arts," Daimyo said, with a wry grin. "Anyway, she spoke of her admiration of the samurai and their ancient practice of seppuku, as well as the World War Two fighter pilots and their use of kamikaze attacks." Daimyo's expression grew stern for an instant. "Despite your harsh words, and actions, her reasoning for what she is considering runs much deeper, Travis. She is looking to be a martyr of sorts, and her main reason for interaction with me is to see what the implications on her soul and spirit would be. Mainly, she claims she can find true nirvana by death at her own hands. This is a most cryptic line of thinking, in my view, but it's been said a long time ago that there is no one path to enlightenment. We all forge our own way, Travis. That being said..." The monk smiled again. "It would be hard, to say the least, for you to express a love as deep as the one you claim to have for your Esther if she has jumped from this mortal coil. As I am sure you know."

Travis nodded, slowly. It was the last thing he wanted to admit, but he knew the truth behind the monk's words. "She does not have the capacity to incite a revolution, at least on a global scale, in her lifetime," Travis said, "But it's as with Leonidas or Christ with her. She's willing to take her death and use it for the greater good, as opposed to allowing her life to be one lived in vain. Or as she said to me in her letter: death before dishonor." Travis shook his head, bemused at the absurd logic. With a smile, however, he realized that it was the same with Esther as it had always been. He shook his head and raised his hands, palms upward, in a shrug. "And I have no idea where she is, much less how to convince her of the insanity behind her thoughts. I just have to do something."

Daimyo smiled and then stood, motioning for Travis to follow him. "I may have a place where you can gather some ideas for how to approach this, Travis," Daimyo said softly, walking though the main sanctuary of the monastery and back out the front. The monk glanced both ways, first left, then right, with a sly grin. Seeing as there were no other tourists in sight, he seized Travis by the wrist and led him towards the very cave where Guru Rinpoche himself had spent three months in meditation. Travis started to protest, but Daimyo just grinned. "Of course you'd protest. It's true, the use of the cave is restricted to once a year by my fellow monks, but exceptions have been made before, Travis. And given the journey you plan to make, and its implications, there is no reason why you should be denied the use of the cave, even if to calm your spirit and offer clarity for a few breaths before you depart to find your beloved." The monk offered one more smile before nodding at the interior of the cave. "You have to let go of that pragmatic nature if you hope to have any level of success, Travis. You know it as well as I do. Make use, and then come to me in my quarters when you finish. Esther has a note here for you, as I said before."

Travis sighed heavily, and then relented. Who was he to argue matters of a holy site with one of the very ones that maintained it? Softly smiling, he made his way a bit into the cave, glancing around, feeling as guilty as a thief in the night. What if one of the other monks saw him and chastised him? His thoughts soon vanished as he found a flat place in the cave. He was sure it was far away from where the Guru himself had been situated, and that offered a small sense of comfort for Travis. At least he wasn't desecrating holy land. He glanced around once more before sitting in the spot, legs crossed, eyes straight ahead, towards the light at the beginning of the cave. He was used to noise and sound, if not from his environment then from the constant companion of his MP3 player in his ears. However, it was his feeling that the situation commanded silence, and so he closed his eyes slowly and thought, just for a few breaths, about what he was to do and how he was to do it.

The wind picked up slightly, feeling pleasant against the new whiskers on Travis's face, but beyond that, nothing happened. Not that Travis had expected anything, but the moment to clear his head had allowed him to set his pragmatic attitude aside and to look at the romanticism and the desperate bravery that his current missive required. He allowed himself to get swept up in the novelty of the moment, and his love for Esther. He seized on these emotions, holding them and melding them into something he could use to drive him to what needed to be done. Eyes snapping open, his face a stoic mask of emotions, and as he stood, he stalked back into the temple, ready for the next note and whatever key to the puzzle that it held.

Daimyo was waiting for him, but Travis gave him little chance to speak. "These are consequences that I've rendered, Daimyo, and it is my honor and my duty that calls me back to my Esther, to do whatever may come. You and this holy of holiest ground have offered me clarity, and for that, I thank you. However, I need you to hand me the note my Esther left here. I have precious little time, and I must learn where she has withdrawn to, and how I am to get there." The look in his eyes was full of excitement and anticipation, of one who knew with what feverish zealotry they must tackle a task.

Daimyo was mildly surprised at this sudden shift within Travis, but he let it pass. Drastic times were known to cause drastic shifts in people, and why should Travis be any different? The monk stepped forward and placed his hands on Travis's shoulders and grinned. "Patience, Travis. There are several things you need to consider. Firstly, did you think I was going to send you wandering into the wilderness of our Bhutan without the proper supplies and an inkling of a clue as to where you are headed? Such actions would be remiss even of a mere mortal, much less of someone who has taken the vows that I have taken. I have the note from your Esther. Sit." With that, Daimyo released Travis and walked quickly to a pack in the corner. With a smile, he dumped the leather satchel before the unsuspecting Travis, whose reaction of surprise registered a quick yelp. "There is everything you will need to survive this trek, Travis. Look it over while I find the note your Esther left with me for you. It shouldn't take me but a moment..." With that, Daimyo rummaged through one of the trunks that occupied the space at the foot of his bed.

As the monk shuffled around for the note, Travis took quick inventory of the items before him, snagging a few from his own packs before rummaging though. The leather pack was tossed aside, of no use despite a rustic look that Travis could find himself liking. His heavy Canopus pack would suit him better. The contents were quite extensive. A small quilt, waterproof matches, and a compass. A pocket knife. Several different maps, some trail maps, and some topographical maps. Packaged rations, and a few small containers of dried fruit. Signal flares. A tarp, to use in making a lean-to, when needed. And finally, at the very bottom, several packs of AA batteries. Travis looked at these with a confused expression, and Daimyo could only smile as he returned to his station before Travis, a white envelope clutched in his hand.

"You listen to music quite extensively, as Esther tells me," Daimyo said simply. "She brought those with her from the States because she knew they were the type that worked your device." Travis smiled warmly, enjoying the fact that she was still able to remember his needs and wants in her state. The pang of guilt was still there, but lessened, as his resolve had allowed him to push down some manner of his own regret for his actions in the last few days. Slowly, he spread the quilt before him and made the rest of the items into a bundle. Pulling all but the warmest of his clothes from his pack, Travis stuffed the improvised bundle in the top. The maps and batteries were stored in the pouch of the pack, for easy access, as Travis knew they would come to the most use. He offered a glance at his collection of little notes, deciding to pack them as well in a side pouch. Perhaps in the coldest hours of night they could provide a source of comfort to him, as well as a strong shot of will that would be needed to press on. He slowly gathered the rest of his belongings and haphazardly stuffed them in the leather satchel, almost laughing at the way they bulged from the top and along the side. He looked at Daimyo with a glare of apprehension. "Would it be okay if I left the rest here?" he asked slowly. "I really doubt I could haul all of this with me to...well, wherever I'm going."

Daimyo grinned and knelt in front of Travis, a playful smile never leaving his eyes. "I had figured you would need to, Travis. I will have your items delivered to your room at the hotel, although I doubt you will have much use for it on this trip. After all, I feel that you will be quite busy." Daimyo smiled again, and handed him the note. It was in the same plain white envelope, but given the weight, Travis could tell it contained nothing but her letter, unlike the last, which had contained passports and visas and the like. Therefore, it was much to his surprise when he opened it and removed a four-page letter. It was tri-folded, just as the last. This time, it was typeset, as if Esther was making sure he could read the words it contained. Travis offered a blank look to the monk, who shrugged. "I have not read it. It was not of my business. She must have written it before she left the States, or perhaps she brought her laptop with her. She could have used a personal computer here as well; the Internet seems to be quite popular among the youth of our nation." With that, Daimyo stood and walked towards the monastery in silence. The letter was for Travis alone; the monk would not muse about or interfere.

Travis looked at the unread letter like it was a bomb, ready to ignite in his hands at any instant. As much resolve as he had built, as much courage as he had told himself he had mustered in his few moments in the holy cave, the note in his hand had brought forth an angry sea of worry, roiling to face him with a swath of anger that could destroy nations. Esther's mental state was unstable, and Travis knew how this wreaked havoc on her human interactions. He had stared it down many a time before. He took a couple of deep breaths and paused, turning the letter over several times in his hand. This was not going to be easy; in fact, given her state beforehand, and her depressed musings from the previous letter, Travis was fully prepared to wince his way through her second entry as well. A few more breaths were taken, and Travis suddenly grew irritated at himself. She was out there, in the Bhutanese wilderness, waiting for him! Meanwhile, he had spent several precious seconds fretting over if he was going to get scolded at in her words. Of course he was! He'd been a fool, a moron, in the way he had acted towards her. What did he expect? The self-scolding seemed to do the trick. Travis turned the letter over in his hands once more and delicately started to unfold it in his hands. He planned on saving this one, just like the last one, and he wanted to make sure it was as intact as possible. There were four pages, Times New Roman font, single-spaced, and knowing Esther, grammatically correct. He could not help but smile at the last; his time spent teaching English had apparently rubbed off on her to the point that she was as obsessive about how she wrote as he was. As the setting sun poured through Daimyo's window, painting the crimson walls an even darker shade of red, Travis bathed in the abundance of light and slowly started reading the most recent in a seemingly never-ending line of tomes, all written from the hands of his one and beloved, Esther Sansui. Travis prepared himself. In a world filled with instant gratification and self-indulgence, it was simply amazing the simple power a little letter could hold, given, of course, whose hands it rested in. Sighing, he unfolded the letter and began to read.

CHAPTER 6

My beloved Travis,

Nine days ago, I left San Francisco for one of the last places we were truly happy together. I realize now I was a total fool for letting you let me walk away from what we had built together. I allowed you to push me away, I allowed what was ailing me to come between us in a way that I should have known, and should have been able to clamp down on. It was not what I wanted. Or needed, for that matter. I have now tasked you with the almost impossible task of convincing me that you can be the man I need, and can be the one and beloved I once knew. And with what little progress your actions have gained you, it has undoubtedly been painful for you. You've been forced to fight inch by inch for me as I've become more vulnerable than I can ever remember. In the end, our love will be stronger for it, but to the lowest circle of hell, it's hard. As it should be. If I were just to hand you what you wanted, like a spoiled child, there would be the fear in me of you reverting to the same overconfident, insensitive, overbearing egomaniac that you grew into at the end. I can't let him come back, but if you have any sense of fortitude about you, you can solve this puzzle, Travis, and you can help me reclaim what it is apparent we both miss.

Basically, I miss how we anchored one another. How we provided balance. How my whimsical dreams, in the beginning, were kept in balance by your pragmatic reality. How we could discuss and negotiate and compromise and in the end, we both were happy with the result. I will keep giving you chances to fix what you have wronged, even if you keep letting chance and chance go asunder, your true feelings and the emotions of my own heart be damned. I can't help it, Travis. As corny and as cliché as it sounds, you are what completes me, you are my center and balance, my hope and light, the soul of my song and the one dearest to my heart. I miss your love letters, I miss the flowers you incessantly bought for me, and so many that we ran out of vases. I miss it all. And I'll be damned if I go without it because of my foolish pride. I'll fight for you, I'll stand shoulder to shoulder to you, I'll take the lead when wisdom calls and I'll defer to you when you are wise beyond my experience.

Forgiveness is a trait I felt I lacked when I left the Bay Area, but with the help of Daimyo, I have found it in myself to provide a path of repentance for you. Now, Daimyo has lectured me on the lessons of unconditional forgiveness, but at the same time, I feel it important to put in safeguards to protect my heart against such abuse once again. You failed, Travis, and at such an astounding level that it makes me wonder if you can ever succeed again.

I hope you can. And, as they say in the movies, hope is a good thing. It's too bad life can't be a fairy tale like in the world we live in as part of the United States. No, Travis, there are harsh realities to our actions, and yet I still hope against hope that you don't have to face final judgment for yours.

Common sense tells me that you will fail, Travis—that you don't even need to bother trying. I'm sure your pragmatic self tells you that I'm just going to keep slipping further into this black pit of my soul, that you'll never be able to live down your deceit. I hope, for the first time in what seems like millennia, that you will allow such thoughts to dissipate, to fall by the wayside as you look for redemption. Can you set your damnable pride aside, my love? Can you overcome whatever may and restore a faith in me that I felt was, as Fitzgerald once said, "…as a boat against the current, borne back ceaselessly into the past?"

As you search for me, Travis, know I slip further into this madness. It is all controlling, all consuming, and I haven't the foggiest notion on how to pull away. I'm not sure what it is you will find when you come to save me; in fact, I often wonder if I know what I was the last fifteen years. I do know I sheltered myself from stones being tossed. I built a wall, an inner sanctum to defend myself from words and deeds that cut like a knife, and that I made sure you were inside this wall with me. I never imagined you'd turn the knife on me.

I know this is unfair to you, Travis, but at the same time, you abandoning me to fight these demons alone, when you say you "love" me, is wholly unfair in itself. Some kind of love, Travis, and yet you wonder why

I am bitter, even loathsome towards you? Well, here is your answer. You're the Benedict Arnold of my heart, and the Judas of my soul. Traitors on that level do not normally get a chance at redemption, Travis, and I am loath to think you should. Then again, why not?

Why not you, Travis? Why can it not be you that breaks the mold? Goes against the grain? There is a good and a bad in all of us, Travis. History hides the tale of how Benedict Arnold fought with valor for the Americans, before inter-squabbling made him a bitter and angry old man, and led him to try and commit treason. His actions cost the United States little; in fact, he died far away from any war effort in London in 1801. Yet so egregious were his actions that even the Brits despised him. I guess nobody likes a traitor.

As far as Judas goes? The man walked with the very son of God, performing miracles and winning souls for the kingdom along the way. We know he betrayed Jesus; this is irrefutable fact, from several sources. How and why are the subjects to debate. There are those who say he was taken by Satan and did it as a puppet. Can Judas be blamed for that? Then again, there are those who say Christ knew of the betrayal and allowed it to happen. Wouldn't that make He who is blameless to blame for the acts of betrayal and the very death of Judas? Is the price of Judas's blood on Christ's head? One account says he did it for weakness of money. That'd equate his sins to those of, oh, about six billion other common day homo sapiens. One theory even suggests that Christ instructed Judas to do it! If that is the case, does that not make Judas a martyr? Should we revere Judas for his traitorous actions instead of condemn him?

You see the issue here, Travis? Any excuse can be made to justify any line of action. But the facts remain. Benedict Arnold betrayed the self-proclaimed "Greatest Nation in History" and was left friendless to die in the bowels of London. And Judas? Judas betrayed perhaps the most perfect person to walk this planet, and for his sins, he died and is no doubt in some endless suffering. Excuses and explanations do not make their actions right. Wrong is wrong, betrayal is betrayal, and the sins unto the ones you love are indeed, still sins.

The difference between these two traitors and the one I love is that Benedict Arnold never apologized for his actions, and neither did

Judas. Arnold spent his last two decades embroiled in land deals and petty libel lawsuits in England; he died an unapologetic traitor, loathed by both sides. Judas took the 30 silver pieces he was awarded for surrendering Christ and, alone and destitute, hanged himself. He never apologized for his actions; in fact, his suicide seems to be more for self-pity than anything else.

The fact is, my Travis, that you are here, in Bhutan, reading this. You have remorse and regret for your actions, and you look to rectify for the wrongs, and to make them right again. Only time will tell if you are to have success or not. It takes a healthy spirit and a large dose of benevolence to forgive actions such as yours, and at the moment I am in possession of neither. Perhaps seeing you again will soften my stance, perhaps it will harden my resolve, perhaps it will force me to cower like a child or to lash out irrationally. I do not know what the future holds, Travis. All I know is that the present hurries on, and time is limited to do what is to be done, and what is to come.

I enjoyed the time and the thoughts shared here with Daimyo, as I am sure you have, but it is time for me to press forth. The maps Daimyo has given you are just rough outlines of where I am headed. One place we were never able to visit was Jigme Dorji National Park, along the Tibetan border. Ha! Tibet, sharing a border with Bhutan, the place where religious oppression and general unhappiness meets the happiest place in the world. God, Allah, Jehovah, Karma, the fates...whatever, must have had a sense of irony when that plan was hatched. Jigme Dorji National Park is a forty-three hundred square kilometers national park in the northwest corner of Bhutan. It is a six-hour journey from where you are now, yet once you arrive at the forests that outline this place of beauty, your journey has only begun.

Despite my mental and emotional shortcomings, you know well that, physically, I am as fit as one could hope for. Chalk it up to years of exercise and a careful monitor of every single thing I allowed to enter my body. Physically, I am more than ready for this journey, and I know quite intimately that your body will be able to handle the rigors of this little pleasure jaunt as well. The hiking, camping, and even climbing parts of this journey should pose little to no problem for you.

But be aware, Travis, there are several other perils. Cold, harsh, bitter weather awaits you, so please, dress warmly. The wildlife there, such as bears and tigers, are nothing to quarrel with either, so by all means, be prepared for such dangers. They are ruthless and wild in the most extreme sense, and will not hesitate to terminate your life force with extreme prejudice if they feel threatened or if you happen to venture into their territory. The sheer rock faces at the hills of the Himalayas are daunting in their own right, and you need to be prepared in every sense of the word if you are to challenge them. This is going to, without a doubt, be a life-altering experience for you, Travis, as I am sure it will be for me as well. I am as prepared as I will ever be, and it is my sincere hope that you are as well.

All the silly, foolhardy clichés we were force-fed in our formative years are being put to trial here, in the remote corners of the Earth. Can love truly conquer all? Is hope really a good thing? Does hope always spring eternal? From where I stand, love cuts deeper than any blade known, yet tucks tail and runs at the first sign of a struggle. Hope is a dangerous, deadly thing, and causes more grief than all seven of the deadly sins together, and, from what I can tell, is worthless. Absolutely worthless.

Just as a general guideline, you'll walk across roughly 500 acres, or close to 70 miles, to get to the basin that leads to the mountains. The terrain is rough and rocky, and I would recommend you arrange a rental vehicle to drive most of the distance through the mountains. Once you leave the forest, you'll be in a large, tundra-based basin, with several areas of permafrost that will lead you up a gradual incline to what I like to see as the footstep to the heavens.

There is another temple, known as Jomolhari, on the plateau, about 12,000 feet above sea level. It is the last temple before one begins the ascent up Mount Jomolhari, a mountain held in religious significance as well as being one of the few mountains that tower twenty-four thousand feet above the floor of the world. It is a breathtaking sight, Travis. Who knows? Maybe it will be the first sight we view together as our love and passion alights anew.

I don't mean to give you false hope, or promises of something I very well may not be able to deliver. But at the same token, I do not have it in me to crush your dreams. I don't want to stop your never-ending struggle against love, against hope, against space and time and everything we are and we are to be. If it's in the cards, and in my heart of hearts, you'll fix this, and we'll see what comes of your effort.

The hands of time and this expedition into the cold may thaw my being towards you, Travis. I know you are coming, and even still, come and come soon. I don't know what the coming hour holds, much less the coming days, but it may very well be that we find what was lost to us in the caves of the Himalayas. It all comes back to my previous question, my Travis: Will this be the finale of our story, or just an interesting footnote?

You always wanted to write, Travis, so here's your chance. Be the hero, take the fool's folly, and find me. The part of me that wants to live is still waiting for you, and hopefully by the time you show, it will be with an open mind and a forgiving heart. Until then, time still turns the pages. And there is precious, precious little time. So little of my light remains, and you are so incredibly far away. They make crude jokes about the great American Novel, but in a best case scenario, our story will be one that is unrivaled in the annals of time, and in the history of romance. And the worst case? Well, it will be something you see, and you will know at that moment what the worst case was.

I love you, and I ache to be with you every hour. I hope beyond hope I am ready to forgive when you are ready for your final repentance. I await you, Travis.With a heavy heart, and a hope that I can forgive myself, and in the process, the one I love so dear.

-Esther Sansui

CHAPTER 7

The letter was hard to read. Of this, there was no denying.

However, Travis had expected such a manic approach to her correspondence with him, in fact, given her condition; he would have been a fool to think otherwise. However, looking past her wordy rants and her willingness to flip flop as it pertained to her desire to live or die, as well as her wanting it to be him that rescued her, Travis could see the bud of hope blooming from her words and thoughts. In his mind, however, a battle was raging. Part of his thoughts remained pragmatic and reminded him with an incessant little voice that the mission had just as much a chance of success as it did of failure. The hopeless romantic within him said to throw himself, and caution, into the wind, to chase her to the bowels of Bhutan, and to find her, cradle her, and save her from herself, at whatever cost. The third voice, and one that Travis was loath to even acknowledge, was the pessimist. The pessimist came with an onslaught into his thoughts with a two-fronted attack. The first argument, and the one that was the most reasonable, was the matter of if she was already dead. What if Esther had managed to commit suicide and all that was left for Travis to find was a body and a shell of the love he had known? This attack he discarded almost as soon as it had attacked; it was Travis's duty to find her, dead or alive. Love commanded as much. Hope commanded as much. Everything he was and everything he hoped to be commanded as much. The second part of the attack was a selfish thought. Why should he go and clean up her mess? As much as the first and the second tied together, Travis would have never confessed to anyone how much he allowed the second thought to linger. It had been her mess, her drama, and by all standards and means, he was detached from her.

Travis shook the thought from his head, tears welling up in his eyes again. She would have never gone this far into her personal madness if not for his foolish actions. No, as much as her thoughts and actions, and even her illness, were hers, he had been such a massive part of her existence that he owed her that forfeit. He had allowed the dependence to grow, sheltering her when she needed it and protecting her from demons that neither knew how to fight. Therefore, it was his duty to make sure that she came out of this. How he was going to do it, he was not sure, but pessimism was knocked awry as Travis began preparing his mind for the journey that lay ahead.

Staring at Daimyo as he crossed back into the temple, Travis started thinking of what would be needed to complete the trip. "Daimyo, where could one rent a car here in Paro? A sturdy one, too; it seems that I am headed off into the wilds to find my beloved." Travis chuckled at the last; in his heart of hearts, he knew these were the words Daimyo was hoping to hear.

The monk grinned, receiving his answer in many more words than was expected. Esther had told the young monk of Travis's pragmatic nature and his art of understatement. With his words, Daimyo was now confident that Travis would be able to follow through with Esther's plan to whatever conclusion it came to. "There are so few available for rent from the reputable dealers, seeing as most visitors are not allowed to trek off alone. Your case is different, because your study visa allows you more leeway than most. For that reason, I think I will refer you to one of my contacts, a friend of mine named Rhek. We studied together in early school before I took up my vocation; and as he is a man of nature and a man of the world, I am assured he can find you a vehicle that will make your journey more passable, at the very least." The monk raised his brows, another thought coming to his mind. Travis stood befuddled as Daimyo started rummaging through the bottom of his chest, searching for something with a furor that betrayed his calm station as a monk. Soon, Travis heard a muffled "A-HA!" as the monk withdrew a silk cloth containing an unknown object from his chest.

Daimyo grinned broadly as he started to slowly unwrap the silken folds. With great drama, the final fold was pulled back, and within was a sheathed sword. It was a katana, made popular by the samurai of ancient Japan. Travis offered a grin of his own, but said nothing. Daimyo was saying enough as it is. "I don't want to send you off into the wilds without any protection, Travis. And seeing as firearms are few and far between here in Bhutan, well, I fear this is the best I can offer you in the way of protection. A word of caution, though." The monk's face hardened; for once, the kind features were hidden under a mask of worry. "This blade is simply to defend. It will not be of much use to you as far as hunting goes, and if you were to come across a large beast such as a bear or a tiger, it is best to flee, and with haste. Although, if you were to happen upon a creature that dangerous, it is fairly certain that it is almost too late." Daimyo grinned wryly at the horror-struck look on Travis's face. "Oh, don't worry. There are very few deaths per year in Bhutan by way of animal savagery, so I feel that you have little to be concerned with. But always be on your guard, Travis, and be careful." Daimyo suddenly stepped forward, and wrapped his arms around Travis in an awkward embrace. "I have no way of knowing what the result of your quest will be, dear Travis, but know this: It takes a big man to admit when he is wrong, and an even bigger one to try and right the mistakes he has wrought. May the spirits of our land watch and guide you as you step off into this journey." With that, Daimyo pulled away quickly, and left the room, almost as if he had never been there.

Travis stared for a long moment at the sheathed blade in his hands. Never in his wildest thoughts had he imagined he would ever draw a weapon, in self-defense or in anger, yet here he was with a lethal blade in his very clutches, prepared for it to be his erstwhile companion on this little journey. Rolling the sheathed blade over in his palms, Travis noted a small leather loop, out of place with the fine decorations of silver and satin that encrusted the sheath. It was a notch to run through his belt, keeping the blade at his side. Travis grinned, and quickly undid his belt, bringing it from the first loop to place the belt at his left side, easily accessible to his preferred hand. As he headed towards the door, to depart into his journey into the unknown, Travis caught a glimpse of himself in the mirror. Fully donned in some of his best hiking regalia, blade at his side, it was a harrowing collision of East and West. The best of both worlds, the most of what great minds from each side of the world had to offer, and yet materials in place for what was expected to be the worst of the human experience.

He could not help but marvel at the contrast. The thing that shocked him the most, however, was the contrast of himself that lay within. This was the very best of him, the most courageous, honorable, and noble of who he was and what he had to offer, yet it was brought on by the darkest sins and the saddest thoughts of the human existence. Travis realized, with a feeling akin to horror, that things had to get worse before they got better, and even more so, he never would have known he was capable of such good if he had not committed such acts of stupidity, had not been wrapped up in his own pride, had not left others to suffer his own arrogance.

With a slight sneer, the erstwhile hero straightened himself in the mirror and spoke. "So begins the long, hard road out of hell, it seems. No more excuses, no more selfish thoughts, no more whining about discomfort or leaving what is difficult to other. And if I want to have what is truly best for me, if I want to achieve heaven, or nirvana, or total peace, whatever it may be, it's high time I walked out this door and made my way to the heaven I so richly desire. And sometimes,

Travis..." A wry grin was offered to his own reflection as he slowly stepped away, heading into the chill air: "...sometimes, it's hell trying to get to heaven."

Renting the Jeep turned out to be the easiest task Travis had faced in his journey thus far. The vehicle's handler spoke perfect English, leaving Travis with the sneaking suspicion that he had been educated in the States. After debriefing the man on who he was, and where he was headed (with the details of why he was headed there spared, of course), Travis quickly settled into the ancient Jeep. Despite its rugged appearance, the vehicle was powerful, with the all-terrain tires showing little wear. It surprised Travis, and yet it didn't. Those forms of tires tended to wear quickly, but, he reasoned, there were few in the native population that would rely on such a vehicle to take them to a terrain as rugged as the one to which he was setting out. Coupled with the undeniable lack of tourists, there was little need for the Jeep's tires to be worn.

A couple of stops were made in Paro to gather up supplies in anticipation of his journey. Several bundles of dry firewood, some of it imported at a heavy cost, seeing as the rocky terrain left for little forest besides evergreen, which tended to be a softer, and therefore wetter wood. It was not a risk Travis was willing to take, being caught in wet, chilly conditions and unable to start a fire because his wood would not catch ablaze. The wood came at a premium, but it was one Travis was more than willing to pay. Several cases of bottled water, three fifty pound bags of rice (overkill, seeing as the vehicle would only be with him for half of his journey, but it was another case of Travis showing an overabundance of caution), and five of the fifteen gallon jugs of gasoline, as the thought of a refueling station in the Bhutanese wilderness was laughable.

And so there he sat, on the outskirts of Paro, as

another breathtaking dawn broke over the ancient city, his thoughts rumbling, realizing this was his last chance to bail, to walk away from the whole sordid mess before it slipped into a realm of which there was no second guessing, of which there was no walking away and letting a dead dog lie. He wasn't worried of traffic; this was the winter months and few people were willing to strike out from the safety of the city into the Himalayan wilderness. In the semi-charmed existence that he had enjoyed for his twenty-seven years, Travis could never think of a time where he was so afraid, so unwilling to do what was before him despite the fact that it had to be done. He could, however, think of troubles in his relationship with his beloved Esther; and although they had been few and far between, when they did happen, they stuck out in his mind. An epic instrumental of Clint Mansell started on his MP3 player just as "One of The Days" by Pink Floyd wrapped up, and Travis closed his eyes and allowed his thoughts to drift back, to the first tiff they had experienced.

It had taken almost a year, a year of banter and dates and handholding and hours spent talking and frank discussions before things moved to the next level. Never harsh words; neither were built for that, but, as with any man, Travis had needs, and while he was willing to wait on Esther, it was not something he was skilled at, despite his pragmatic nature. It wasn't that he felt as if he was being strung along; it was simply that his patience, like that of any man with the same biological needs, was wearing slightly thin. As it was with Esther, the step was taken on a whim, without warning, with results that, while surprising, Travis felt that Esther had been prepared for all along.

He had received a text as he was walking out of a criminal law class (strange for an elective, but Travis felt it would be a good thing to take if things got too rowdy at a pub one night). He had set Placebo's remake of the eighties pop classic "Running up That Hill" by Kate Bush as her text tone, and as the eerie chords and ghastly vocals emanated from his pocket, a grin crossed his face. Certain biological needs aside, the time he had spent courting Esther had been the highlight of his college experience, and while we wasn't exactly a braggart, he had let the few friends he had made on campus know that, yes, indeed, he was seeing her. Mick and Brian were two of those friends, and as the text tone went off, they both rolled their eyes and stalked off in the opposite direction, shouting playful banter as they went.

"Travis Saint Croix, nineteen eighty-four to two thousand and seven, died running to the whims of his girlfriend," Mick shouted. "We'll have that engraved on your headstone!"

"Or better yet, we'll put on it..." Brian followed up. Whatever Brian was suggesting was lost in the distance, although knowing Brian, Travis thought as he gave them an exaggerated wave, playing along with their banter, it was some of the more perverse acts one could mention in a eulogy.

Once they were safely in the distance, plans to go drinking that night extinguished, Travis pulled his phone from his pocket. Grinning, he selected a couple of buttons to read the message. As the message brought itself up onto the screen, his grin of elation soon turned to a frown, then to an outright look of worry. Normally, Esther's texts were long and poetic, or filled with quotes from some of their shared heroes of history, but this message was so blunt, stark and... un-Esther-esque that the first thought to come to Travis's mind was that something was deathly wrong. It read:
GET OVER HERE. RIGHT NOW.

As he read it for what seemed like the millionth time, Travis shoved his phone in his pocket, not bothering to respond to the text. Something was deathly wrong, and he had not the time to ask what. Frantically, he sprinted to the bike rack that held the ten-speed he had recently purchased, as some vague, subconscious desire to appease those so concerned with the environmental movement at San Francisco State. He kicked himself for such short sightedness now. The bad news was the bike was fairly new, not broken in, and given that Travis had barely ridden one since his childhood, his conditioning on the particular mode of transportation was not the best, to put it kindly.

The good news was her apartment was less than a mile away.

That, coupled with the fact he was carrying very little in the way of books, and Travis pushed off, pedaling with a fury that surprised even him. The path to her dorm on campus was flat, and at this time of the day, mercifully lacking a crowd. The short ride took less than three minutes, and as Travis dismounted the bike, he allowed the thing to roll forward, crashing noisily into the bushes as he sprinted towards the steps of the ancient rustic building. One of the aluminum wheels bent, and the bike was disabled.

Not that Travis cared. As he sprinted up the stairs, he discarded the backpack, the leather and books making a noisy bang against the concrete of the front stoop. Books slid from his backpack and scattered slightly, but he could not have cared less. Esther's building was an old one, and Travis was thankful that the common door was left unlocked by a lazy trustee of one of the many sororities that seemed commonplace on every college campus. Esther's room was on the third floor, at the end of a long hallway, on a floor that, oddly, was lacking tenants. Off-campus housing had become all the rage, and even though it was a trend that Travis had allowed himself to be caught up in, Esther was at San Francisco State on a scholarship, one that included her room and board. And while her mother had left a small inheritance when she passed, Esther lived on a shoestring budget, never over-indulging, never allowing herself to extend beyond a self-imposed weekly stipend. It only made sense that she would restrict herself to the ancient, and free, housing provided by the state funded university.

Travis sprinted down the hallway, soon realizing that, while he had been in her two room flat before, he had only been in the sitting area in the front, not the intimate privacy of her bedroom that lay beyond. As close as they had come, and as much as their courtship had been old fashioned, and patient, it was of little surprise that she had hidden the most intimate of her domains from him. Sliding to a stop at her door, Travis breathlessly grasped at the knob and twisted frantically. Nothing. The door would not budge. Fist clenched, Travis pounded on the wooden frame of the door, his fist a sledgehammer, thudding home the finality of the absolute panic that had risen in his being.

"Esther?" Travis called timidly, the tone of his voice a sharp

71

contrast to the fury of noise coming from his fists striking the door. No response.

"Esther?" Travis said again, louder, more urgent, unsure how to reconcile this real fear he was facing. No response. His response went beyond simple panic, into the full on terror and dread of the unknown, a sickening sense that left him beyond desperate. Irrationality set in, and Travis stepped back, planting a foot against the door with a violent kick, knocking it from its hinges, the door flying into the space of the outer room in a terrific, violent explosion of glass and splintered wood.

Travis stood at the entryway of her dorm, shocked, not willing to accept that he had actually kicked her door in. Shaking his head, Travis entered the apartment and looked around. There was no visible sign of her in the entry room, and for a split second, Travis worried that she was not there, that he had misunderstood the context of her message—or worse, some horrid, unknown fate had befallen her. Frantically, Travis pulled his cell phone from his pocket and re-opened the message. Staring at the screen, Travis read the same stark words from her over and over, as if he somehow stared long enough, their content would change, or a deeper meaning would come to him. Nothing changed. The screen simply stared back at him, reading:

GET OVER HERE. RIGHT NOW.

Travis slowly slid the phone into his pocket again, a growl of frustration rising from somewhere deep in his chest. She was not in the front room, this much was for certain. Shaking his head, Travis studied the door to the bedroom before him. A shaking hand went to the doorknob, jitters not only from fear, but also, for reasons he could not deduce, from excitement, from anticipation. He was in uncharted waters, untested territory, and the thought of what lay beyond had teased the more perverse parts of his mind for months now. Slowly, the knob turned in his hand, and Travis shoved the door open, breathless, terrified to see what awaited him.

Black. A color uncompromising in its starkness, as unchanging as the stones of the field and as dark as the very soul of man itself. It was the first thing Travis noticed when he opened the door. The black curtains made of a heavy drop cloth, dense, blocking out any light from the singular *outside window and dulling the appearance of amethyst-hued walls. Candles, close to two hundred, adorned any surface that would hold them, including each post of the heavy, oaken four post king bed that took up a goodly expanse of the room. Black silken draperies hung from the ceiling in a rough, four-post star pattern, adding to the dark, seductive quality of the room. Black silken sheets, no comforter, lay elegantly spread across the expanse of the mattress, and in the middle lay Esther. "It took you long enough, Travis," she breathed, her voice as bells chiming as a playful tone took her voice, despite the overall darkness of the room.*

Travis stood, bewildered, unsure what to say. Part of him wanted to lash out at her, not physically (as he could never strike her), but with words, sharpened to a fork with bad intentions, to let her know exactly what he thought of her little façade. However, a better part of him was enthralled. Most intimate experiences in college were rushed, drunken escapades, with little emotion and little flair for the dramatic. And while Travis was driven by the same needs as most men, he was different in the fact that he could appreciate the little nuances of a romantic episode. Not that he was emasculated or unwilling to play his part as the male in such an arrangement, as Travis was far from the type to cater to masochists. However, as with all things, Travis saw sex as an art, something beyond simple penetration. Playing the dominant and submissive roles were both an art form in their own right, and unlike most things in his life, Travis was not keen to play an average role in such matters. This side of him won out, and his voice was tempered, cool, as his right arm snaked behind him, shutting the door. "Things such as this cannot be rushed, sweet Esther," Travis deadpanned, brown eyes locked onto her.

Her response was coy, almost cooing, as she purred in his direction. "I fear you owe me a new door," she teased.

Travis smirked. "Is that the only thing you fear?"

Esther offered a soft smile. "There is much I fear, my Travis, yet those worries seem to vanish once I am in your presence."

Another smirk, followed by a raised brow. "So is that why you send ominous, vague messages? To send me into a frenzied rush into your presence?"

The smile never wavered, although Esther looked away for a

73

moment. *"You know it is not in my nature to be forward, Travis. Although, judging by the door, you seem able to play your role to perfection."*

Travis slowly paced to the side of the bed. *"Sit up,"* he commanded, and Esther rose, kneeling on the bed before him as he stood sideways. Her head bowed, eyes on the darkness of the sheets beneath her. A light breeze entered the room, blowing the dense curtains back, making the flames of a good number of the candles dance as a small amount of light filtered in from beyond the draperies. An artist's touch could not have made the scene more foreboding, or romantic.

Travis raised an arm, gently placing a finger under her chin. *"Look at me."* Travis said simply.

Esther did as she was commanded.

Travis offered a sideward glance, a strange grin playing at the corners of his mouth. He took a moment to admire what she was wearing. Three simple bands of black silk, covering all of the necessities yet leaving little to the imagination. It was, in a word, stunning. Of course, so was everything else about her. Part of him wanted to shout her down, to lash out for sending such a message, one that left him full of worry and dread. That part of him, however, was small, and fleeting, and quickly dismissed as he brought the icy stare of her blue eyes to meet the warmth of his brown ones. And sure enough, as his eyes were no doubt conveying a storm of emotions, so were hers. Anxiety, nervousness, and yet at the same time, passions—unbridled, uncased, and aimed at him. It was strange for Travis, in the world of quick exchanges and fleeting relationships, to have someone desire him so strongly. In doing so, it stirred up desires within him that he did not know existed. Not only to own, to claim, and to retain, but to coddle, to protect, and to honor. Travis stepped away from her, drinking in the emotion of the instance before walking to one of the bedposts. He gently blew out a candle. *"Once I make you mine, Esther, it is to be mine and only mine. No desires for another, no longings for a taste, a flavor of something different. Outside these walls, we are equal in the eyes of the world, but within our den of decadence, you belong to me. Completely."*

Esther slowly made her way to another corner of the bed and

blew out the candle that was perched precariously on the post. "Then I expect the same, Travis. I may belong to you, but you may not claim domain over another. What we do within our lair belongs to us and us alone. I am not a whore, nor am I a plaything to toss aside. I won't stand to being made into a harlot in the eyes of our comrades. Beyond that, yes, I belong to you and you alone." A smile played at her lips. "Now, are you intent on blowing out each of those candles?"

It was almost too much. Focus was hard enough to hold when one was driving the ancient roads of the wilderness of Bhutan, but when such thoughts occupied one's mind...well, Travis decided he needed to pay attention to the path ahead before he lost control of the vehicle and ended his journey before it started.

Travis squinted and stared up at the sky. The sun had moved quite a bit, and was making a mad dash to the west, leaving brilliant red and yellow streaks of fire as it parted company with the Bhutanese sky, headed, no doubt, for their adopted home of San Francisco. How long had he been sitting there? Travis shook his head, feeling a sudden chill. The Jeep was built to handle the rugged conditions but was far from airtight, and cold crept in from a hundred different directions. Travis opened the door and stepped out, ambling clumsily across the hard packed snow to the back of the truck. He coughed lightly as his lungs adjusted to the chill air, and reached for one of the red cans full of gasoline. Its contents were soon emptied into the gas tank and Travis took a section of hose he found in the back of the truck. The first section was run into the first of the four remaining cans, and then divided among all but the last. Duct tape provided an airtight seal, and a siphon system was set, so as the truck burned off fuel, the rest would be siphoned down into the gas tank. The last can was left for Rhek, who would be along in three days to retrieve his Jeep.

Travis hunkered back into the Jeep, plugging his iPod back into the cigarette lighter. It would be one of his last chances to give the device a full charge before he departed on foot, a chance bought by the fact that he had driven like a man possessed to reach the entrance of the park. In doing so, he had arrived too early, as the man Rhek had arranged to bring an alpaca to carry his supplies was still a day away. The wait irritated Travis, but was one of necessity. He could not carry his supplies alone, and while he knew he had to be patient, the thought that Esther was already dead left him mortified. "Ash to ash, dust to dust, fade to black..." he sang along with Metallica as he ambled up the hill before him.

CHAPTER 8

The sign before him was made of a far sturdier wood than the forest contained, and had been in place for well over half a century. It was stark in its appearance, warning:

Jigme Dorji National Park
Closed for the Season.
Death Awaits Those Who Would Venture in Alone.

Travis stared at the sign for the moment, squinting into the last traces of the sun. On the bottom of the sign was a manila envelope, partially covered with blown snow and hidden to anyone not looking for its existence. "TRAVIS" was scrawled onto the front, in Esther's handwriting, no doubt distorted by the chill weather he was encountering. The wind howled and screamed a thousand veiled threats at Bhutan's wayward traveler, each shriek more ominous than the last. Scowling, Travis ripped the envelope from the sign and ambled back to the Jeep.

Slamming the door shut, Travis was thankful for the heat as he pulled his snow-caked gloves from his hands and discarded them on the passenger seat. Hands still shaking, Travis opened the envelope and withdrew the pages within.

The first was a simple charcoal and parchment drawing, no doubt done by Esther's hand. Both beautiful and macabre in its appearance, it was a simple, shadowy view of Esther, below the very sign from whence the envelope hung, with the word DEATH darkened almost to the point of blurring. Travis shuddered at the ominous painting for a few breaths before grinning. The parchment, for what it was worth, was the closest he had been to Esther's touch in ages, and he was prone to enjoy it.

After several moments, Travis set the simplistic

artwork aside and reached inside the envelope to gather the other page. This was photo paper, and of a higher quality. The piece had been folded into fours, and only unfolded when it was time for it to be paired with the parchment within the envelope. With a wince, Travis realized what it was. A flyer, created by his hand, to call for the resignation of the dean of San Francisco State University. If there was any instance that could be pointed at as the catalyst for Travis's dramatic shift in character, and as the jumping off point for the demise of Travis and Esther's relationship, it was this. Travis turned it over slowly in his hands, deep in thought again, wondering how in the blue hell he had let his own ego ruin things…

Five of them sat, gathered in a rough semicircle around a fire on a remote section of beach in Half Moon Bay, about forty-five minutes south of San Francisco Proper. Travis had not been this incensed since his father's suggestion his blood reeked with cowardice. Well, perhaps not that poetically, but when it came to his father and their disagreements, it was easier to handle if Travis added his own wordy flourish to their quarrels. "The Dean. Of all people, of all parts of America, of all COLLEGES," Travis sneered, unhinged at the perceived misdeeds of Felix Jones.

Jones had been dean at San Francisco State for eleven years, and, unnoticed to all but a few, minority enrollment had dropped by sixty-seven percent in his tenure. San Francisco State was one of the few universities in the country that had fewer minority students than it did when Brown vs. Board of Education was handed down by the United States Supreme Court. In uber-liberal San Francisco, nobody thought such a thing was even possible. However, two students in a feminism class, Elizabeth Richardson and Nicole Brinson, had uncovered these facts, as well as the fact that minority students, especially African Americans, were rejected in favor of white counterparts at a rate of almost three to one. To top it all off, most of the white students chosen over their minority brethren were less qualified to attend.

Now, seeing as San Francisco was a well-known hotbed for progressive activists, it was no small wonder that this had not been noticed before. However, it was not the fact that such profiling existed that called this gathering to order. When confronted with the data and with a demand for answers, Felix Jones did what nobody expected: he grew defiant. "Regardless of test scores and grade point averages, Negro students simply do not have what it takes to survive in such a challenging academic environment," Jones had announced to a shocked assembly of student body leaders, university chairs, and political figures. The mayor had compared Jones to a terrorist. A state senator had pointed out George Wallace as an example. There was outcry for Jones to be terminated at the least, and, at alternate moments, castrated, hanged, and tarred and feathered. However, the hands of the Board of Trustees were tied. Jones, a former civil litigator, who, unknown to the University, had represented radical churches, the government of Somalia, and, in one instance, a pedophile set free on a technicality, in libel suits, had used his vast knowledge of litigation and legal contracts to insert a one hundred-million-dollar golden parachute for himself in case of termination. Even worse, the parachute applied whether he was terminated with or without cause, and only became void if Jones resigned. Facing a strapped budget, and with costs rising and tuition income falling, the University had no choice but to let Jones continue in his job while legal remedies were sought.

Travis was, to say the least, infuriated, and although he would never admit it to Esther, he had not been sleeping. A week's worth of stubble covered his face, his eyes sagged and were puffy, and he was irrational, tense, and unpleasant to be around. He paced in front of the group, back and forth, back and forth. The tension was thick—so thick, in fact, that you couldn't cut it with a machete. Travis growled, and slumped to the ground, crossing his legs and sitting, Indian style, to face the gathering. Interlocking his fingers, he twisted his hands back and forth for a minute before looking up at the group and offering a wry laugh.

"As we sit here, in as much mental turmoil as physically possible, or at least, as much as Felix Jones would like to see us in, the part that angers me is that there is nothing we can do about it." Fingers tapped against his chin, and then a hand ran across the length of his face

as he pressed on. "The sad part is, there is a lot to like in Felix Jones. Rare is the man, indeed, who stands for something and sticks to his guns, while ever so bluntly thumbing his face at authority. It's not who Felix Jones is that bothers me so much as this ideal he stands for. I hate this idea that black students have any less a right to an education that we do. I hate this idea that Felix Jones knows better than you and I do about who should attend here and who belongs somewhere else. He doesn't, but he is better at playing the game, at politicking, at getting exactly what it is he wants because he knows what it takes to get it, and that he's willing to have no moral code, no compass of what's right or wrong, in order to have things in the manner that they should not be. He's vilified us, in his own mind, to justify his wrongs, to make them into rights. We can't take him down with conventional methods; he's made sure that every 'i' was dotted and every 't' was crossed, he's closed every loophole, and in the eyes of the law, he's bulletproof." *Travis grinned, and let his words hang for a minute.*

Elizabeth and Nicole lit up at the same time.

"So you're saying…" *Elizabeth started.*

"…that we should look beyond the eye of the law?" *Nicole finished.*

The words saturated the thoughts of those present for a moment, and Travis grinned again. It was then that Esther decided to speak.

"Travis, you can't just break the law; you run the risk of getting suspended, kicked out of school, arrested…"

Travis jumped to his feet, his eyes a storm of emotions, anger rising in his voice as he spoke. "Esther, SHUT UP."

The unplanned outburst shocked those in attendance, leaving Elizabeth and Nicole half expecting Esther to fire back, to storm off. Instead, much to the chagrin of everyone present, Esther simply bowed her head and muttered a soft "Yes. Of course."

Travis never cracked a smile; in fact, if anything, his face hardened. His eyes burned with a fire that could lead him through the darkest moments of hell, lines forming on his face, turning his glare into an icy stare of determination. Travis stomped a few steps forward into the darkness, spreading his arms, palms facing forward, as he shouted into the night. "We won't be held down, and the likes of Felix Jones will not cast us aside. Things are not the way they used to be, and I will not stand idly by as we watch the devolution of our kind. What is this, nineteen fifty-seven? This university is ours, has always been ours, and if it means prison, if it means censure, lawsuit, or damage to my being, I will not stand idly by and allow every idea we held dear when we enrolled at SFS to be trodden down and debased into the mire, Esther. Civil disobedience is just the beginning of our war on Felix Jones." With that, Travis paced into the night, leaving a hurt and bewildered Esther to trail slowly in his formidable wake.

Travis pondered that day—the day he let the likes of Felix Jones ignite a blue, cold, bitter flame of hatred into his soul, an all-consuming flame that led him to scorn anyone he saw as trying to stand in his way, including the one he loved: Esther. What Felix Jones did angered him, still angered him to this moment, but given what he had built with his beloved, he should have used the bond with Esther to his advantage as opposed to allowing how he felt about matters outside his control to deconstruct what he had worked so hard to get. However, the thoughts back at the monastery came back to him, and, with fuel and daylight burning, Travis knew this was no time for shame.

The page was folded and stored in his pack. Travis kicked back, propping his feet on the dash as the MP3 player spewed forth "I'm Comin' Home" by City and Colour. He barely had time to set the alarm on his watch before his eyelids grew heavy, and he drifted off into what was, thankfully, a heavy, dreamless sleep.

CHAPTER 9

The hike into the snow started early, and, despite the gravity of his mission, Travis could not help but feel a tiny twinge of excitement, a sense of adventure, and a flicker of hope still springing eternal. This was, after all, an odyssey of sorts, and Travis was about to trek through a wilderness that was rarely explored. The thought alone was heady, almost too much to take in.

"Snow shoes would have been a wonderful investment," Travis muttered to himself as he broke a fresh trail through the drifts. The effect the wind had on the piles of white powder was astounding in places, building drifts in places close to ten feet high. Sometimes the snow was packed and hardened, and Travis would climb each little hill and descend into a snow-made gulley, a thousand different landscapes temporarily made by the frigid conditions. In other places, the drifts were nothing more than fresh powder, easy to sink into, and shifting in size as winds blew the snow to and fro. In some cases, Travis was still able to hike through the terrain, but in some instances he would detour around, or, on occasion, plow through the mountains of snow.

The base of the mountain was a five-day hike from where he had parked the Jeep, and Travis estimated it would take a solid week's trek through the park to where he was headed. In a pure physical sense, it allowed Travis to test the limits of his endurance, to see exactly how far he was willing (or able) to push the fibers of his physical being. A unique challenge, this, and one he was soon relishing. However, the downside was that Travis was left alone, moody and introspective, with his own thoughts, and the weights of his own lies and sins. He dared not use his MP3 player; the device had a limited battery life, and there was no telling when he would reach a point where he could charge it again. If he ever did, he told himself once, before pushing away such dark thoughts with a mental shove of desperation.

Refocusing, Travis descended another hill of snow onto an unexpected surprise: a camp, of sorts. There was a small lean-to, facing downwind, as to protect the meager belongings of whoever resided within. A fire had been burning, and recently, as displayed by the small pile of ash, aglow with embers as the evening sun began its lazy descent behind the Himalayas in the distance.

Travis took in the sad little scene with morbid fascination. Who in the blue blazes would be living in the very depths of this frozen, wintry hell? Not just living, but surviving, and functioning of their own accord? It was almost as stumbling into someone's house, uninvited, and being afforded a very personal, and very painful look, into their own life. On the same token, however, this was Bhutan, home of little outside invasion and even less scenes such as this. After all, the Happiest Nation on Earth had little to offer to scenes of despair and to scenes of a desperate mind.

Travis stood for several minutes, unsure what to do, until shaking his head and rousing himself from a haze of thought. He whistled a loud, shrill whistle that was absorbed by the adjoining snow banks, and, at least initially, offered no response from within the camp. Travis stood and waited before offering another whistle, a low, mournful sound that was in sharp contrast to the one before. Something stirred from within the lean-to, and Travis was soon faced with a lithe, tall, androgynous young man. At least Travis thought it was a young man. Standing a wiry six foot three, and of weight of about one hundred and forty pounds, so hollowed out was this young man that Travis considered for a moment that he may have a translucent quality to him. The lad was adorned in white furs of some undeterminable animal species, perhaps a snow fox, or even a polar bear. The cut of the cloth was quite unlike anything Travis had seen in Bhutan, and this led him to deduce that the young man was not a local. A closer study revealed a rounded face, with high cheekbones, and eyes of deep blue. His hair had been dyed blonde at one point, but an undetermined amount of time had faded the coloring, leaving it with heavy specks of brown. Slavic was the first thought that came to mind, but Travis was leaning towards Nordic when the lad spoke, letting loose a high-pitched torrent of what was undeniably Russian.

Travis caught a few wisps of what was spewing forth. Back in high school, there had been a foreign exchange student, Vlad. The poor boy had been plucked from a former Soviet Bloc state when his father had turned state's evidence in a spy case. Arms were twisted, hands shaken, threats made, and the father, a scientist, had been offered immunity and a permanent visa in exchange for testimony against a rogue fringe group of Chechen rebels that were bent on terrorizing the United States. Vlad had been a swarthy sort, and took to American football quickly. Travis had been a captain of the defense his senior year, and had took it upon himself to explain the nuances of the game, insomuch as he could between the boy's torrent outbursts of violence, filled with Russian expletives. In some of his calmer moments, and when able to suppress a laugh, Travis had exerted the meanings of some of the more colorful phrases from the boy, a few of which were being tossed his way at the moment by a waif of a man that had absolutely no business in the Bhutanese wilderness.

Upon being called something along the lines of a goat fornicator for what seemed like the thousandth time, Travis burst out in a fit of uncontrolled laughter. He had not intended to, and as his body roiled and shook with misplaced screeches of a jovial man, the Russian youth stopped his torrent of profanities and looked at him as if he had sprouted a second head. Travis, for his part, tried gamely to stop laughing, but his body would simply not cooperate. It was as if his body had been seized by depression for too long, and was forcing him to remember that, yes, he was still human, and that there was still much in the universe to laugh about, whether he wanted to or not.

Finally, the lad tilted his head to the side and proclaimed, in heavily accented English: "Do you make it a habit of wandering into a foreboding wilderness and mocking those that wish to die?" The laughing stopped, and Travis returned the boy's stare with an inquisitive one of his own. Two things had caught his attention. One, despite the heavy accent, the syntax and choice of words were of a highly intelligent youth, one that had studied the language to the point of perfection, accent aside. Secondly, the word death had rung through the air, carrying all of the heavy weight of the gong, dark and foreboding in its haunting, single note melody.

"Too much death," Travis muttered to himself. He was sick of hearing about it, sick of thinking about it, sick of discussing it. And yet, in what was supposed to be this location of eternal happiness, the Reaper kept making his presence known to him, pervading his very existence with a common theme that no man wished to carry as a burden. He shook his head and sighed.

"I am not here to mock anyone. In fact, the thoughts and actions of those around me mock who I thought I was." Head still shaking, Travis extended a hand.

"Travis Saint Croix, from the United States, by way of San Francisco. I've wandered into this wilderness to fix a mistake that I am unsure can be fixed. And what brings you into this white hell? Surely you kid me when you say you come here to die?" Travis stared at the youth, hoping against hope that the wording had been a joke, yet knowing in his heart of hearts that the lad had been deathly serious when he said what he said. The tone, the inflection, the defeated body language. He had seen it a thousand times in his beloved, yet it had taken

85

until now for Travis to realize that his Esther had been living a very real form of torture.

The youth offered a limp, ungloved hand, and Travis had to wince at the very real signs of blackened frostbite on the limb. "Zvaid Stalin. I carry the names of two Russian revolutionaries, yet I have all the backbone of a jellyfish." It was a weak attempt at a joke, and yet Travis managed a smile. The small gesture seemed to warm the lad, and he continued to speak, making no move to pull his hand away. "Mother Russia is my home, and I am here by way of a city known as Irkutsk. Perhaps you are familiar with it?" Travis shook his head, offering a negative response while allowing the lad to speak. "Well, my hometown sets within a short distance of the Mongolian border, as a part of the frozen tundra of Siberia. Just a little over three thousand kilometers from here. San Francisco, you say?" Zvaid's eyes perked up, and he allowed himself what Travis could only assume was his first meaningful smile in years.

Zvaid's eyes clouded with shame and despair, and Travis could almost feel the desperation, the hopelessness roll off the man. He turned away quickly, although Travis could see tears welling up in his eyes. "I've come here for, as we say in Mother Russia, a 'Каникула смерти.' It's what you folks in America would call a death vacation."

Travis's eyes opened wide at such a suggestion. "You mean to tell me you've come here…" His voice trailed off, unable to confront suicide again, in another grotesque form.

Zvaid brought his gaze back, shaking his head at what Travis implied. "You are thinking self-destruction? Typical, from an American. You are a queer folk, one that tends to glorify the destruction of self through the indulgence of sex and drugs and self-pity. No, I am here, of sound mind and of my own volition, to die of AIDS. I figure that if I am going to go anyway, I am going out on my terms, my style, my way."

The old Sinatra song popped into his head and for a

fleeting moment Travis was sidetracked, pondering why he had not put it on his MP3 player. Some kind of cliché-based thing that prohibited it, or something. He shook his head. "But why would you die alone, in the Bhutanese wilderness, as opposed to at home, surrounded by family? Or by your friends? Perhaps a…" Travis stopped, putting the connection of his appearance and his affliction. "Perhaps a lover?"

Zvaid smirked before raising a brow. "A lover? No, my friend, I fear that I could never be happy with just one 'lover.'" The youth sighed, and let out a self-deprecating laugh. Eyes skyward, Zvaid refused to look at Travis as he spoke. The verse had been memorized, dwelt over, and in reality, Zvaid could not have found a way out of the consequences held therein. Call it the Catholic guilt of his forefathers, call it the internal self-loathing of a childhood, but the youth had found a scapegoat. Himself. "Leviticus, the twentieth chapter and the thirteenth verse: 'If a man lies with a man as one lies with a woman, both of them have done what is detestable. They must be put to death; their blood will be on their own heads.' Leviticus, the eighteenth chapter and the twenty-second verse: 'Do not lie with a man as one lies with a woman; that is detestable.' Now, do I believe that some Old Testament nonsense that was wiped from record from Gentiles by Christ is the reason I am dying? Of course not. But, my friend, there is something to be said for gluttony." With that, Zvaid shook his head, disgusted not by the bend of his carnal desires, but by the sheer overindulgence of them.

Travis smirked, slowly shaking his head. Blunt, brutal honesty would drive the fragile eggshells of an already warped mind past the point of insanity in this instance, and he knew he would have to choose his words wisely, lest there be more blood on his head. Brow raised, a wry grin on his face, he turned to face the youth once more. "I never knew gluttony to be an unforgivable sin, in regards to either food or sexual partners, regardless of sex. And by sex I mean male or female, not the act itself. No double entendre intended." Laughing at his own joke, Travis approached the youth, nodding at the tent. "So you plan on staying in some of the more hellish conditions known to mankind until you simply fade away into nothingness?

Zvaid shrugged. "Why not? While Mother Russia has a form of universal health care, much better than whatever it is you Americans have, it seems that in a country as conservative as mine, one is looked down upon for enjoying the homosexual side of things. Some doctors outright refused to see me. Others would play a shell game, where I would make an appointment and for some reason or another, I would always have it cancelled, or delayed, or referred to another practitioner. Sad, isn't it? Per capita, we have more doctors and health care providers than any other country, yet I could not get these fine doctors to provide me with the treatments that could prolong my life, due to some age-old homophobic, provincial prejudice. That, my newfound friend, is where you Yanks have the upper hand. At least you have laws to protect you from discrimination. In Russia, if they can find a reason to practice their hate, they will. Hate, beliefs, fear, you name it. Would you care for something to eat? I have plenty, and this may be the last time I have someone to dine with." Zvaid nodded towards the fire. "It's a bit primitive, but it will fill your belly."

Travis nodded, grimly. "As long as I am not being an imposition, I would be more than happy to dine with you. What is on the menu?"

Zvaid grinned. "I'm the one dying, and yet your face is grimmer than mine. Well, then, we have a couple of options. Seasoned rice, or perhaps some of the meat of a Takin. This old brute was a solitary male, destined to wither away and die in the coldest portion of this white hell, just as myself. I ended his misery." Zvaid nodded towards a rifle. "Granted, violent games of sport do not fit your stereotypes of gays, but in

Russia, you do what it requires to feed yourself. I only moved to the city after I found out what I was. Before that, it was the countryside, where we grew our own food and killed what we could not grow."

Travis paused. The Takin, as he knew from his previous research trip, was the national animal of Bhutan, one held in high spiritual regard, and rumored to only exist in the tiny, landlocked nation. "Mythology holds that to eat a Takin is bad luck." Travis grinned. "That being said, I am not one to let old wives' tales dictate to me what it is I am to eat. Besides, if legend holds true, and my mission fails, or I am wounded because of this foolish choice, what am I going to do, kill you? It's not as if you shoved the meat down my throat…" Travis realized too late the damage his words would cause, and he shook his head, as if he was not able to believe he had said such a thing. "Zvaid, I am sorry," he stammered, unable to look his newfound comrade in the face.

The Russian youth stared Travis in the face for a long, singular moment. It was as if the Reaper himself had crept into the conversation, and was holding pause long enough to make Travis wonder if he had shoved another over the edge. Slowly, Zvaid started laughing, growing and swelling in volume until it reached a full-blown cackle—light and wheezy, given his health. His eyes were watering; tears froze almost instantly to his gaunt, thin face. Travis simply gawked as Zvaid tried to compose himself. "I am sorry, my new friend, the look on your face was priceless. Not to mention the perverted little image that came to mind when you mentioned shoving meat down your throat. Oh my!" Zvaid offered, giving his best George Takei impression, which was mediocre at best. "Look, Travis, I spent enough time of my life being hurt and ashamed by the comments those made about my death. Family. Doctors. Those I thought to be friends. If here, in the Bhutanese wilderness, listening to my own death knell as it moans against the trees, I can't find humor in what is said by someone who did not judge me on first glance, then I have no right to wish for another breath from whatever forces it is that control the universe, the sun and the stars, the rhythm of earth, wind, and sky. Come, let us feast."

CHAPTER 10

Human contact, genuine warmth, and friendship were the last things Travis felt he deserved on this little journey into his own personal hell. But despite the fact that he was preparing to stare down demons that not even he knew he needed to face, Travis could not help enjoying himself in Zvaid's company. The youth was brash, funny, coarse, crude, and yet a warm, gentle soul, one that was not expected in this hellish corner of frozen wasteland, yet well received. They feasted on Takin and rice, and while the creature's predisposition to eat salt made the meat taste over-seasoned, with rice and the surprise of wine, Travis gorged himself and shared many stories with the youth. When he told of the rebellion at San Francisco State, Zvaid's eyes danced and showed the look of a patriot that would have stood up to a raging wolf for the sake of the equality that Travis clumsily sat out to provide. When he spoke of his father, Zvaid listened with a pointed interest and offered his limited insight on handling parental affairs. As with most folks from the country, they had led a simple, straightforward life, Orthodox of some faith or another, and had little understanding and no tolerance for Zvaid's yearnings for those of his sex. They spoke of the history of the world, of the great triumphs of man, and the great downfalls of those with enough greed to see the lesser wither and die away. And when Travis told the youth the story of Esther, and what he sought to do, Zvaid cried, and offered kind words as Travis did the same, baring his soul in the wilderness to a stranger he would never see again. It was therapeutic, and Travis told himself this was the last of tears he would shed until Esther was in his arms once again. The midnight hour found them lounged by the fireside, wine in hand, on the barren earth of the lean-to, slightly inebriated, stuffed, and warmed by the flames of the small fire.

After a long silence, Zvaid spoke first. "I guess if one was to pick a time to pass from this old world, the here and now would be perfect. An old doomsayer preached to me once about the last and evil days of the world." He coughed, a fit that was prolonged, only passing with a long, gurgled pull on the wine. "He was right, Travis, but not for the reasons he thought. There is a God, and I am sure he has issue with what I chose to be, but trust me, it's not my choice to embrace the love that dare not speak its name that has us on the brink of Armageddon. No, men war over tiny sandboxes in God forsaken wastelands in the Middle East, spending billions of their generated dollars to depose and install oligarchs that know little of what their people truly want. We all run out to placate a minority, any minority, simply because we notice that they are, in fact, a minority. The last thing we notice is true beauty, in all of its forms, and the first thing we look at is skin color, religious claimants, and the like. People seem so eager to be the judge against what they deem wrong. It's sad, really. Providence and, on a lesser scale, evolution and the maturation of our species has allowed us the ability to reason, and yet, for some reason, we are in such a hurry to devolve. It's as with you. Granted, what you did is disgusting, yet at the same time, you see your mistake, filthy in your sin, so to speak, and you seek to rectify it by whatever means necessary. It's a rare quality in someone nowadays: nobility. Cling to it. As for me?" Zvaid looked at his blackened hand and grinned, using the other to take another pull on the wine. "I freely take my punishment for my sins. AIDS cannot be fixed. I grin and bear it, as you would say, and I prepare for that long walk into death."

Travis sipped his glass and stared into the dancing flames for a long second. Fire: it warmed you, and within the depths of white and orange, Travis could see destinies fulfilled and destinies yet to be conquered. "Yet some of our destiny is in our hands, friend. I cannot fail mine. I sat here for a good piece this eve and questioned your desire to die, and yet, if I find Esther and she's gone, or worse yet, I never find her…" Travis paused, and took a sip. "Well, I would be lying if I said I did not consider the same thing you are. I sit here, and wish I could dissuade you from this death mission of yours, and yet I know if try, I will be complicit in a lie that I keep telling myself. Sometimes, life isn't worth living."

Zvaid raised a hand to stop him. "Wrong, comrade. Wrong. Life is always worth living, even a fading, withered existence in the Bhutanese wilderness. If you find your beloved, as I pray you will, then you have the rest of your lives to live, to hold, to help, and to love. And if you lose her? Well, it's a white blank page, Travis. You can write a quick, short sonnet that brings what you had to a roaring finality, or you can decide what to be, and go be it. The brightest flame burns quickest, Travis, and your flame may not be ready to die, regardless of what Esther chooses to do. Sometimes, we wallow in the muck before we crawl out and move forth. Sometimes darkness is hidden in the light. Don't take this philosophy lightly, nor my prayers. It's the first prayers I have offered in ages. Now, shall we turn in?" Zvaid laughed at Travis's hesitation, rolling his eyes lightly. "I'm not going to try and seduce you simply because we share a lean-to. As ruggedly handsome as you are, I would not wish this infectious bile upon anyone and besides, something tells me if I tried, it would be a fight that I lost, and rather handily. Not that the thought hasn't crossed my mind. Oh my!" Zvaid let out a loud belch, one that very much challenged the feminist swaying he exuded, before bundling down and rolling over. "Goodnight, my comrade. To the stars…" Whatever poetic thought that was forthcoming was forever lost to the night as Zvaid started snoring.

Travis sat, staring into the smoldering ashes of the fire,

trying not to burst out laughing at what Zvaid had just said. A thousand stinging retorts were on the tip of his tongue, but there was no need to address the back of a sleeping man. Travis simply shook his head, smiling, before adding wood to the fire, and settling down to sleep.

Felix Jones grinned. The pot had been stirred, the proverbial hornet's nests kicked, and he was in rare form. Unable to distinguish himself in the mainstream world, he had become a rallying point, a hero to those extreme elements that, for some reason or another, clung to the notion that some were better than others, and that by separating the races, equality through discrimination could be achieved. Standing at the mike, he railed on.

"America has gone soft! It seems that everybody wants a trophy for participating in life, so that we can all go home and pat each other on the back and coo and coddle one another and somehow convince ourselves that a mind that is less equal to another is deserving of the same opportunity simply because they are black." Jones sounded good on the stump, Travis admitted to himself, and if not for the extremist views he held, he could have held a wonderful career in politics. The thought of Hitler and politics came to mind, and Travis could not shake the similarities. Glancing over at the soundstage where a friend stood, one that Travis had cajoled into taking the sound gig for Jones's rally, Travis nodded to give the go ahead. It was time. If former generations had rallied behind leaders and protested against Vietnam and inequality behind great leaders, then it was time for Generation X to take the same role. Some leaders were born great, and some had greatness thrust on them. As for Travis? He was going to reach out and seize greatness himself.

The audio tech hit a switch, and Jones's mike went dead. There was a long silence, for ten seconds or so, and Jones screamed at the soundman, who proceeded to twist knobs on the soundboard and looked confused, playing his part to perfection. Suddenly, he looked down, and grinning, he pushed a button.

Disturbed's cover of the Genesis hit "Land of Confusion" hit on the public announce, and for a second, the crowd, a great majority being hecklers who wanted to see Jones deposed, milled around in noisy confusion. Travis smirked, took a deep breath, and stepped through the curtain. Black jeans with a black T-shirt, a black beret topping the ensemble and giving Travis an almost sinister, militant look. There was a microphone in his hand, and after allowing the music to pound on for a few notes, he slowly raised the microphone to his mouth. Seeing he had the attention of the gathering, Travis allowed a look of incredulity to come across his features as he opened his mouth. "Now, I'm not the smartest crayon in the box, by any means, but am I wrong in assuming that this sort of racism was condoned as unneeded, reckless, and, for the most part, stupid almost fifty years ago?" Travis cocked his head to one side in mock contemplation, and stroked at a goatee that did not exist on his chin. "Or have I jumped in a time machine and traveled back to the past? No, no, no, that can't be it, because there are both Caucasians and Negroes here." The word Negroes was accented with a heavy dose of sarcasm as Travis stared holes through Jones. Travis pointed at a gentleman in the first row. "I mean, Professor Williams is quite black, and quite qualified, and surely not the victim of these loathsome conspiracy theories about the softness of America that you sit here and spin, vile invective that you put out as truth. Or how about Markus James, he of professional football fame?" Travis pointed at a man in the rafters. "One of our most famous alums, and a man who has donated close to a million dollars in the past three years to the humanities departments here at San Francisco State. How come his money isn't too black for you? I mean, wouldn't taking his scholarship donations be paramount to taking lesser money? Or since his money is the right shade of green, that makes it okay." The crowd quickly saw what this was, and started laughing and cheering. As the appreciation grew, Travis soaked it in, allowing it to build to a dull roar before turning and staring straight at Jones. Finger pointed, he spoke again. "You are a disgusting man, a shell of a bygone, tragic era in our history, and I'll be damned if anyone is not admitted to this school because you have a xenophobic fear of people of a different race." Travis sat again; legs folded beneath him, Indian style, on the stage and sneered. "And I challenge anyone to move me from this stage. I'll remain here until this man resigns."

Jones stared at Travis, flabbergasted for a moment. He had expected opposition, sure, but not such that was so violent and so brash. He took a step towards Travis, and then stopped. There was a look in Travis's eyes that gave the Dean pause. For a moment, for one glorious moment, he froze, realizing that the crowd was buying every point Travis had made. He was now a rallying point, and there was not a single move Jones could make that would be the right move. Arrogance won over, and Jones almost scowled as he took the mike. "You forget something, punk. This is MY gathering and MY assembly, and you are now trespassing on University property," Jones snapped, and two uniformed members of the campus police stepped forward, both watching Travis with a wary eye.

Travis moved. "I'm not moving, clown shoes. I've cast the pearls of truth before you, and it's your decision to still wallow in the mud. But remember this. I'll win."

The university police stepped forward, bringing themselves to a stop only when they were behind Travis. They stood, rigid for a moment, before Bobby, a friend made during the second year of Lit, whispered out of the corner of his mouth: "Travis, trust me, we're with you, but we have jobs to protect. You know I take my classes for free because I am employed here."

Travis knew that allies were at a premium in this instance, so he started looking for a way out. In a book he had read, one of the characters had managed to surrender without a struggle, while making a scene, and Travis decided it could work for him as well. Standing, he threw the mike at Jones's feet and started shouting. "I guess David Duke and James Earl Ray can be visiting professors next semester! Are they going to start issuing white hoods and Nazi armbands at freshman orientation?" He shouted on and on for a few seconds, all the while sliding his hands softly behind his back so that Bobby and his fellow officer could cuff him without a scene. It was a small gesture, but one that would come to benefit him later on.

CHAPTER 11

This was not the first time Travis's own shouts had stirred him from slumber. It had been Esther's primary complaint from their relationship—how violent and aggressive his patterns of sleep had been. Pillows and blankets strewn about, shouting, screaming, tossing and turning, and even thrown punches were the norm for his nightly excursions. In these moments, it took Travis a moment to regain himself from the reality his dreams had produced, and even in the Bhutanese wilderness, this was no exception. He was covered in snow and chilled before he realized where he was, and that Felix Jones was more than ten thousand miles away.

Travis shook the fog of sleep from his mind and rolled back towards the fire pit. The heat source had burned back down to embers, and he spent a moment gathering his thoughts before building the fire back up. He was simply too cold to regain sleep, and as the first streaks of dawn met the star riddled sky, Travis knew sleep would be impossible. Glancing at his watch, he realized he had slept close to seven hours, so in that regard the timing of his dreams was impeccable. Pulling his knees to his chest, shivering as the fire roared back to life, Travis slipped his headphones on and flipped through the tracks before settling on a playlist filled with nothing but classical music. There were the greats, such as Bach and Mozart, as well as some sprinklings of modern composers such as James Horner and Michael Kamen. The wordless void of the arrangements allowed Travis to interpret them as he would, and he marveled at how he always heard something new, something different, regardless of how many times he had heard the song.

It was in this state that Zvaid found him when he rose,

physically exhausted from the toil the disease was taking on his body, despite the long hours of hard sleep. Shaking the fog from his eyes, he grinned at Travis, a rather weak attempt given his physical state. "To paraphrase you Americans, a ruble for your thoughts?"

Travis smirked. "They're not worth that much," he started, removing his headphones. "Besides, as you learned last night, my thoughts are rather singular, although I have spared a few minutes for your dilemma this morning. I think you should head home, Zvaid. Regardless of the sins of any man, woman, or child, they deserve to die on their own soil, surrounded by the friends and family that love them. And well, if you do not have friends and family, at least you have the soil of your forefathers. This, I must add, has to be more inviting than this winter wonder land of Bhutan, the beauty of the white death be damned." Travis smirked and picked up a handful of the snow. "Besides, it's not the tourist season."

Zvaid sat for a moment, taking in Travis's words. Slowly he stood, and scattered the ashes from the fire they had burned the previous night. "Travis, I cannot promise you that I will return to Russia." A weak smile followed. "But I will at least consider it. I still have a few weeks before I would die, and this…" Zvaid held up the frostbitten hand. "Well, there is no fear of gangrene in such cold conditions, and I have kept the rest of my body fairly safe. So I take it by your words and actions that you will be departing today?"

Travis stared at the dead limb with morbid curiosity, but let it pass. Standing, Travis let out a long, exasperated sigh. There was no sense in debating it with Zvaid; it was not his fight to fight, and he sensed the decision was made long ago. The mere fact that Zvaid had placated Travis's concerns by giving them consideration showed just how much the youth had appreciated his companionship. "Very well then. And yes, today is the day that I leave you. Just as you have your own sins to atone for, I must go and face mine. Hopefully…"

Travis stared into the depths of the Bhutanese forest and offered a sad little smile. "Hopefully, penance awaits me."

The cave was cold, and damp. *The Cave of Winds*, Esther had christened it. It was little more than a hollowed out chamber, deep in the bedrock, three yards high and about 20 yards deep. She had considered calling it the Death Chamber, but seeing as death was not a certain thing, she relented, allowing for the far more poetic name. The name suited the cavern as well, as fierce winds whipped through the opening, hollowing out channels in the rock. At times, the sounds of millions of years of Mother Nature's work were beautiful, serene, and peaceful. At others, when the black wind howled and pushed at the mountain with a desperate desire to destroy what could not be destroyed, the sounds were hollow, foreboding, and disenchanting.

It was here that Esther built up a small fire, the channels in the rock ventilating her small fire, preventing the smoke from choking the life from her lungs. As she worked, she pondered a small step out, but relented. Unbeknownst to her, a few climbers, and a few locals, had spotted her on occasion, and while nobody was sure she was there, rumors of a white ghost maiden had started in local lore, and such rumors, if substantiated, would lead to a search. Although she had no knowledge of the rumors, she was not naïve enough to think she could go on living (or dying, she thought) unnoticed if she left herself out in the open.

Next to the fire, Esther hummed a soft tune, one written on a guitar, as soft and warm as the tropic air of the Caribbean. The music kept her warm, at least in her own mind, as she argued back and forth with herself, slowly rolling a cyanide capsule in her right hand. Frowning, she put the capsule back in its case, and sank into a sitting position.

Not yet, she determined. She would give Travis a few

more days. He would find her.

At least, she hoped he would.

The rest of Travis's morning was spent helping Zvaid gather more wood, leaving the youth with an ample enough store to last him through three winters. They boiled water, leaving the lad with a purified supply, and somehow Travis was shoe horned into helping with a small bit of cleaning and laundry, using melted snow to clean things the best they could. Finally, neither could delay what both knew was coming, and it was with a slow apprehension that Travis gathered his supplies.

Neither was comfortable with long goodbyes, but once Travis was situated, he gave the youth a sidelong glance before a quick hug. They disengaged quickly, and Travis said goodbye as he turned to walk deeper into the Bhutanese wilderness.

"Travis?" Zvaid shouted once he had walked about fifty yards.

"Yes, Zvaid?" Travis answered, turning on one heel to face his friend, one more time.

Zvaid grinned. "I hope you find her."

Travis offered a wry smirk. "Thanks. I hope you find yourself, my friend."

CHAPTER 12

Travis was astounded at how a day could seem like a lifetime. He started at a brisk trot, which slowed to a walk, which slowed eventually to a lethargic pace. The map was leading him to Esther, regardless of how often it seemed like he was walking in circles. Despite the beauty of his frosty hell, the scenery rarely changed, and Travis swore he saw the same tree close to a thousand times. At times, his music accompanied him, and at others, he sang aloud, unafraid of whatever terrors nature held for him. More often than not, though, he trudged along in silence, his mind consumed with thoughts of both victory and defeat, of triumph and despair, of fear and loathing, as well as of smug self-satisfaction. All roads of thought led back to Esther.

Just as the sun started to settle in for its daily slumber, he found it. The note was in a beautiful pink envelope, one that Travis recognized without pause. He had purchased the stationery for Esther, both laughing at the time at how he indulged her feminine side, and how she adored that he had done so. It was pinned, at the top and bottom, with a rusty nail, held to the trunk of a deadened, barren tree, one that had met its untimely demise at the hands of lightning. The cold, dead, brown starkness of the nails was quite an aesthetic contrast to the stationery, and the sight flooded Travis's mind all too quickly with despairing thoughts of Esther's death, and the paradox that lay within.

Ripping his mittens from his hands, Travis cocked his head sideways and grimaced. As he tossed them idly aside into the snow, he reached up and gently worked the letter free of the nails, trying not to rip any of the keepsake as he did so. Despite himself, he grinned, and brought the letter to his nose.

When he had bought the stationery, it had been accented with the scents of lilac and jasmine. The scene still lingered, and the combination was intoxicating, even in the desolate wasteland he found himself in now. It reminded him of her. Her scent, her taste, her laugh, and the way her eyes danced. It was enough to make him fall in love with her all over again. A certain, almost childish eagerness gripped him, and he tore the letter open with zeal. A few neatly folded pages fell out, the stationary matching the envelope, the neat print she took a great pride in exploding from the page. Finding a stump nearby, Travis dusted the snow from its surface, and slowly began reading the words she had left there for him.

Travis,

I do not blame you.

I do not blame you for your faults. I do not blame you for wanting to obtain something that few are privileged enough to obtain. I do not blame you for seeing a chance at leadership—at doing what was right, and taking it. I cannot speak to your reasoning; that is something that you and you alone have to look at and decide if what was gained was worth what could be lost.

Along the same vein, you cannot blame me for wanting what we had. When you were simply Travis, our essence was simple. I smile at the hours I spent, watching you hum along with some song. I grin when I think of how you used to read, used to devour books, over and over again, lest you missed something the first time through. It still makes me laugh to this day, thinking of you muttering in your sleep, incoherent, yet focused and sincere in what you were saying.

It also still hurts me to think of how, once Travis became "TRAVIS!" and your headlines grew to be larger than life, you cast me asunder. I was an object of affection. I was loyal and steadfast and willing to offer you whatever counsel my life experience could, and yet you were unable to separate the two. The line in the sand was blurred. Your own vision of who you were became distorted.

I cannot fault you, however, for the demons I face. It was never your fault that my father was more of a sanctimonious jerk than you could ever hope to be. As bad as you got, you never approached that level, yet the second you expanded on the simple formula you had made for yourself, in my eyes, you became him, and it made me hate you with a bitter passion that I did not know I was capable of.

For a while, I blamed myself. I had a need for something, a complex yearning that I tried to break down, over and over. I wanted you, and just us, and yet my selfish wanting consumed me with a guilt that was evil and harrowing. It puzzled me how you laid everything I cherished to waste; however, I only pointed the finger at myself. Maybe, in some small measure, it was my fault. Maybe I should have bashed you over the head and pulled you away when you got in so deep that you could not deduce which way was up and out. You were acting like someone I didn't want you to be, and someone I knew wasn't you. You had slipped into a self-centered monster, and I became convinced, at least for a while, it was my fault.

Somehow, I found the will to carry on. Freedom was a farce, a tale made up to convince us our minds could not trap us. It's the same with material possession. None of it really belongs to us. Land, title, cash, names, property, nothing. It was simply given to us to use while we were here. I needed you. Not medicine. Not therapy. No gadgets or tools or prizes or baubles or anything else one would think they wanted.

I was greedy for you. It's as simple of that. I wish I could have found a way to reconcile what you had become and what we had been before. It's the truth when they say love is as the ocean, the ebb and flow, the flotsam and jetsam, the hide tide and the dry shore. Our love goes on and on and on and on and on, at least in my mind.

Learning to live, and forgive, has almost killed me, but here, in Bhutan, within my darkest hour, I have found hope, in you. I have no doubts that you are reading this letter. I want you, not just the man that you were, but the man you've become as well. I will leave you to your thoughts when you need them, and I will be there to provide whatever you need. I know that to have you in any manner as I had you before, I have to not only make myself subservient to you, but submissive to my own desires as well. I have tried for too long to make it all about myself, and at the end of the day, it is not just about me. It is about us, and I have to go about fixing us, not just fixing you.

If you subscribe to reincarnation, as I do, then the love between us is simply borrowed between the two souls that we are now bound to. They have been in love for eons, despite whatever roles they have played, despite whatever obstacles and deeds of mistrust they have borne. We, in our physical bodies, have to reap whatever the crop of misdeeds they had sown, long before our time.

I do not know where we go once we are reunited, or how we get there, yet I do know that I am willing to forge the trail with you. We could end up as the Mormons, with their own little slice of heaven out in Utah, or we could end up as the Donner Party, eating each other so that we could sustain our own selfish existence.

Either one sounds acceptable to me. Just as each country has to pay debts for their wickedness, just as Germany has to carry the burden of the Nazis or the American South carries the burden of the Civil War, so must you and I carry the burdens of what we have done to ourselves, to each other, and to our relationship. It's not ours to destroy, yet it is our duty to make it right.

> *I am willing to shoulder my partition of the load. Are you?*
> *Counting the hours until you take me into your arms once more.*
> *Yours, beloved for once and for always,*
> *-Esther*

While the distance that separated Esther and Travis was less than ten miles, according to Esther's mind, it was a lifetime. Desolation was her companion, despair her constant reminder of what might have been. About the same time that Travis was reading her latest musings, Esther was again by the fire, contemplating the little pill. The red capsule of potassium cyanide, known to cause death within seven seconds. It was the end of Hitler, nine hundred souls at Jonestown, Alan Turing, and several unknown CIA and KGB operatives. The black wind of despair howled against the opening of the cave, singing nothing but a mournful tone of despair as Esther warred with herself over the decision.

She had suffered for far longer than she would ever allow herself to admit. The heavy blanket of anxiety, the darkened veil of depression, had been her burden to carry since as far back as childhood. The darkness within courted regions of her being that she never knew existed. It left her paralyzed with fear at times, and yet at others, it pushed her to force a blade against the porcelain veneer of her own flesh, just to see if she still felt pain. She did, always, of course. The pain gave her something to live for. It gave her a drive to push forward, even to see if the pain could be multiplied. When thresholds were reached, Esther then sought to see if the power of pain could be harnessed, even manipulated, to affect those around her. It was a sick little game she played at times. However, it was her only grasp to sanity. Quietly working in the background, the analytical side of her brain recorded data, observed, and used the weaknesses of her own mind to turn out tomes of worthless data. Data she could not comprehend, yet data of which she was sure held use to someone studying something... somewhere.

She had learned to cancel the pain, block it, and ignore it. She no longer wept for those that had gone. Her mother, her father, assorted friends and acquaintances, gathered and discarded over the years—and Travis. They had all passed from her life, and with the sole exception of Travis, she saw no need to grasp to those that were dead and gone. They were discarded from her life, as if she could simply no longer feel. In truth, it was a defense, this pain blocking, one she was using to protect herself. It never occurred to her that once the pain was loosed, she would be consumed by it, but once Travis had betrayed her, it burned from the crown of her head to the soles of her feet.

Travis had seen her grief, and all he could do was ask

all the wrong questions. His undying belief in what he had become caused Travis to pound away at her, using all the wrong tools. In trying to make things better, he had made them worse.

Esther stood and pulled her fur-lined cloak close to her flesh as she walked past her small fire to the entrance of the cave. Long spells of silence were the norm here, in the Cave of Sorrows. She was not apt to talk to herself, and besides, conversation was not a strong suit. As she approached the labyrinth-esque opening, she hummed. "Redemption Day," by Johnny Cash. Cash was not someone she had listened to much, but she had stumbled across the track on Travis's iPod. She recognized it as a cover of a Sheryl Crow song, and while she had enjoyed Crow's version, Cash's had become a bit of an obsession. Maybe Cash's disjointed voice, full of years of heartache and sorrow, resonated with her on a deeper level than she liked to admit.

As she stood at the opening, the wind kicked up again, and she could feel the first hint of cold dampness. Snow was coming. Another barrage of days without sunlight, without warmth. Another unbridled attack on her being, of her hopes and wants being collapsed under the fate of rough winds. The sensations of the upcoming storm were exhilarating on her soul. The implications of what was to come dropped her into a point of despair she knew not existed. The weight was unbearable, at least by her standards.

She walked back to the fire, slowly, still humming. Nothing about her demeanor betrayed what she was suffering at the moment, nor did any of it betray what she was about to do. This was from years of schooling her actions, the way she stood, the way she held her face, even the way she breathed. She would never let anyone know what she was suffering, except for Travis. It was her burden; it was hers to suffer and to bear. Hers and hers alone. Travis had been the only one privy to her turmoil, and he had used this knowledge to rip her asunder, she had decided.

Sitting by the fire, wrapping the folds of the cloak about her legs, she gathered the capsule in her hands and contemplated it. Esther, when she desired, was able of a certain charm, of flirtatious cloying that could have even the most faithful of the male species eating from the palm of her hands. Some of it was sex, but a vast portion of it was a certain assumed goodness, sweetness, and innocence that only Esther knew didn't exist. That was how she had obtained the capsule. She had convinced a pharmaceutical student who had done an internship at the Centers of Disease Control (and had carried an unspoken crush on Esther for years) to procure it for her under the false pretense of an experiment. She had rationalized using the young man as revenge for his subtle attempts of trying to pry her away from Travis.

Her eyes turned back to the opening of the cave. The last hit of daylight was vanishing outside; darkness was creeping to seize at her despair once again. The pain was too much, she decided. Travis would just have to understand.

A tear rolled down her face as she raised the capsule to her mouth. "I'm sorry, Travis." Esther muttered as she bit down on the capsule, the bitter taste engulfing her taste buds. She was seized with drowsiness, but before she slipped under, the last three words of the Cash song flooded back into her mind.

Freedom. Freedom. Freedom…

CHAPTER 13

The amount of time he spent on the stump was far longer than he would have liked. Esther's letters were a Pandora's Box of contradictions, of spacing and emotions that made no sense to the rational mind. To those, however, that had insight into the beauty that madness could possess, it was poetic and torment, a rise and fall of love and desolation that was crushing to the human spirit. The sun had crested over the Himalayas and into the coldest depths of night before Travis was able to uproot himself from the spot he was occupying. The note held promise that he dared not allow himself the luxury to contemplate. The fact that he may actually succeed was a heady thought, to say the least.

The wind chilled him, snapping him from pleasant thoughts back into the reality that surrounded him. There was barely enough gray light of dusk to make a camp, and Travis set to his task with a fury that belied the weariness of the conditions of his new every day. Unfolding the tent from his pack, Travis cut several long posts of bamboo, each in the area of six feet long. They would serve as the supports of his structure, placed at several points along the edge and the center of the tarp, to keep the temporary shelter from collapsing under the weight of any snowfall that might make its way to his campsite. Travis whistled as he worked, Esther's note lifting a burden from his soul. Hope, as dangerous as it was, had begun to creep back into his being, and he was determined to feed it until it could be fed no more.

Travis grinned. The shelter was finished and ready for use. Unrolling his sleeping bag, Travis whistled softly, allowing his thoughts to wander. With their combined careers, time was often found for travel, and they did quite a bit of it. The trip to

Savannah, Georgia, where they had spent a week making love on the beach, under the palm trees. There was another weekend where they had traveled the entire course of the Pacific Coast Highway, or Highway One, as they fondly referred to it. Travis had just received his motorcycle endorsement, and the four-day jaunt had taken them from Leggett, where Highway One started, to Orange County, where they spent several hours visiting some scenic areas for photographs. Beautiful photos, ones that Travis cherished. Photos of Half Moon Bay, the Albion River Bridge (California's last wooden bridge), and many other beautiful images, a wonderful trip that both had enjoyed.

Rolling out his sleeping bag, Travis slowly stretched towards the sky. Another smirk plastered his face at what he considered a job well done before he stretched out onto the bag. His need for shelter being fulfilled, Travis turned his thoughts to lighter matters. He had been an avid reader, and given where he was at the moment, some of his favorite adventures came to mind. *My Side of the Mountain,* Jean Craighead George's novel was the first book he had read in fifth grade, been the inspiration of such adventures. It had been ages since he had read it; however, the tales from Sam's adventures had not left his mind. Look at him now! Just like Sam Gribley, off in the wilderness, dependent on nobody but himself.

A sobering reality hit. Travis was only out here playing Boy Scout because of the severity of the mistake that he had made. His reckless globetrotting had little to do with any sense of adventure, or bravery. He was simply trying to right a wrong. It wasn't the first time Travis had taken the precarious trip down what would be Hero's Lane.

The chess players stared intently at the board. Although the opponent is on the other side, it is common knowledge to any player that your biggest opponent is the pieces before you, the light and dark warriors, representing good and evil, all the while blurring the line between.

The player on the white side picked up a pawn, setting it down again as he contemplated his move. He was dressed in Soviet era relics, muted browns and greens that dulled his features as much as he dulled the room. The only thing that betrayed the beautiful mind within was his eyes, brilliant pools of deep blue that rose and fell as he contemplated his next move. Suddenly, a smirk crossed his face. "You know, Robert, it's as Vitali Klitschko once said: 'Chess is similar to boxing. You need to develop a strategy, and you need to think two or three steps ahead about what your opponent is doing. You have to be smart. But what's the difference between chess and boxing? In chess, nobody is an expert, but everybody plays. In boxing everybody is an expert, but nobody fights.'"

The second figure never looked up, instead choosing to stare intently at the ivory pieces. He made not a movement as his blandly dressed opponent moved his piece. "Knight to E7," Ivan said proudly. Robert, dressed in a long, flowing black cloak, hooded, stared at the board intently. His pawns had been left in a bloodbath thus far, but most of his power pieces still remained in play. Ivan was intent on capturing his queen, it seemed. Why not let him have it? Ivan was fairly easy to bait, it seemed.

Robert sighed as if frustrated and laid the trap. "Queen to C8. Check, Ivan."

Ivan grinned, thrilled that he had managed to capture Robert's queen. "Well, comrade, I'd say this is an unsightly turn of events for you, no?" Sweeping the piece away, the Russian grinned as he waited for his opponent's move. It would be the final time he was offered any joy for the remainder of the game.

Robert pounced. In the next six moves, he managed to capture a knight, a bishop, two rooks, and a pawn. Every time Ivan tried to lay a trap, Robert evaded it; every time Ivan pursued a piece, he instead found himself retreating. Soon, he could retreat no more, and he stared in stunned anger as Robert announced, one again, "Mate. The game is over. If you move in any direction, the king is mated, and you lose."

Ivan stood, flustered, having no idea what to do next. With a guttural cry, he unsheathed his sword, and made a frantic, desperate lunge at Robert.

Robert had no time to think. He simply reacted. The dagger left from somewhere beneath the fold of his robes, and embedded itself right between Ivan's eyes. As the Russian began an exaggerated death fall, Robert smirked and spoke in a disjointed, hollow voice, his warm brown eyes shining: "And you forgot the words of Mao, my friend: 'Revolution is not a dinner party, nor an essay, nor a painting, nor a piece of embroidery; it cannot be advanced softly, gradually, carefully, considerately, respectfully, politely, plainly, and modestly. A revolution is an insurrection, an act of violence by which one class overthrows another.' You shouldn't have been angry at me because you made the foolish mistake of risking your kingdom on a chess game." Ivan had dropped his crown dead center of the chessboard, and Robert, throwing back his hood, gathered it up, a grin tugging at the corner of his mouth. "Checkmate."

The lights brightened the auditorium, and there was a light smattering of applause. Travis looked over at the director first, then Esther, grinning the entire time. "Well done, Travis." Art, the little British chap who headed up the theater department was beaming. This strange fusion of cultures, where Game of Thrones met <u>Spassky</u> vs Fischer had been his crowning achievement in what had been an unremarkable career at San Francisco State, and Travis and the others involved were trying to see that the diminutive English chap went out in a blaze of glory. Esther was there for moral support; she had little interest in the theatre. However, things had been strained between her and Travis, and this was one way she knew of to spend more time together.

Travis helped George, who was playing Ivan, to his feet. The two shared a rough embrace and grinned. "I guess we'll knock 'em dead opening night," George said softly, his natural voice a soft contrast from the haughty Russian he had played.

Travis laughed, muttering in agreement. As the stage crew cleaned up, his eyes went to Esther once again. Her presence there was comforting, as theatre seemed to put Travis outside of his comfort zone. Hopping down from the stage, Travis headed towards Esther. "So, milady," he said offering an exaggerated mock bow, "how was our performance?" He would not hear her answer.

Without warning, the doors burst open to the theatre. Elizabeth, one of the beachcombers that had been enthralled with Travis's bold words, almost sprinted down the aisle, a look of righteous indignation plastered across her face. Esther looked up with a start, her mouth left in a half-formed 'o.' "That son of a bitch!" Elizabeth screeched. Her green eyes were dancing, aflame with anger. Gathering her breath, she straightened and crossed her arms on her chest. "That backwoods, ignorant, no good, racist son of a bitch!"

Travis raised a quizzical brow at her, but in his gut he knew exactly about whom she was speaking. "What in the blue hell are you talking about, Elizabeth?" Esther's jaw had relaxed, and as much as she didn't want to admit it, she knew exactly who Elizabeth was referring to as well. "Felix Jones," Esther muttered softly, rolling her eyes, and turning away from Travis.

Travis saw the subtle hint of resignation in Esther's eyes, but said nothing. Instead, he looked to Elizabeth. "What has he done now?" Travis asked, his voice an octave lower, monotonous, foreboding.

The scowl never left Elizabeth's face. Unlike Travis (and to a lesser extent, Esther,) she was prone to wear her emotions, however trumped up on insincere, on her sleeve. "He's barricaded himself inside the Hall, and he's refusing to come out until all the 'impure' elements are off campus. The rat bastards on the Board of Trustees have yet to find a way to get rid of him."

Travis winced, and his reasons for doing so were twofold. First, he thought himself to be rid of the whole Jones mess. His arrest had led to a misdemeanor disturbing the peace charge, a small fine, and an admonishment from the judge for 'drawing attention to the ramblings of an idiot.' It was the prevailing view at San Francisco State that by allowing Jones to rant and ramble on with his special brand of vile invective was to let him talk himself from importance. They eventually hoped he would simply go away. The second issue was Elizabeth. Despite the harsh words and aggressive behavior, Travis found he had an attraction for her. It was, of course, of the basest and most carnal type, but he found that just because he was able to call the attraction for what it was, that did not mean that he could suppress it. Shaking his head, Travis set aside all carnal thoughts and glared holes through Elizabeth, only offering a short, bitter glance to Esther. "Alright, let's go."

Esther stood, and grabbed Travis by the arm. "Please, Travis," she began, staring him full in the eyes for a second before lowering her gaze to the floor. "Please. He's a babbling idiot, but even idiots are known to do things that put the lives of others at risk. Let him be." Travis slowly looked down at the hand that was on his arm. The look of resolve on his face flashed to rage for a moment, before a calm serenity crossed his features once more. "Of all people, Esther, as a minority and a woman, of all people, I would think you would understand. Let go." Without giving her a chance to comply, Travis yanked away. "We'll discuss this later." Sneering, he flipped the hood of his costume over his head. "Let's go, Elizabeth."

CHAPTER 14

For a world that has grown cynical and cold, it still holds a sense of ironic humor that how, in our most desolate of moments, we tend to notice the small details of the moments that define us. How, for example, a star athlete notices a singular noise in a crowd right after the largest moment in their career, whether it be a blaring horn or the simple, undulated scream of joy that only a child can unfurl. Esther, despite the fact that she carried around a soul older and more broken than even the eons of time, was no different in this regard. For a capsule of what was supposed to be cyanide, the little pill did not have the intended effect.

Initially, she had thought herself passed into some sort of afterlife. Heaven or hell, purgatory or nirvana, perhaps the beginning of reincarnation, she was unsure. Her hair chafed lightly against her cheek, and while this irritated her, she dared not move. If she was about to stand judgment, the submissive, the masochist inside of her would rule the day. A pebble dug into her exposed thigh at some point, and with a slow build to despair, she realized that she had not passed on, but was simply waking up from whatever effect the pill had wrought on her.

A low moan started somewhere in the base of her throat, and Esther would have surely thrown herself into incoherent sobs and screams of frustration had she been able. However, the pill she swallowed seemed to have left her parched, dehydrated, and for all she was worth, she could not bring any more noise from her throat. The iron will of survival took over any thoughts of self-destruction, and slowly, painfully, she started to crawl towards the small basin that made up the fresh water spring of the cave.

Springs. They were an amazement of nature all their own, she thought, as she inched towards the water source. The spring in this cave had spent millennia forcing its way through the hardest of bedrock, millions of pounds of sheer mass that formed the most breathtaking mountains in the world. It left her in awe how the water, in its infinite patience, had waged its own private war with the sheer forces of gravity, time, and mass, and had won. The water here was refreshing, a cool spring that Esther had found herself staring into for hours on end, waiting for Travis to be of men or of mice. It had become her shrine, her oasis, the basis of the essence that flowed through her. As she babbled on for hours, sometimes in a mindless drone, others in an incoherent fit of gnashing teeth and pitiless shouts, it had listened, consoled, taken the role of a silent partner in her struggle. When she was of right mind, staring hopefully in the cool depths of the pool, it had mirrored her hope, fed her desire to live. And now, when she simply needed nourishment, it would provide.

Reaching the lip of the spring, hidden between two boulders—boulders that stood sentry over the world's greatest treasure—Esther almost threw her face into the clear, cool water that lay before her. As tasteless as we know water to be, at this moment, to Esther Sansui, in the Cave of the Winds and Ice, water was milk and honey, it was prime rib at the Four Seasons, and it was the finest bottle of Italian wine. It was the manna of the gods. She drank greedily, inhaling all that she could handle. Only when she was struggling for air was her thirst quenched, and she pulled reluctantly away, almost wishing she could have just become one with the water, ending what she saw as the remnants of an already pathetic existence.

Her head drenched, Esther shivered in the ice and stone that entombed her. Despite the fact that the cave had been home in her last and evil days, for most of its existence it has been just that, a dark and desolate cave, only somewhat lighted and never warmed by the constant refraction of light from the ice that garnished its every surface. Instinct took over, and Esther slowly rose, bracing herself as best she could on the slippery cover of ice, and slowly made her way to the fire pit.

Fire. For as much as water was the essence of life, fire, and how to make it, how to control it, how to use it and meld it, may very well have been the greatest discovery of all of humanity. Fire had given Esther warmth, had helped the blood course through her veins, and had cooked and prepared her food. As she tossed wood into the pit, Esther reasoned that, although the cost of making fire was greater than that of discovering water, and although the danger was far greater, humanity had found a way to make the reward outweigh the risk. Fire powers our cars, warms our homes, melds our iron and steel into our whims, and protects us from the terrors of the world.

The flint and steel shaking in her hands, Esther struck the stones against one another until, at long last, a spark caught some kindling, and the fire sprung to life. Unlike water, fire depended on the forces of either man or nature to sustain it, and it was for this reason Esther concluded that water was mightier than fire. Man favored fire because he could control it, but at the end of the day, fire could not harm water without an intermediary. However, throw a bucket of water on a fire, and what do you have? "Ashes to ashes, dust to dust," Esther muttered, finishing her thought aloud.

As the fire grew, slowly warming the air that surrounded her, Esther realized that she was filthy. Any pretense of self-destruction gave way to the feminine desire of cleanliness, and Esther inelegantly stripped down nude. Nobody had searched this cave in the weeks she had been there, and the only person likely to find her there was Travis, and, well, there wasn't anything there that he had not seen before. Gathering up another robe, this one quite a measure heavier, Esther sat down next to the fire, knees pulled to her chest, slowly rocking back and forth as she waited for the heavier robe to warm her.

Her mind wandered. What, exactly had that pill consisted of? It was powerful enough to knock her out, yet given her deteriorating physical state, a simple sedative could have done that. Given that, despite the parched feeling, there was precious little in the way of side effects, she could only assume that it had been just that. That slimy little chemist! It could have been his personal little home brewed version of Nyquil for all she knew. In the end, he was just another depraved slice of humanity that Esther could muster up little rage against. Regardless of what the pill had been, it did not have its intended effect.

The fire warmed her aching bones, loosed up tightened muscles, and helped her relax. She had long ago subscribed to the theory that there was no such thing as coincidence in the world. Hope, as it did, sprung eternal within her once again. Maybe it was meant for Travis to find her, to fix what had gone asunder, and to make right was wrong.

Either that or she was simply immune to cyanide. That little rueful thought brought the faint curl of a smile to the pout of her lips, and within a few moments, Esther was humming a soft lullaby, falling asleep in the warm, soft folds of her robe, dreaming of Travis.

Thundersnow. A winter thunderstorm. A thunder snowstorm. The Winter Anger of the Gods. Call it what you will, it's a relatively rare kind of <u>thunderstorm</u> with <u>snow</u> falling as the primary <u>precipitation</u> as opposed to <u>rain</u>, sleet, or hail. It typically falls in regions with extremes, such as large bodies of water or strong upward drafts. High mountains can also do the trick, and in Bhutan, there was an abundance of such peaks. Aesthetically, and in its results, it is not much different from any other type of thunderstorm, although the top of the <u>clouds</u> are usually quite low.

The scary thing about the Winter Anger of the Gods is that, in Bhutan, the dense quantity of snow held in the clouds muffles any thunder that would give away its arrival, right up until the moment that the storm lashes out, bringing down all the sound and the fury of whatever god it is you chose to fear. Winter storms have this sneaking effect on even the most aware, and a wayward traveler in Bhutan can find themselves in a four-inch-per-hour disaster without warning, with hurricane force winds and temperature drops of more than fifty degrees signing the death warrant of even the hardiest travelers. For someone who is in a state of slumber, the arrival of such a nightmare is almost certain to lead to death.

Travis was in a lean-to he had constructed, enjoying the warmth of the burning embers as he dozed, unaware that nature was preparing to unleash the blunt force of her rage upon him. His first warning was the branch, ripped asunder from one of the very trees providing him shelter, to come crashing through the canvas that shielded him from the hellish elements. The sudden impact sent searing pain through his leg, and he woke with a start. The leg would bear a nasty bruise in the near future, but it was Travis's blessing that the damage was limited to just that.

Scrambling, Travis climbed to his feet, deftly dodging the embers from his scattered fire as he stood. The winds forced him to brace his ground, roaring full force into his face, all the while instilling terror into his soul. Just as the winds slowed, giving a moment for respite, thunder roared in the small clearing, announcing the full terror of the storm with a chorus of demonic voices that would have riveted even the bravest souls in place with fear.

The moment passed, the winds roared forth again, and Travis was sent head over heels by a seventy-mile-an-hour gust that would have toppled a man twice his size. The lean-to collapsed, not standing a chance against the full fury of the storm. His supplies scattering, soaked to the bone and chilling fast, Travis swore to the sky as he struggled to his feet once again.

He would have been better suited staying on the ground.

Without warning, the fierce winds ripped another branch from one of the great trees. Splinters flying, the branch stayed attached at the break, sending the branch hurtling full speed at Travis. He was unable to avoid it; indeed, he would not be able to recall the moment of impact as long as he remained alive. There was a thud, the taste of blood, a scream—Travis heard the sound, but would never learn that the noise had come from him, and then, in the middle of the storm to end storms, nothing but blissful silence.

As is the course of nature, Travis awoke some time later. His head screamed curses at him with a vengeance normally reserved for a lover's quarrel, or a political spat. He opened his right eye. Squinting, Travis stared at a point in the distance, struggling to focus. How long had he been lying in the snow? His joints ached from the cold, but his blessing had been in the nearly two feet of powder that fell while he was unconscious. Coupled with his layered clothing, he had been insulated from the horrors that the storm had wrought throughout the forest. Tree limbs and the frozen corpses of animals were scattered about, some in view of where Travis lay.

He stood, or rather, he tried to stand. The second he went to rise, his head seized him with a horrible pain. This was far worse than any hangover he experienced at San Francisco State. Shaking, he pulled himself to his knees. Why could he not focus? Looking down, Travis saw in horror the limb that had struck him. Just beyond it, where white snow should have been, the earth was stained crimson.

Bile rose to his throat as it slowly dawned on him what had happened. With a grimace, Travis clutched the great branch and pulled his head away. Pain—indescribable pain—

twisted through his being and, unable to contain it any longer, he vomited. Once his stomach contents graced the white snow, Travis pulled himself into a sitting position, knees pulled to his chest. His vision was focusing in and out, slightly off kilter. He avoided looking at his assailant for as long as he could; however, necessity soon won out, and Travis slowly turned toward the limb. In a cruel twist of fate, his vision suddenly sharpened, and with an awestruck horror, he knew for sure why he was unable to focus his sight.

For staring at him, the light faded from its gaze, impaled on a smaller offshoot of the main limb, was his right eye.

As he faded into the warm oblivion of unconsciousness, Travis realized for the first time in his life why the eternal embrace of Death, he being the final lover, held such an appeal to his Esther.

CHAPTER 15

The door flew open, containing the power of the east wind and the fury of the seventh circle of hell. The skies outside shook with thunder, with the lightning providing a macabre, over-dramatic backdrop to what was quickly becoming the largest talking point in the nation. The talking heads, both left and right, weighed in, the right taking the rare stance for the First Amendment and the ones on the left longing, for the first time in their careers, for the death penalty. Politicians weighed in, from city council people up to the Vice President of the United States. Support had poured in for both sides from such faraway places as Tunisia and Oman. Marches formed outside the campus, black clad Panthers and white robed Klansman alike bickering for attention, and crowing with empty threats of violence from an era thought long dead.

All the while, Felix Jones stood and watched, a sly grin on his face. He was writing his place in history, no doubt, and while he would be hated, and even loathed, he would have his place nonetheless. He relished the attention in much the same way a serial killer insisted on taunting a terrified public through their letters. It wasn't so much about the cause; while Jones thought minorities to be substandard students, he didn't necessarily hate them. They were simply a pawn in his game. The sad truth of the matter was that although America had done everything to separate themselves from their hate-filled past, within the dark heart of evil men, hatred still lived, and would continue to breed as long as a culture of fear was allowed to run amok.

Such fears were perfect for an extremist like Jones to feed off.

Jones made a point to straighten his tie. After all, if he was going to have an enemy, his convoluted views suggested that he do his best to look better than they. It was the same well-dressed theory David Duke had unsuccessfully used back in the 1980s to try and mainstream the Klan. Jones was convinced that it would have worked if Duke had possessed the same deft touch that Jones assumed he possessed.

Jones strolled to the overcrowded podium, one rigged with enough microphones to host a Presidential debate. Fox News was there. MSNBC was as well. CNN, C-SPAN, Current TV, it was a veritable who's who of political channels. The local news had, at first, been denied access to the podium, until an intense round of hand wringing and hellraising had made for more holes to be drilled and more microphones places. Local affiliates for CBS, NBC and two for ABC had wrest spots away from half a dozen others.

Stuart Avett was the local beat reporter for KCBS-12 in Oakland. A good-looking fellow in his thirties, he had set aside the old school strong-arm methods of local field reporters and had unabashedly played on his warm face, and liberal leanings, to grant himself access in places where most reporters could not. Higher placement was a dream, just as it is with any reporter, but in his thirties and in place for six years at one station, Stuart knew that time was running short. He needed a break. And by playing both sides, he would find one in what would become known as the Felix Jones Standoff.

Jones had decided to play tribute to Governor Wallace. The Board of Trustees had yet to penetrate his contract; and by commitment, and under fear of suit, he was still gainfully employed by the University system of the state of California. Lawsuits were pending; in the meantime, a friendly conservative judge from Orange County had granted an injunction to keep Jones from being terminated. Most of the state screamed; those in Orange County hid in shame and distanced themselves from the judge. The judge himself was eighty-three, a longtime donor to conservative causes, and on the brink of retirement. He didn't give a damn how the gossip ran; in fact, it was nice to see his name in print one more time before he was put out to pasture.

This knowledge, coupled with his own twisted Messianic views of himself, made Jones press forward with his plan. Stepping to the microphones, a well-tailored, conservative brown suit hanging from his frame, Jones straightened his red tie and pointedly cleared his throat.

"Let me make something very clear to all of you. This is not just about trying to raise the academic standards of this sorry school. No, San Francisco State cursed themselves a long, long time ago. It is a curse to be

nothing more than a middle of the road school. It's a curse that regulates what was one of the finest research universities in California to one that accepts mongrel hordes of liberalized idiots, allowing them to skip to and fro to their classes, eyes squinted, backs wet and pants around their knees without will or wont to what their true purpose in being here is: to learn."
So far, so good. He had managed to insult three races in one sentence, not to mention the queers. He hated the queers almost as much as the rest. Shaking his head, he gathered his thoughts. *"At one time, only those who could afford it, or the best and the brightest, got into college. They came because they could afford it. Because they earned it. Because they deserved it. Nowadays, all it takes is a student aid department and a check on the box of any one of the so-called minorities listed on the admissions form. I saw it, several times, where a well-qualified and self-sustaining student was denied for some jerk kid on financial aid, simply because the jerk kid was black."* Not true, but it sounded good. Jones pressed on.   *"Admission standards have been lowered, just for the blacks. Financial aid has been thrown at the Hispanic kids. Every Asian and Middle Eastern kid only has to ask for a student visa, and they're here, learning things to smuggle back to Red China, or even worse, things to hand back to al Qaeda for their next terrorist attack. Is that what you want?"* Jones was rising to a fever pitch, and sadly, some of the crowd was in agreement. *"You want the future of higher education dumbed downed so that some urban street thug soldiers can claim to be the next Tupac Shakur, only with a college degree? You want a bunch of little Mexican cartel punks running back across the border, using the education WE provided them to streamline their drug trade? You want China to get an inner working of our finances so that they will come and foreclose on this popcorn stand we call America? Guess what? We'll become the insurgents on that day! And what about North Korea? I guess you folks are in a hurry for them to have the bomb, after all. And let's not even get into the towel heads! I guess you all want the Coit Tower to suffer the same fate as the World Trade Center!"*

A chorus of boos followed, and Jones knew he was standing on the line. He lowered his hands, urging supporters and detractors alike to settle back into their seats. Thankfully, the detractors still far outweighed the supporters. Jones took a sip of water, wiped his brow, and spoke *again, this time in a much calmer voice. "I'm not here to incite hatred. There may be some of you, however, that mark me as xenophobic. You may say that, as a nation, we have moved past such hateful rhetoric, such blatant stereotypes. I say this to you: The problem America now has is this system of entitlement. We've gone from a system that rewards those that work hard to one that allows everyone to be on the same footing, regardless of the effort put forth. SAT scores matter not. Grades matter not. Hard work, dedication—none of this matters. At the end of the day, all that matters are a name, a student loan, and a dark hue of skin, and we fling the doors wide open for you. Seventy-two point four percent of Americans are white. Yet, only fifty-three percent of students here are white. The other forty-seven percent are Negro, Hispanic, Oriental, or Persian. It's not my place to worry about those forty-seven percent. They're going to get theirs, regardless. I have to worry about restoring the balance. I have to worry about rewarding hard work. I have to worry about the best and the brightest. And that is why I'm here. I swear an oath, to everyone here in attendance and everyone at home. I will not leave this building. I will not resign from my post. I will not waver, I will not step down, and I will not walk away. I will fight for the majority of those here, and by God and by Christ we will stop this system of rewarding the weak and the non-evolved in favor of those who stand high above the muck, high above the slovenly minds and bodies and souls. This country and this university is sorely lacking in leadership, in bold ideas, and in decisiveness. Affirmative action was a mistake when it was instituted, and it's a mistake now. The governor of this great state has said he will remove me by force. Well, in honor of the great Governor Wallace, I say this to the state of California this day! Affirmative action was wrong then, it's wrong now, and it will be wrong forever. Come on down, Mr. Governor! Move me if you must, or if you can." With that, Jones stepped back from the podium, arms crossed, a sinister look on his face, one of pure hatred, mingling with smug satisfaction.*

The crowd exploded in a chorus of boos, and Jones encouraged them. He was a perfect target for their righteous indignation, and he relished the role. The few students in agreement with him were quickly shouted down by the majority, and the entire arena was teetering on the edge of a riot.

The auditorium went dark.

The crowd fell silent, teetering on the edge of panic. A spotlight, from high in the rafters, shone on Jones as he stood on the stage. As hard as he tried, it was simply too hard for him to stand resolute, and those with a keen eye could see him tremble. A second light hit the entrance, and there was Travis, cloaked all in black. A well-placed A/V student handed him a microphone, and Travis started slowly strolling down the center aisle. The first quarter of the way, he said nothing, just paced slowly as Elizabeth and Nicole followed, not in the spotlight, but very much a part of it. As he reached the halfway point, he finally spoke.

"So that's how it is, Felix? Those of us that are not what you quantify as normal are denied our fair share? People like Martin Luther King, like Malcolm X, like Che Guevara, like the Dalai Lama, like Mahatma Gandhi, fought for nothing because some fool in California decided that he knew what was better for the majority? And what about people like me, Felix? My girl is half Asian." Travis paused, and noticed with a twinge of anger that Esther was not around. He should be able to point out how open minded he was, damn it! She was ruining everything. His eyes narrowed as he stared Jones down. "And let's put that aside." Travis paused, tossing his hat to the side. "My face has nothing extraordinary about it. My eyes are plain and brown. Same with my hair. I am of average height, of average weight, of average intelligence, and average grades. There's nothing amazing about me. Yet, for some reason, I'm more entitled than my brothers and sisters in humanity?"

Travis had reached the edge of the stage. "Let me explain something to you. They've been trying to knock me down my entire life. I'm too short. I'm too small. I'm too slow. I don't have what it takes. But that's not me, Felix. I work, I fight, and I study so that they cannot take what belongs to me. They can't take my heart, they can't take my mind, they can't take my soul, or my being, or my essence. They can't replace what makes me who I am. It takes work, Felix. Not skin color. It takes blood, sweat, tears, every ounce of effort I can muster to make it, and every bit of honor I have not to haul off and knock every one of those giant teeth down your arrogant throat. Esther says I have an enormous ego, and I'll be the first to admit, sometimes it's insatiable. As I've gotten older, I've learned how to control it. Of course I have, and of course I've aged. I put aside childish things, and I've laid down my arms of anger in favor of being a noble, civilized creature."

Travis went to step up to the stage, but was stopped by a security guard, a black dude named Clint. Travis cocked a brow. "You're going to stand in my way while he stands here and calls you everything but a nigger, Clint?"

Clint smiled. "Just wanted to make sure you made it up safely, Travis." With that, Clint stepped aside, allowing Travis to pass.

Grinning, Travis walked up onto the stage, the microphone still in his hand. "That's the beauty of it, Felix. Twenty-six years. Twenty-six years of wisdom, twenty-six years of understanding, twenty-six years of love and regret and hate and honesty and everything that makes a man a man, not without a little punishment and random acts of violence sprinkled on top. My deeds will hopefully live on today. I want to live and prosper long after the records of this have fallen, long after the newspaper print has yellowed and dissolved into nothingness. I'll do whatever I have to do to ensure that not only my legacy, but the legacy of any student here, regardless of race, creed, religion, nationality, sex, sexual preference, or bubblegum flavor, lives on into the eons of the future, into the annals of eternity. We are San Francisco State, and we will be remembered. Our actions here today are how we will be remembered. They speak much louder than words. How we progressed is marked down into record, and believe you me, Felix, we will leave our mark and it will endure forever."

The crowd erupted, but Travis was not done yet. He was going to provoke some of the very violence he spoke of, come hell or high water. Grinning, he pulled a cigar from the folds of his jacket. Jutting it between his teeth, he struck a match no more than six inches from Jones's nose. Looking down, he noticed Jones's shoes. "Those things are huge, Felix. Are you a clown in your spare time?" The words were no sooner out of his mouth then he blew a huge puff of acrid smoke straight into Jones's face.

In no less than a moment, Jones lost everything he had achieved. Anger boiled over from within, and without thinking, he finally committed an offense worthy of termination. Reaching back to the plantation, with all the sound and fury of a madman, he slapped Travis full on the face, knocking the cigar from his mouth. It rolled noisily across the stage, still lit, setting under one of the ancient velvet curtains that adorned either side of the arena.

Travis recoiled, a huge red welt spreading quickly across his features. He paused for a moment, and then, without warning and with a fury that was greater than even Felix Jones on the stump, he kicked the man, full on, directly in the temple.

Jones hit the floor like a dead weight.

If every life is an arc, then it stands to reason that every life will, at some point, reach both its base and its zenith. Each man, woman, and beast, it seems, is destined to stand on the highest metaphysical peak and sing praises to whatever god they choose. On the same token, however, each is destined to sink to the lowest of whatever hell they could imagine has existed.

For Travis, these moments happened within mere breaths of one another.

It's been said that we fear not because we are nothing, but we fear because we know we are all. It is also said that the mere measure of a man is how he handles both his best and worst moments, and that what makes a man noble is the mere ability for compromise.

Unflinching, uncaring, uncompromising, Travis allowed what should have been his finest hour become the shallow pit of his own hell.

Almost immediately, Travis felt hands around his waist. In his heightened state of anger, he turned around and let a backhand fly.

It hit Esther full on in the side of the face. She went down slowly, a delayed reaction brought on from the combination of the strength of the blow and the fact that the one thing she had always seen as unspeakable had just happened.

Travis whirled around with a fury, trying to see who would dare lay their hands on him. Seeing that it was Esther, he wavered on his emotions, back and forth, between anger and despair. In what would be one of his last salient monuments of sanity, despair won out. The façade dropped, and, filled with sorrow, he quickly dropped to a knee, to check on her condition.

He should not have bothered.

Before he could utter a single word, Esther broiled over with anger, hurt, depression, and loss. Travis striking her was the proverbial straw that broke the camel's back. "Don't touch me!" she snapped, causing Travis's hand to recoil in fear.

"Esther, I had no idea…" Travis managed to stutter, but it was too late. Too late to apologize, too late to atone for what was the death knell of their relationship. Esther, in control as always, bit down on her own anger, swallowed her pride, and stood, raising a hand.

"Save it, Travis. I'm leaving."

The crowd was oblivious to what had happened. They were too riled up by the kick that felled Felix Jones. Avett, being the reporter he was, had managed to get KCBS's live feed hard wired into the video system, and the encounter played on, in a loop. Travis glanced up at the screen. Jones's slap had been like a boat paddle against a dead fish, and Travis slowly felt his face, the heat still radiating from the spot that Jones had slapped. As he watched, the replay of the kick he had delivered to Jones, despite, everything, he could not help but smile. The second the kick made contact, Jones had momentarily straightened before crumpling in a frumpy heap at Travis's feet, left arm still extended in the air, as if offering a salute to a general that nobody but Jones could see. It was a classic fencing response, one of the key indicators of a concussion. Travis admired his handiwork for a moment more before turning back to Esther.

As loyal to her word as the sun was to rising, she was gone. Travis thought to give chase, but circumstance would stop him. Elizabeth and Nicole stepped up, cheering, acting the fools, and all the while blocking his way to the exit. Then with a cry, Elizabeth froze and pointed to the curtains behind Travis.

The once-forgotten cigar decided to make its return. Flames were slowly crawling up the side of the curtain. Leaping to and fro, they licked at the ceiling with acrid, black smoke, and as others noticed, chaos ensued. There was an immediate stampede to grab loved ones, belongings, and, for a couple of opportunists, whatever goodies were left at hand by those fleeing: laptops, music players, wallets, purses, and cash became fair game as the mass of humanity streamed towards the exit.

Travis, not wanting to hang around to see what damage the flames could offer him, decided to make an exit out a side door to the left, hitherto unnoticed by the fleeing mass of humanity. As he steamed for the exit, Elizabeth and Nicole in tow, he glanced back at the stage.

There lay Felix Jones, knocked out cold, completely oblivious to what had happened to him, or to what was going on. That part did not so much bother Travis; Jones had made its bed and now he could sleep in it. The fire was moving slowly, and there was a good chance Jones could make it out alive. Travis was not in any hurry to play hero to such a man, anyhow.

Travis would have walked away from the gathering completely unwounded emotionally if not for what happened next. For the rest of his days, he could rationalize his actions towards Jones, and to a lesser degree, towards Esther. As he turned to exit, he saw a figure out of the corner of his eye, moving towards the still unconscious Jones.

From their earliest days, reporters are told that they are there to record the news, not to be a part of it. However, in the days of the twenty-four-hour news cycle, actions by people such as Anderson Cooper had changed the way reporters acted in the field. It was not so much a desire to be the story as it was a certain school of New Age news keepers that were willing to break down all walls of professionalism to walk whatever path they saw morally fit. Perhaps Stuart Avett was seeking his big break, or perhaps, despite his flaws, Avett could not leave someone to burn to his death. Regardless of his motives, Avett made the decision to try and save Felix Jones. He almost succeeded.

Almost.

Avett reached Jones's body and instinct took over. He reached down and picked the man up, draping him over his shoulder. The classic fireman's carry. He stumbled slowly towards the exit, unaware of the side door that Travis watched from. Avett was stumbling around blindly, ready to succumb to smoke and heat. By some miracle, he was within ten feet of the front door. A few more steps. Seven feet. He staggered a little bit more. Five feet. The smoke began to overcome him and he fell to his knees, inching along with every bit of iron will in him to live. Three feet. Then two. Never a religious man, Avett began whispering a prayer under his lips, begging whatever god it was that was out there to help him to his goal.

Providence was almost delivered. Then again, it is a requirement of balance that evil sometimes wins out.

There was a loud crack, and one of the giant wooden beams that held the roof in place collapsed, fracturing under the enormous amount of heat. The beam hurled itself down, and for a second, Travis watched in utter horror, as it went on a collision course. Days later, Travis would recall hearing Avett scream, only to be told by other parties that the voice that had been screaming was his own.

The beam had knocked Jones from Avett's shoulders, crushing his skull and bringing a cruel finality to one of the darkest chapters in San Francisco State's history. Avett was pinned, the beam across his legs. Everyone else had managed to escape, and fire sirens wailed in the distance. The heat in the room was unbearable, and Travis coughed, tears streaming down his cheeks from the smoke as he watched Avett try and pry his way loose. Avett glanced up, moaning like a dying animal, and in his desperation, caught sight of Travis.

"Help!" Avett cried

Travis did not move and the smoke grew thicker, the flames higher and hotter.

"Help!" Avett shouted again, fear etched on his features, the finality of the situation finally dawning on him.

Tears streaming down his face, Travis stepped through the door, into the cold night air. He shut the door behind him.

CHAPTER 16

It was Travis's turn to awaken, only to be startled by the fact that he was still alive. His body screamed in physical pain, and hours spent lying in the snow had led to him almost being frozen to the ground. The nightmare of the last moments of Stuart Avett's life had hurt him far deeper than any physical pain, and something deep within him snapped.

Travis stood, catching a view of his eye, now frozen, still benignly staring back at him from its perch on the limb. Madness, brought on by a combination of the cold and his storm of emotions, brought Travis to the brink of hysterical laughter.

"What're you staring at?" Travis bellowed, the combination of the cold and his own pain slurring his words ever so slightly. "Look at you, so smug and arrogant, over there on your new perch. I kicked Felix Jones's head off his shoulders! What's a little eyeball like you going to do to stop me, hmm? You like being on that stick, apart from me and on your little own? I'll give you what for!"

Whirling, Travis looked around, finally settling on a smaller branch that had fallen off during the melee of the storm. He stalked towards his detached eye, and with a grim look of determination, reared back and swung the stick with a Ruth-esque swing.

One thing he managed to forget was that his equilibrium, as well as his depth perception, was askew because, well, his eye was stuck to a tree branch. He missed, spinning wildly around in the snow, flailing at the air until his momentum took him to the ground.

He rose and swung again, this time channeling the spirit of Bay area great Willie Mays. Strike two, and this time he landed face first in the snow. He screamed in agony as snow packed itself into the empty eye cavity, almost freezing him from within.

Travis dug at the socket, pulling out as much of the ice and snow as he could, before composing himself and preparing for one more swing. Being from Tennessee, he thought back to all the wonderful Braves games he had taken in, and the 1992 National League Championship Series came to mind. Little used Francisco Cabrera, two outs, bases loaded, Braves down 2-1, 2-1 count. Staring off into the distance, Travis could almost see Stan Belinda staring down the barrel at him as he prepared to throw a fastball right by him. Travis steadied his hands, which were apt to betray him in this hellish cold. Nothing but him and the ball. With an anguished cry, he swung. As he swung, he could replay it in his mind's eye. The ball connecting with the bat, going over the head of a flailing Jay Bell. Justice scores easily from third! Bonds gathers the ball, which he would have had a lot sooner had he listened to Andy Van Slyke and moved in when Cabrera came to the plate. Flipping Van Slyke the bird had cost Bonds possibly his best chance at a ring. Bonds uncorked a mighty throw! It's high and down the 3rd base line! Sid Bream, perhaps the slowest player in Major League history, lumbers towards home! He slides! Safe! Braves win! Braves win…

Sadly, Cabrera would not connect in this instance. Travis missed, and by a far greater measure than his first swings.

He lost all control. With a tortured cry, he charged the eye, the stick in hand, and began flailing away with every reserve of energy he possessed. Somewhere in the middle of his rage, he connected, sending the offending ocular organ flying deep into the Bhutanese forest, forever lost to the ages. Victory! Travis charged through the forest, leaving everything but his small pack at the camp, stumbling blindly, screaming at whatever God was responsible for his pain and anguish. The memories of striking Esther, of letting Avett die, of all the hellish mistakes he had made in his twenty-seven years were too much to bear. Pain and regret coursed through his being. The cold was bearing down, and soon, Travis was delirious with fever. He cried, he screamed, he moaned and smashed his fists against any offending trees in his path. Finally, with a soul-piercing sob of utter despair, Travis sank down at the base of a great tree, knuckles bleeding, still fevered and utterly exhausted. Tears poured from his one remaining eye. He had forgotten the questions, and any answers were but a faded memory of yesterday.

He sat silently, sobbing, as he pondered his next move. His pack! Travis reached in and pulled the sword out from among the folds. There was only one thing to do. But could he do it? Could he take the final step that he had been so critical of Esther for wanting to take? Pain and morality warred with one another, wasting time, taking up space in his thoughts until he could bear it no longer.

"SHUT UP!" Travis shouted into the darkness.

Standing, he gathered his composure and unsheathed the sword. He stared at the blade for a long moment, catching in its reflection a hollow, one-eyed shell of what had once been a decent man. That seemed to set his resolve.

Travis placed the point of the blade to his stomach. Glancing up at the sky, he muttered, "Forgive me, Esther."

He took a step forward, and the blade penetrated his clothing. He could feel the cold steel against his flesh. He paused, and prepared to take another step forward, when something off kilter caught his attention. Something was…off about the surface of the tree. His eye adjusted, and as the light of the rising sun caught the edge of the envelope, Travis dropped the weapon. His heart went from the lowest of the lowest circle of hell to his own personal nirvana in the space of a heartbeat.

She had left him another letter.

He seized it, crumpling to the snow in a joyous heap. He clutched the letter to his chest, crying and humming to himself, trying to find his center.

He managed to compose himself, fighting exhaustion and a host of emotions. The letter was still clutched to his chest. Travis wrapped it in his pack, not willing to lose it to the elements. He took the time to bandage his battered knuckles. He built a fire, and watched as the leaping flames pulled him back from a place that very few men come back from. Using a small mirror from his pack, he winced as he shredded a shirt, using the strips to wrap an angular bandage, much like a bandana, to cover where his eye had once been. Blood seeped against the wound, but at least he would be safer from infection and obstructions.

Sighing, Travis reached his warmed hands into the pack and removed the note. It was about the same thickness as the others, and Travis hunkered into his nest of fabric, determined to stay warm as he prepared to read the next epistle that Esther had left him on this journey.

October 15th, 2007

The Law Offices of Baylor, Backmann, and Lambert

555 West Main Street
San Francisco, California 94101

415-555-1212
415-555-1213 FAX
LawOffice@BBL.com

LAST WILL AND TESTAMENT OF
Esther Sansui

I, Esther Sansui, a resident of San Francisco, California, being of a decaying and eroded mind and memory and over the age of eighteen (18) years and not being actuated by any duress, menace, fraud, mistake, or undue influence, do make, publish, and declare this to be my last Will, hereby expressly revoking all Wills and Codicils previously made by me.

I.   **MARRIAGE***: I am not married, nor do I have any children. I have been committed to Travis Saint Croix, in mind, body, and spirit, for the last several years.*

II.   **EXECUTOR:** *I appoint Travis Saint Croix (despite his betrayals and his wretched ways) as Executor of this my Last Will and Testament. My Executor shall be authorized to carry out all provisions of this Will and pay my just debts, obligations, and funeral expenses. He shall also be responsible for letting others know how his very actions led to my demise, coupled with a staggering failure by the American medical profession.*

III.   **BEQUESTS***: I hereby bequest the following property to the following person(s), given that they survive a demise that will no doubt be brought about by my own hands:*

A: **My Mind***: I hereby leave my mind to the neurological research team at San Francisco State University. It is my sincere hope and prayer that my brain may be researched to see what may be done to prevent others from falling down the hellish spiral that I find myself entangled in. Although my Executor, Travis Saint Croix, holds a vast swath of responsibility for my demise, the pain that ills such as depression leaves on one's being can no longer be ignored. Therefore, it is my sincere hope that my mind can be used to further research into this vital field.*

B: **My Body:** *Although the Executor, Travis Saint Croix, was given my physical essence to do with what he pleased, he abused and lost said privilege when the staggering debts of his transgressions became too much to bear. Therefore, I wish to return my body to the Earth, and not complain about it. In Tibet, as in Bhutan, there is a* practice known among the Buddhist faithful as a sky burial. The body, after death, is ritually dissected and fed to the birds. The bones bleach in the sunlight, and eventually return to dust, thus fulfilling the circle of life. Therefore, after my mind is sent back to San Francisco, I want my body to be disposed of in this manner, as to not be a burden unto anyone else.

C: My Soul: The soul is a complicated matter, and one that neither Travis nor I have any experience with. I was never one for religion. I had no doubts that there was a God, but given my desperate state of mind, I never felt connected to a God that I felt was supposed to be benevolent in all of my affairs. Besides, what kind of Almighty allows evil men to either profit or slay in His infinite name? As far as my Executor, Travis Saint Croix goes? Well, I just assume he does not have a soul. Therefore, I leave my soul to whatever higher power is the right one and I hope with all my being that He/She/It understands, and shows mercy on it.

D: My Heart: I have spent the last several months warring with myself on this issue. Love starts with trust. To be loved is to never want for affection, to never fear what protects you, to never be rejected. I have experienced all of these things from the one I was supposed to love—my Executor, Travis Saint Croix. Yet, as the sun sets on my final hours in this wretched world, and I grow stronger in what must be done, I can't find it in my being to take away from Travis what he lost. My heart will always be his. This cannot be disputed, as much as I wish it could.

E: My Physical Belongings, my property, and my money: It is impossible for me to care any less what happens to my belongings. Burn it all.

IN WITNESS WHEREOF, I, Esther Sansui, hereby set my hand to this last Will, on each page of which I have placed my initials, on this 15th day of October, 2007 at the Law Offices of Baylor, Backmann, and

Lambert, 555 West Main Street, San Francisco, State of California.

━━━

Had that been the only page within, the fragile state of Travis's mind would have no doubt collapsed, leaving his mission uncompleted. However, there were other pages available, and Travis began to read again.

━━━

Travis,

It was my hope that you would never see the attached document. Perhaps if I had better control over my own emotions, we never would have come to Bhutan. In that regard, I was the one that failed. I was the one that made the egregious mistake of thinking I could resist doing what it was that I was destined to do. Some people are destined to lead quiet normal lives. Nobody writes books about their lives, simply because nobody wants to read something serene and peaceful.

The world is filled with drama queens. They've all become a bunch of clamoring fools trying to grab their fifteen minutes of fame. You see it every single day. Some idiot frat boy, parading around behind a reporter as they do their job, thinking every hip thrust and thumbs up will somehow bring him closer to Internet immortality. Every other post, on any social networking site, is either a slew of vile invective, a diarrhea of the mouth about agreeing with their own views, or, and much more commonly so, disagreeing with someone else's view that they find abhorrent. Some people need blogs, walls, and reams of pages of words and prose to do so; others do it in quips of one hundred and forty words or less. Never mind that they would never say such things to anyone's face; the fact that they seem bold and fresh enough to do it in public seems to be all the justification they need for their own righteousness. It's a bold and fresh piece of something, that much be assured.

Unlike the rest of the world, who only seem to wallow in unhappiness as a means to make themselves happy, I fought a daily battle with unhappiness. It was not of my doing, nor did I present it as something that I wanted the world to know about, much less something I wanted their pity for. I never had any social networking account. I never went online, seeking to let out a torrent of emotional turmoil, so that I could be coddled and mocked at the same time. When I hurt, I locked it in. I internalized it, and I dealt with it the best I could. I tried therapy, something I managed to keep private for years and years. It did not help. I tried medicine, forcing down whatever little remedies that the doctors had concocted as a way to force me into the mainstream of society. They failed, at least partially because of my own sabotage. I could not fathom how turning me into a mindless, drooling zombie was going to make me better. I cannot wrap my mind around how making our world dependent on a bunch of unnatural chemicals is going to make it a better place. It seems that they want to take the last visages of humanity and twist them up into some kind of drug addled, altered race, easy to control, with no real focus on how to fix us.

They say we are ill, but I say it is they that are ill. Ill with want. Ill with greed, poisoned by their insatiable desire for power, for profits, for the chance to have one more dollar or one more ounce of gold than the next. They've stopped looking at us as human beings, and started looking at us as livestock. We're cattle to them. We're lobotomy rats, bought and paid for experiment dolls. They control the doctors, because they will cut off their funding and shame them as quacks if they do not force the next pill down our throat. They control the hospitals, running the public sector out of business in favor of private, profitable hospitals that care less about the invalid and more about the invoice. They control the airwaves. I mean, what place does a commercial for an anti-depressant have during a family sitcom? A football game? The State of the Union Address? They're shameless whoremongers of greed, of everything that is wrong with the human experience.

And you became one of them.

The issue of Felix Jones wasn't your hill to die on. It wasn't yours to take point on, and it damn sure wasn't yours to take into your own hands. Your actions and words on that day led to Jones's death. I won't sit here and say that I am sad that Jones is gone, nor will I condone what you did in regards to him. But another man died that day. That day will live forever in infamy, emblazoned on your soul, and mine. Avett, for all of his desire to do exactly what I just condemned, did not deserve to die for his actions. And while you may not have pulled the trigger, while you may not have stabbed or shot or bludgeoned him, your actions led to his death, all in the line of him trying to do what was right. Felix Jones was abstract to him, just a point to report on, and perhaps in his own way, to rally against. However, when humanity stepped back in, when he saw the crumpled heap of a shell of a man, and not just some cause, he did what we should all hope we should be able to do in the face of adversity. He tried to save him.

He failed.

I have no idea why he was destined to fail. I have no idea as to the magnitude of sins he bore that eventually led to his demise. But at the end of the day, when all the news was reported and all was said that had to be said, Felix Jones and Stuart Avett had no control over how they went out. Heroes or villains, angels or demons, pariahs or martyrs, they lost the decision on how their days ended. The control was wrested from them by a society that thrives on the macabre and the extraordinary, all the while failing to honor the normal, the just, and what truly matters. Granted, you played a part in their demise, but it was a small part, and while you share blame, the fault is not all yours.

If anyone is to be held accountable, it's this sick fascination with the morally bankrupt that we have. (I speak of us as human beings, not necessarily you and I, although your actions do tend to lend to the theory that you subscribe to the same insane school of thought. But I digress.) It is this fascination with the fact that we can play God, that we have the right to swoop in and do away with any injustice we have. When are we going to learn that sometimes we're meant to suffer so that we may grow stronger? When are we going to learn that sometimes we have to survive the fires so that we are harder than steel when they rise up against us again? When are we going to learn that sometimes it's hell trying to get to heaven?

You don't get to control how hate and love are used in the world. You don't get to control how things will start and how they will end. You don't get to control how others live their lives. We all have a basic, fundamental right to make our own decisions, to do things as we see fit, and to have our own moral compass. We control ourselves. That's it. And when we try to step in and control the fate of others, people die. It's a role we have no right playing, and it's a space we do not belong in. We have a right to ourselves, and that's it. And when others take it upon themselves to try and take our right away, we have to be willing to do whatever it takes to keep that right.

You felt like you had to kick Felix Jones in the head. I felt like I had to go to Bhutan.

I will not be like Felix Jones. I will not be like Stuart Avett. I don't have much, and the day you took your love from me, I was left with even less. But I have control over how my story is written, and how it will end. And that is one thing I will not allow you to take from me. It's my life; it's my soul, my heart, and my body. It's not your call, it's mine, Travis, and you have no idea how much that liberates me, after so many years. I can stop you from deciding how my story will end. The only thing I cannot stop is the ever-intervening hand of fate, which is the reason you are reading this letter.

One of two things comes to me. Death or Travis. Behold, they both come, and one comes more quickly than the other. Even so, let them come. Let the one that is destined to win take their victory, and let the other weep and suffer over their loss, wondering what happened so that they may have failed in the manner they did. Of course, there should be no wondering. If Death wins, well then he finally got from me what he wanted for years. The right to dance the last dance, the right to allow me to be released, to miss the pain and suffering and agony and sorrow. It's a tempting offer, an offer that I have wanted to take more times than you will ever know. No weariness. No waking hours. Just the peaceful serenity of sleep, in some lonely mountain cave in Bhutan, loved and owned by one of the metaphysical, of the spiritual.

It makes you wonder why I haven't taken Death's offer before now.

These letters were written along my journey to the cave, and my mental and emotional states have been up and down, to say the least. The journey took me far less time, so most of it was spent with pen and paper in hand. I've had time to ponder many things, Travis.

The one recurring theme is that hope springs eternal.

As much as I want death, seek death, and even desire it, a larger part of it wants my breath of life, my drink of water, and my hero back. (That's you, silly.) I know if you find me, my kingdom will be at hand, and my mistakes will be forgiven. I saw the remorse that rocked you at Stuart Avett's funeral. I denied that it was anything more than you chasing every second of your legacy. I denied it with every fiber of my being for as long as I could. I put it off as an exercise in arrogance, in fraud, in you not being able to let it go. Only now, on this trip, have I seen it for what it really is.

Your return to humanity. You're finally walking away from what was not your role to play.

Hope springs eternal, Travis. I await you.

-Esther

CHAPTER 17

Travis sat for what seemed like an eternity. The guilt of the Jones-Avett incident, as it was called in U.S. media, was now blunted, dulled by Esther's words. He had made mistakes, that fact could not be denied. But, then again, so had others. Jones had signed his own death warrant by trying to incite hatred and fear in the very hearts of the youth that had grown up without it. Travis's actions were a unilateral rejection of those beliefs, one final nail in the coffin of the racial hatred that had haunted the American psyche for so long. Jones's death, while unfortunate, had sanctified those who had begun to question their own feelings, and had probably saved other lives. As for Avett? Why he wanted to save Jones in the beginning was incomprehensible to Travis. The mere fact that Felix Jones could have survived his sins against humanity was grotesque to Travis. Avett's heart could not be questioned. His judgment, perhaps, but not his heart. Travis, however, took solace in the fact that the decision to endanger himself had belonged to Avett. He wrote his final chapter, regardless if Travis had closed that door, or had walked through it.

The human spirit had revived itself within Travis. He was going to reach Esther, to atone for his mistakes, to let the rains of righteousness wash away whatever sins he had committed against her. She was offering penance, forgiveness, and atonement, whatever it was to be called. He would be a fool not to take it.

Travis took stock of himself. His eye was gone, ripped from his head. He was certain he would spend the rest of his days impaired by its unceremonious departure. All eight of his knuckles were a swollen, grotesque mess. A few were split and bleeding, still others had bark embedded in them, and the largest on each hand were split down to the bone, the stark white making a macabre contrast to both his bruised flesh and the little rivulets of blood that had traced the length of his forearms, finally pooling at his elbows. His face was bruised and swollen from the tree limb, and unbeknownst to him, he had fractured both his ocular socket and his nose. In short, his face looked like a swollen, grotesque ball of discolored putty.

He looked like he had stepped in the ring for twelve rounds of boxing with Mike Tyson, only Tyson was not wearing gloves.

That was just the damage to his face and hands.

His entire body ached. Joints that he did not know existed screamed with the agony of overuse, malnutrition, and pain. His legs were sore, his feet swollen and bruised from the rocky terrain. The whole experience had pushed him to a physical limit that he did not know existed in him.

Mentally, he was much worse for wear. Never a big fan of self-doubt, the feelings of failure, of despair, and even of suicide had made Travis doubt himself more than ever. He was able to forgive himself for Stuart Avett's death. He was able to forgive himself for what he had done to Esther. This was a new level of self-hatred, a new level of questioning what was right that shook Travis to his very core. The lost eye, the breaks and bumps and bruises were something he could overcome. The crippling despair, the lingering self-doubt and self-loathing was something he was not accustomed to.

Overcoming such failures was not an option. Pushing back down a festering illness such as this was not something that could be done, at least not with the resources that lay within. In all, Travis reasoned, the only way for him to become himself again was to find Esther, and do whatever it took to reunite the pair. Granted, he could not help but roll his one good eye at himself. It was turning out like a pathetic romance novel, where the sad protagonist continues to seek the affections of one who may or may not want him, but in turn does not want anything to do with wanting themselves.

He spent many hours at the base of that great tree, in complete peace and utter silence, contemplating what his next move should be. Part of him, the only rational part that still existed, pleaded with him to pack up and get the hell out of Bhutan. There were plenty of beautiful girls. Hell, there were plenty of regular girls that he could settle down with and start a family. He could leave San Francisco and head back to Tennessee. He could head to any city in any state. Denver. Atlanta. Boston. Anchorage was even a possibility! He could find a woman, settle down, start a family, and bury his sordid history from San Francisco. The greatest thing about having fifteen minutes of fame was that it ended. It was so easy. So incredibly easy. In fact, it was almost too easy. How in the blue hell had he evaded charges? Was Jones such a universally reviled figure that even those who upheld the law were loath to bring Travis to justice?

Best not to dwell on it. After all, all of his future paths, at the moment, rendered the matter moot.

With a sigh, he reached into his bag and pulled out a plain cotton t-shirt. Slowly, with sore and shaking hands, he ripped the shirt, tearing it into several strips about two inches wide and a foot in length. His first option was to pursue Esther, and do the right thing, and for him, this was still an attractive option. The second option was an attractive option too. Buried deep in his pack was a unit called a PLB, which stood for personal locator beacon. A PLB was a global distress beacon, commonly seen on boats that tended to fish and travel in rough waters; however, PLBs had become common among hikers. The one in Travis's pack weighed less than half a pound, and was smaller than his cell phone. The beacon could be activated at any time, and would alert the local authorities that someone was distressed. Travis had spent quite an extra bit of money making sure that GPS coordinates for Bhutan were loaded into the device. He had registered the device with

Bhutanese customs on their last trip to the country, and it would also send notice to NOAA and SAR, two groups in the States that would be able to alert the Bhutanese authorities to whom the beacon was registered. The emergency contact was an old friend named Jeff, from San Francisco State, who had managed to stay away from the entire Felix Jones affair. However, Jeff had been briefed on Travis's trip, whom he was going after and why, and if NOAA or SAR contacted him, he would be able to relay information. The system was all digital and included a strobe light. Travis could be rescued in a matter of hours. This nightmare would end, and he could turn the rescue of Esther, if it could be called that, over into the hands of those that knew what they were doing. The nightmare, for what it was worth, would end, and Travis would be missing little except his eye.

His eye, of course, and his honor. Travis took the straps and piled them one on top of another until they were half an inch thick. With caution, he picked up the impromptu bandage and wrapped it diagonally around this head, coming across his eye at an angle. The exposed socket was covered completely, keeping out the cold and other elements. Grimacing, he took the flexible collar from his shirt and pulled it down over the crown of his head, using it as a means to help hold the bandage in place.

Oh, the temptation was there. All he had to do was flick a little switch on the device and a little beam of radio waves would hurtle itself towards a satellite orbiting hundreds of miles above his head. Bhutan would be a thing of the past. Esther would become, slowly, a faded memory, a brief little aberration in what would otherwise be a normal life.

The rescue beacon was in his hand, shaking. The side of him that still deferred to logic was waging war in his head, bound and determined to win a battle for the physical being that was known as Travis Saint Croix.

With a soft curse, Travis lowered the beacon and

shoved it back into the bag, taking care not to set it off.

He wanted nothing more than to let her go. However, try as he might, he simply could not. A soft whimper evaded his lips and escaped into the night air. Why? Why had whatever great power in the universe decided to both bless and curse him with such a bond to Esther? The thoughts he had thought, thoughts that made him want to abandon her, had made him all but physically ill. He could not let her pass from his life. He could not move on and walk away. He could not gather himself up and take the short walk back to sanity, despite knowing the other path diverged into his own trials of madness and into his own self-destruction.

Fact of the matter was, Travis reasoned as he stood, gathering his surroundings so that he could ponder his next move, his existence depended on hers.

Now, if he could only find his way out of this cursed forest...

Looking northeast, Travis could not believe his eyes. There was the rising sun. Right above the tree line.

A tree line that was at its end. He had managed to navigate Bhutan's forest of death and despair. In the one place where people in Bhutan came to die, he had walked out alive.

He had passed through the Sorrows.

CHAPTER 18

    Travis stared at his dad for a moment, incredulous. "Enlist? Look, Pops, I've known for quite a while that you were a little out there, but do you honestly expect me to run out and sign up for a career path I've never given a moment's consideration to because of some events that happened in New York City? Any other time, you'd be spouting off about how much of a trash hole New York is. There's enough hopeless war mongering in this world without me adding my piece. I'm not going to enlist for anything. Not now and not ever." Clenching his fists, Travis set his jaw and prepared for his father's wrath.

    He should have prepared better. His father's speed betrayed his many imagined ailments, and without warning, the old man had Travis pinned against the wall. Gripping Travis's collar in his hands, he was literally face to face with his son. He sneered. "You're just like any other coward that has run from defending these colors. Hell, you're just like that draft dodging nigger Muhammad Ali, aren't you? I should take you out back and shoot …"

    Those were the last words the old man got out of his mouth. Perhaps it was from being pushed around, perhaps it was the threat of dying for a cause that he did not believe in, perhaps it was hurt, the simple pain of being dehumanized by one of the people responsible for bringing you into this world. Tears, pushed out by anger and sorrow, blurred his vision as he swung. The left hand came from left field, and landed on his father's nose like a bomb. Blood splattered across the elder Saint Croix's face, turning his face into a macabre pale and crimson canvas. He fell to the hardwood floor like a stack of bricks.

    In war, soldiers rarely give pause to what they are doing. Their heinous acts, while sometimes heroic, are all done in the sense of ending the life of another, whether it be in order to preserve their own life, or for a cause that they see as beyond their singular existence, benefitting the greater good. Travis had no idea why, but the second his father hit the floor, he was over him, like a wild animal stalking his prey. His father made it to his hands and knees, rocking back and forth on all fours. He was muttering curses, threats, the sort of primal growls you'd expect from a wounded animal fighting for its mere existence. The only problem was he had knocked Travis on his back one too many times. Travis was bigger and stronger than the one who saw to rule over him and he was not going to give him another chance to hurt him. With a sneer, Travis delivered a kick to his father's ribs. The point of his boot meeting flesh was sickening, giving off a loud and disgusting crack to let both parties know that something was broken. Travis delivered another kick, the second just as hard as the first, and the old man crumpled over to his side, curled up in the fetal position, almost whimpering.

Eyes filling with tears, Travis spoke with a primal rage that betrayed his raw emotions. "All you've ever been able to do is mooch off others while claiming some higher order, some greater calling. You strut around and tell people that you're the closest thing to perfection that they will ever see, and that you're the greatest thing going on God's green earth. You know what I see, Pops? I see the crumpled shell of an old man, one that was not going to be happy until he forced his own flesh and blood into being what he was. You know what the difference is?" Travis knelt next to his father's head, grabbing a handful of hair and sneering as he brought his father's eyes to meet his. "The difference is you're a pathetic bag of hot air that would have no idea what standing up to anything is. When push comes to shove, when it comes time to do what is required of all of us, you don't stand up; you stand aside and hide behind some justified shield of an excuse to keep from making the hard decisions." He brought the old man's face, wide-eyed with astonishment and fear, eye to eye with him as he spoke. He was shouting now, loud enough to be heard three generations back. "Is this the reason why you shoved this on me, Pops? So you could justify the way you treated me? So you could make it okay to the world for holding me to higher standards than you did yourself? You forced this take, this whole no-holds-barred, take-no-prisoners thing to a whole new level. One you cannot reach yourself, and yet the second I have enough gall to push back against your wild-eyed conspiracy bullshit, you decide to lay your hands on me. I've messed up, and I know I don't have the courage to sit there and innocently kill people with a gun, in the name of a higher calling that I've never heard. How selfish of you, you pitiful fucking shell of a man. You dried up, withered up old bastard! You selfish ass! I hope you burn in hell for this shit!"

Travis slammed the graying head against the floor one time before releasing it, staring at the blood that had congealed between his fingers before he spoke. He lowered himself down even further, lying on his stomach parallel to his father. When he spoke again, his voice was almost a whisper. "We all die eventually, Pops. I don't have any plans of dying for a group of fat cats that care nothing about me. Now, this may be the last time we speak, this may be the last time you want to see me, because I sure as hell have no desire to see you again. Maybe in the future, but not now. So, it would be remiss for me not to tell you this. This insanity, this madness that is the Saint Croix madness, dies with me. I'll make myself a eunuch before I ever let another child from this arrogant, self-righteous line come into the world. There are plenty of children out there that I can give a good home to. Hell, maybe if I decide to get married, I can find a wife who will share her last name with me, and we can put this madness to a rest. I want no part of it. Your line dies with you. And I'll see to that."

Travis slowly pushed himself from the floor. Part of him was disgusted with what he had done—disgusted that the old man had finally goaded the one reaction out of him that he had wanted. The old man rolled over to his back and grinned up at the ceiling. Despite the pain, and the streaks of blood that were running down the sides of his face to the floor, he grinned, gasping for air. "So there it is, boy. You've finally learned what it is to lose it. You know what anger is. You know what it is to hate."

Travis had turned to walk out the door. Every fiber of his being told him to walk away, save for one part. As loath as he was to admit it, there was a small yet insistent part of him that had enjoyed the sheer brutality of what had happened. It was violent poetry, something he had wanted to do for a long, long time. At this moment, he had gone as far as he could have ever seen himself going. He allowed this part of him, this unnamed feeling, to egg him a little further. "Hate? Any hate I possess will die with you." Rearing his leg back, he delivered a kick right to the old man's crotch. He could almost feel the old man's testicles pop as he *screamed in agony. He spat in his face for good measure, and then walked out the door, slamming it as he went.*

———————————————

The memory was not one that Travis was particularly fond of reliving, but it was one that he knew that he could not forget. It was one of two times in his life that he had become exactly what he swore he would never be. The other time had been in that auditorium, with Felix Jones and Stuart Avett. He had destroyed his relationship with his father. That in itself was not a great loss, but it was still something he regretted. Had he tried harder to appease the old man...Travis shook such thoughts of regret from his mind and tried to forget the whole thing. The whole situation was too heavy of a burden for him to carry at the moment.

His surroundings did precious little to help. Jomolhari was an icon of beauty, a towering, snow-covered goddess that made the Himalayas the breathtaking wonder they are. The mountain rose almost five miles into the heavens, crossing the point where man was able to breathe and most birds were able to fly. Airplanes had to be pressurized to make breathing viable at this height. Yet there she stood, along with seventy-five of her brethren, towering over the worlds, the masters and rulers of our universe, as well as the benevolent giants, the unmoving, courageous foundation that is mankind's gateway to the heavens. Men had stared at these mountains with wonder and amazement, with courage and hope, seeing the ladder to their dreams, all the while vaguely aware of the graveyard of brave souls that littered these great giants. Few things outside of religion had led men to salvation and natural death. It is little wonder, then, that the Buddhists of Bhutan and Tibet see the peaks as holy, as blessed by the sacraments of their gurus and their enlightened.

Jomolhari was the altar on which Esther was to sacrifice her love for Travis. Jomolhari was the great wall that

Travis had to climb to reunite him with the only thing that made sense to him in the world.

All that lay between them was a series of windswept plains that made the forest Travis had just departed from seem like a magical wonderland. Not much grows in the barren tundra that surrounds the base of most of the Himalayas, and the land on any side of Jomolhari was no exception. It wasn't that the land was devoid of life. Many herd of yak, led around by their tired-eyed yet faithful shepherds, dotted the landscape, patches of brown, white, and black wool in a sea of brown grass. Settlements dotted the landscape to and fro, some still standing, some left behind by chieftains and hordes long passed from the land. The Paro Chhu river intersected the valley at points, finding its origins on the mountain and yet having been around long enough to take a gentle, rolling path to its destination, some places rushing with rapids and others moving along at barely a trickle, betraying the fact that this river had been around far longer than man of any stripe had settled here. Most people took a circular route, approaching the peak in a path that rounded the trip from the north and ended it at the south, back towards the south and civilization. Travis, however, had traveled in a straight, dissecting path since the start of the trip, and he was loath to change such a habit now.

Calling the valley a wasteland did little justice to its own peculiar brand of desolate beauty. The surroundings were born of the north, of cold winds and colder snow. The place bred hard men and women, hearty people who spent every second in a race to beat the cold. That was not to say the people here were cold people; despite being born of ice and iron, they were a benevolent people, as was commonplace in Bhutan. They never hesitated to help someone, whether it be friend or visitor, and they did so with a glad heart and without expectation of favor. Oh, there were exceptions, as there are in any culture, but unlike so many others, they were just that—

exceptions as opposed to the rule.

Travis knew, however, that he was to forge this chapter alone, to go his own way and press towards the finality of whatever Esther had in store for him. In all honesty, he had thought little about what would happen beyond retrieving Esther; so much had happened in such a short time that the thought of anything beyond his next few steps was exhausting. He had little clue to the end game, what it was, or how he was going to handle it. What if she had regained her madness and was willing to leave with Travis, only to go her own way once they parted? What if she refused to leave the mountain? What if he arrived, only to be too weak to depart from where he was, destined to die in a cold, rocky tomb?

The thought of finding Esther dead was not one that crossed his mind. He simply could not cope with worrying about that.

Betrayal and desolation. A sound and a fury, this whole matter was riding to a wave of finality. Figuring he had spent enough time standing around and pondering, Travis reached to the back of his skull, making sure that the bandage that covered his eye wound was secure. Some of the crimson blood had soaked through the bandage, and this was a source of worry for Travis. He was outputting energy much faster than he was putting it in, and the extra trauma to his body would do little to help keep his reserves in place. It was a race now, a race of time and energy and wits, and Travis needed every resource he had to succeed.

Thankfully, the ground was soft enough to manage, without being too soft to impede his progress. The weather, while far from comfortable, was warm enough to allow for aching joints to move a little freer. His pace quickened a little, and Travis actually managed to whistle as he walked, beginning his slow trek from the valley. The high grass was pushed aside easily enough as he stepped, and for the first time in several days, Travis saw hope and promise in what he was doing.

There was nothing wrong, in his view, of looking at the issue with a sense of pragmatic hope. He had made it this far, so perhaps Daimyo was right. Perhaps the winds of fate and destiny, the great karmic scale, the divine intervention of whatever god Esther chose, was leading him to do what was right. Oh, there had been sacrifices, something he was quickly reminded of when he brought his hand to his head, to re-adjust again and again the damp bandage that covered where his eye used to be. But iron was forged in steel. The will of man had proven time and time again that it could survive the most hellish of circumstances, to come out victorious and triumphant on the other side.

As he marched across the valley, Travis saw himself as another example in this great human experiment.

CHAPTER 19

As it often had been in the turbulence that consisted of their relationship, while Travis was taking the view of the bigger picture, Esther was still trying to figure out the riddle within. Although she had contemplated taking her own life several times, this had, by far, been the closest she had come to success. Despite her suicidal nature, Esther was not the type to seek attention. She had shunned the advice of doctors and shrinks and psychologists and even spiritual advisors without a thought. She had told very few people of what ailed her. She didn't spend time spouting off longwinded diatribes on some blog, or some wordy, self-important post on social media, or even a quip in a text message. She didn't have a dark sense of humor; in fact, although the daily specter of death haunted her very existence, it had never found a way to pervade her art, or her entertainment.

On the flipside, even though she had fought against death by living, she had thought, for the longest time, she was simply existing, and not truly living. Before Travis, she had not spent much time traveling, and even less enjoying the arts. She didn't obsess over a particular detail or scream with righteous indignation at some injustice, whether real or perceived. She was not big on social groups and gatherings. She didn't give holidays or birthdays or anniversaries or even the deaths of others more than a passing thought. It wasn't an obsession with her own sorrow; if anything, it was a reflection of the bleakness of her own condition and a realization that if she ever bothered to break down those walls, it would lead to the chance of others to be hurt by something she saw as inevitable. In essence, she protected others by protecting herself.

She stirred, nature rousing her out of a confused haze

of half dreams and confusing nightmares. The cave was old enough and high enough as to allow for a decent sense of cleanliness and privacy without the sharing with wild creatures, and as she eased into the deeper darkness to relieve herself, Esther was grateful. There was little filth to be found on the cave walls, and despite the nature of the spring that provided her with water, there was nothing to be seen in the way of plant growth. Perhaps a few stout bugs, used to the cold extremes, but the cold and elevation kept out even the hardiest of creatures.

Matters of sanitation complete, Esther walked back to her fire in a haze. The wood had burned down to embers, and while she had a fairly sizable stockpile (for which she had paid a handsome price), she still saw common sense in preserving what resources she had. If Travis succeeded and found her, there would be no way of knowing what condition he would be in. He could be starved, injured, frostbitten, even dying of hypothermia. Fuel for the fire would be a resource that was in demand in those situations, she reasoned, and although Travis had been a pig-headed fool, she had dragged him into this mess. In that situation, if he succeeded, it would be on her to preserve him. The weather at this elevation was unpredictable, oxygen was in short supply, and they could be weather-bound for days. It could take a huge supply of wood to keep a fire warm enough to preserve them.

Shaking her head, Esther absently reached for a small bottle from her supplies. Hand sanitizer. She had just relieved herself, and well, even in death, she was not a creature to be unclean. She squeezed a small amount into her hands and rubbed them together vigorously for a few moments. If she had, in fact, come here to die, then by no means would it be because she had decided to skip on a little personal hygiene. *More than a little*, Esther thought with a small smile. For reasons known only to her, she had brought two giant bottles of the stuff, to use to refill the dozen or so smaller bottles that had also made the track.

Chuckling, Esther finished rubbing her hands, enjoying the antiseptic smell of the cleanser. It was a sharp, alcohol tinged smell...Esther stared dumbly at the embers for a moment. That was it! The hand sanitizer! If the flames died out and starting the fire was an absolute necessity, then perhaps she could use some of the gel as a catalyst to restore the fire.

Eyes dancing with hope, Esther gathered herself up and walked over to the large pile of dry, seasoned wood that was stored within the cave. She selected a small branch and returned to her station beside the fire pit.

A smirk on her face, Esther sat the small branch before her. Digging into her packs, she pulled out one of the larger bottles of the gel, grunting with an effort that betrayed how weak she had grown. Squirting a large dollop onto her hand, she worked feverishly to spread the liquid before it dried. Once applied, she reached into the pack for the small butane lighter she had brought along, in case the embers vanished for some reason and making another fire was a necessary. She stood, putting the lighter close to the stick while extending her body as far away as possible, as if the stick might go off like a small bomb. Closing her eyes, she struck the lighter and opened them to see the stick engulfed in a tiny blue flame. The flame spread slowly, but before long, it had engulfed the entire stick. Esther watched with a small creeping of joy as her little experiment proved to be the key in another way of surviving, if indeed she was destined to survive. As the stick continued to burn, she slowly heaved a couple of dry logs onto the fire and built it up once again.

Sinking down next to the fire, she watched as her little stick danced with flames, slowly shifting from blue to white-yellow as the sanitizer burned off and the wood took its natural course as fuel. She had figured it out, she told herself with a gentle smile, and if for some reason she needed to be the hero, she would. Travis was coming, after all.

Reaching into her pack once more, she pulled out a candy bar. Munching away happily, she could see hope for herself. If she could learn fire, then perhaps this learning to live, as opposed to existing, would not kill her, after all.

Despite the circumstances that had brought him here, Travis could not help but enjoy the sheer natural beauty that was an integral part of Bhutan. The closest thing he could compare his current surroundings to was the windswept plains of Wyoming, a place he had visited as a child, his mind holding only disconnected memories of the barren beauty therein. He had not visited this section of Bhutan in his previous trip. Sadly, school had called him back before Esther had ventured this far north, and it was with a tinge of regret that Travis realized what he had missed out on. It was not so much that he had neglected to spend time with Esther; if anything, he had been a little too constant in her every day, to the point of dependence. It was a simple regret, of missing the simplicity of the tranquil existence of the few Bhutanese hardy enough to survive this area.

There was so much natural beauty to behold here. Rivers, fairly young by the planet's standards. Several outlets and a couple of major branches began their journey here, runoff from the extreme peaks and meltwater from millennium-old glaciers feeding them on their long, winding journeys. For the most part, these streams were slow moving, yawning, tranquil little pools, moving along without the urgency of some of their larger cousins stateside. These basins, despite being in their infancy, provided a fresh drink as well as the life force for the local yak. The water here was cool, clear, and clean, harmed neither by the runoff of urban population centers or the harsh elements that churned up sediment further down the Indian subcontinent.

The plains held their own sort of majesty. Dry reeds covered the few spots that were dotted with high vegetation—reeds that, at this time of year, were bleached a light tan from drying and freezing out. They were of stiff construction, rough and firm to the touch. Despite the layer of permafrost and the harsh environment, they had adapted to thrive in this landscape, providing a molded sea of brown for Travis to navigate. Although the ground froze every night, and, for the most part, remained frosted this time of year, it was of a sandy loam, pleasant to touch and, with the proper preparations, not uncomfortable to sleep on.

There were a few wintergreens spread about, mostly measuring in the size of a small shrub. The little bushes dotted the landscape to and fro, able to spread out shallow root systems and thrive where their larger tree cousins could not penetrate. The deep emerald green of their foliage blended into, as opposed to contrasting with, the browns and blacks of the grass and mud, and painted a muted yet beautiful landscape for Travis to transverse. A few grayed boulders, coupled with scattered patches of snow that refused to melt, completed the simple yet beautiful landscape.

From the plains, the ground rose violently, moving from the rolling foothills where few of even the hardiest of man and animal inhabited, on up into the gigantic mountains themselves. Bhutan, along with the rest of the Indian subcontinent, had rammed unceremoniously into Southeast Asia millions of years ago and created a series of rocky crags. Time, along with heat and pressure, had pushed these growing giants skyward, to a place so high in the heavens that the men who found themselves in the area at the dawn of intelligent life had no choice but to think that the peaks were holy unto themselves. The government of Bhutan to this day respected the holiness that their ancient brethren had bestowed upon the mighty peaks, issuing laws that forbade sport mountaineering on their side of the Himalayas. Although Tibet, the British, the

Italians, the Germans, and finally the Chinese had ignored Bhutan's desire for reverence of the peaks, some of them had remained virgin, and Bhutan, in fact, is home to the world's highest unscaled mountain.

Sadly, Jomolhari had been scaled before the tiny nation could stop it, but the climbs had done little to decrease its holiness in the eyes of the faithful. The Bride, as it was known locally, towered close to five miles above sea level, providing a majestic backdrop to Travis's journey. A hazard to anyone who dared brave it, the steep peak was a harrowing, breathtaking blend of gray, blue, and white. The hard rock that made its foundation inched up every year as the land masses pushed together every hour, extending its hand higher and higher to the heavens. The blue from the ancient glaciers and the white from the centuries-old snow capped off one of the few places where a man could not be sure where Earth ended and the heavens themselves began.

Thankfully, the stars handled that. Save for a few lamps used by the local yak herders and the occasional purplish smoke plume from one of their quaint little huts, there was little to obstruct one's nighttime view of the skyline

What a majestic view it was! Millions of stars dusted a sky that was darker than even the evil hearts of man. Despite the snow, the tundra and high plains were scant of precipitation, the land being too far inward to feel the effects of monsoon season. It was a stargazer's dream, one of the few places where many a feeble attempt at light did not outshine the pure, awe-inspiring spectacle of what nature provided. Nary a star was missed, nary was there a constellation that could not be easily identified by even the most rudimentary of sky watchers. There was, to use a tired cliché, no place like it on Earth.

Night shifted to day once more, and Travis plodded along with only a hint of where he was going. Hours ran together, the brilliant white haze of the midday sun blending in with the airy blue of the sky, dawn shifting to noon and back to dusk with a brilliant explosion of pinks and purples, all making even the darkened gray hue of the scattered clouds seem a little brighter. A post card could not have done the scene justice, yet so absorbed in his own thoughts and pain was Travis that even the brilliance of raw nature could not grab his attention.

Oh, his thoughts still drifted to and fro, but there was little of importance that came to mind at this point in his trek. Thoughts came and went, and while they drifted from Esther to Jones to Avett to the States to some of humanity's greatest mysteries and back again, in a circle, they were just that: abstract thought. There was none of the earlier self-loathing, none of the violent anger, none of shame and regret. Remorse had been set aside, and hope had been cast away like a ship at sea. A great measure of time was spent refocusing his vision. The missing ocular appendage had thrown his vision askew, making things seem that they were much farther to the left than they truly were. After several bumps and near misses with foliage and stones, Travis soon figured out how to adjust his field of vision, to compensate what was no longer a part of his being.

Matters of vision aside, Travis had become just another moving mass in a great sea of matter. When he was tired, he would stop and sit for a few moments, always making sure to pull several handfuls of dry reeds loose from the ground. The dried grass made a wonderful seat, keeping his clothing dry against the muck. After a few breaths, Travis would stretch his tired, sore muscles and rise to walk again, always taking a moment to adjust the bandage on his head. When he was thirsty, he would stop at one of the many little pools that dotted the landscape, or occasionally at the big river itself. Unlike their relatives down in India, the rivers in Bhutan were given similar reverence to that given to the mountains, and there was no fear of contamination when one decided to partake. Sometimes Travis would use a cup, other times he simply thrust his head into the cold waters, drinking his fill while the shock of the glacial runoff woke him from the perpetual state of drowsiness that he carried around. When exhaustion prepared to overtake him, he would finally concede and build a small shelter, burning a fire to keep warm as he slept with the frost nipping at his face.

If Travis's story was building to an uneasy crescendo, then Esther's story was roaring forth to a finality that, while predictable, still made for a macabre scene. In her addled mind, it seemed like ages since she'd arrived in Bhutan, although it had only been a matter of a few short weeks. The cold stone walls of the cave had long since ceased to be any sort of comfort, instead growing to resemble the walls of the tomb that would encase her forever. Where she had found solace before in the peace and solitude of her own thoughts, now she found the desperate ramblings of the insane. The voices that spoke to her in her head were of many tongues, some calm and reassuring, some angry and violent, some sad and despondent, and even a few that were apathetic to her situation. There was little she could do to stop this spiral into madness. The more she tried to reach back and grasp reality, the further away it seemed to pull, content to leave her as she had long desired, trapped in a foreboding land of nightmares and half-truths. Self-loathing was now a way of life. Madness was the only one she could count on.

So on the madness went, taking a little of her each time it forced her to the brink of self-destruction. There was a desire to live, a desire for peace and happiness somewhere beneath all of the desolation. Each time, however, she seemed to close in on regrouping, it all fell apart, to leave her wailing in sorrow before whatever god it was that found such perverse pleasure in torturing his children in this manner.

Her thoughts, much like Travis's, were no longer centered in reality. Somehow, her pain was relieved through abstract musings. She wondered if this was a reincarnation of a past life that had inflicted pain on others, only to have the mental anguish return several generations later. Perhaps this was punishment for the fact that she was born in sin, the product, as much as she hated to admit, of a Scandinavian playboy who felt the need to shoplift the goods of her whore of a mother. Not that she loathed her mother for what she had been, or what she had done; in fact, it was something that Esther had considered herself.

Mental illness is a tricky thing. People often wonder how even those who are the most beautiful amongst us struggle with the demons of self-loathing, not realizing that, more often than not, it is society's expectations that drive us to the dark places we seek. The images of what is supposed to be beautiful are driven into our collective conscience on a daily basis. Young women are often encouraged, subconsciously if not directly, to mistreat their own person in the name of vanity and beauty. Body mutilation, once a crass, third-world punishment for those that did not meet the standards of religious extremists, is now something that is practiced in order to make oneself a more suitable, and sought after, companion. Women (as well as men, to an extent), go larger here, smaller there, more pronounced here, a different color or shape there, all in an effort to appease the insistent little voice that tells them that they are not good enough.

Despite her raving and unique beauty, Esther was no different. Such traits were sometimes deadly even in those of the soundest of mind. One thing that helped others, however, was the resolve to do something about what they perceived as ailing them. With Esther, hesitation and indecisiveness only seemed to compound the matter. The rest of the world could take a drink, take a drag or a hit, and things were better. They could have surgery or bring themselves to vomit up a perfectly good meal. Their action seemed to placate their fears, or better yet, expound on them to a point where they actually sought help.

Esther was the textbook definition of someone who was paralyzed by her own submissiveness. So paralyzed was she by the thought of independent action that she found herself reveling in the role of a slave—often, but not always, quite willing to do whatever it was that someone else commanded her to do. In the arena of academics, this suited her well, as she was constantly striving to please those who taught her. This was viewed in a vast majority of cases as Esther simply being a willing pupil. In a scant few others, it was seen as her playing the sycophant, taking any level of appeasement in order to gain the grade she desired. None could understand her total commitment to what was a very real slavery, at least in her eyes. She expected to be miserable, to be subservient, and even to be slave-like, because it was the only thing she could see as being pleasing to others.

Her thoughts often turned, in these hours, to the omnipresent God that everyone seemed to think was behind all of creation. Was her role preordained by Him, an existence that was, by her standards, all too much to bear? Was it something that she had control over, and, as everyone had tried to tell her, was something she could snap out of? Was it all just a cesspool of chaos? The last was what truly terrorized her. If God had no control, and she had no control, then what evil force of the world was driving her to the brink of the very insanity that she so feared? There were no answers, just more questions, and with more questions came more fear, more nightmares, and a stronger desire to die.

One thought, however, was stronger than all the others. Lying on the stone floor, staring up at the gray lid of what was to be her tomb; Esther was consumed with the thought of how she was going to end it. In a fit of rage, she had pitched the cursed container that she thought contained cyanide out the door of the cave. For all she knew, the damned thing had fallen off the side of the mountain, or, if she was lucky, off the very face of the earth. She had not brought a firearm; any wound from such a device would leave her disfigured and unsuitable for Travis to view. Even in these last and dark moments, she still wanted him to adore her as he once had, and she simply could not see him doing so in the macabre scene of a violent death. Such thoughts also eliminated immolation, not that she had the materials and the skill to burn herself alive. Many thoughts had been given to hanging, and there were several suitable rock formations that could be used to lace a rope around. With a simple leap off a nearby boulder, the deed would be done, and she could finally close her eyes and take whatever peace the universe would give her.

She thought for a while that the solution was in place, until she thought of the rock giving way and leaving her to crash to the floor, severely wounded but undying. Then what? If Travis somehow found her, alive but mortally wounded, was he to haul her from the cave into the elements in a vain attempt to save her? The thought made her shudder. She did not wish to be any more a burden than she already was. What if he never came and she was to sit there for days, even weeks on end, defecating on her person, stuck in a situation from where she could not move, and dying in a disgusting pit of filth? This thought scared her even more.

This left two possible choices, neither of which was attractive. The first was to walk from the cave door and throw her person down the adjacent rock face, almost a mile to what was to be a sure and very messy death. This solved several problems. It left the locals with one less body to dispose of, as on most Himalayan peaks, bodies in dangerous places were left to the forces of nature to decompose. Their retrieval was simply too risky for the living, and what did the dead care? Secondly, it spared Travis from having to view her disfigured corpse. Hopefully, in this case, his last images of her would be one of where he viewed her at her most beautiful, as opposed to the sick, suicidal shell of a person she now was.

The second choice was amongst the folds of her robes. Therein lay a blade of the same style and color of the one Travis now carried, but smaller. Most Japanese blades came in sets such as this, but for Esther, the size of the blade held its own meaning. It was the tale of the greater and the lesser, the leader and the follower, the master and the slave, the dominant and the submissive. Her blade was smaller than his because it was in her nature to be less than he was. Travis had been her anchor, her rock, her constant, and her universe. It was not in her nature to cast him from her existence, despite her ravings in the letter that had been left for him. She needed him. Even in the end, even as her eyes closed one last time, she would need him.

The blade had been sharpened to a razor thin edge, and Esther removed it from the folds of her silks with great care. Unsheathing it, she caught a ragged view of herself in the reflection of the polished steel. Oh, how she loathed herself. How the hatred boiled right underneath the surface of her skin. She should have been better, she should have tried harder to please him and make him want her to the point that he could never part with her as he did! She should have stood beside her rebel, her outlaw, even when he crowed and ranted and tried to take on a role he was not suited for. She should have given him the credit and adulation he so desired, she should have made herself available to him physically, mentally, spiritually, and emotionally. She should have done what she was destined to do, instead of raging against a yoke that was so befitting of her. Staring back at that reflection, she hated herself. She hated the hand of fate that had made her this creature. Alas, try as she might, she could not hate Travis. There was nothing left to hate.

The blade slipped from her hands as she sank to her

knees, another pitiful wail coming from deep within her chest. There was simply no energy left to rage as she had before. Instead there was just the soft sobbing of a defeated woman. Silent tears slid down her cheeks as she asked herself, not for the first time, how she had become so withered and worn. She had no more room for deep musings, no more desire for context and rationale. She was alone, in a tomb of ice and rock, in an isolated cave thousands of miles away from everyone she knew and loved, save for one. Here, in a small pocket of the Indian subcontinent, in a nation that few had heard of and even fewer cared about, she was slowly losing a fight she was destined to lose from the beginning.

Malnutrition and exhaustion stepped in to once again pull her from the edge of destruction. Slowly, surely, she sank to the cave floor, curling herself up in a ball, small and insignificant to the rest of existence. Her thoughts began to blur and soften, finally relaxing enough to where they were not causing her so much pain. The edges blurred, the nightmares began to fade, and soon Esther was without thought, a shell, barely pressing on her existence because a small part of her natural being willed itself to live. When all had faded to dark, when all the screams and voices faded into the wind, when night finally crept onto her vision, she slept.

CHAPTER 20

For years, Bhutan had avoided any contact with most of the world's superpowers. Part of this was out of deference to India, its staunchest ally, and in a sense, its protector. The country had no standing armed forces to speak of; in fact, several treaties had, at one point or another, given India full control over all matters of national defense for the tiny Buddhist nation. In that spirit, and cautious after seeing Tibet overrun by China, Bhutan was much more interested in keeping relations with the superpower in the south as opposed to the one in the north.

Along the same vein, Bhutan was determined to keep its identity as the last true Buddhist nation in the world. The Christian minority was not recognized, and the country had taken a shift towards a national language. The borders were kept tight, with a two hundred dollars per day tariff for every foreign visitor. That, coupled with a refusal to allow outside investment in business, and the little country had long been of little interest to the United States.

It wasn't that the United States had any issue with what went on in Bhutan. The country was peaceful and quiet, was not chasing arms, was not saber rattling at any time, and was not providing Russia and China with another ally in thwarting the United States and their goals. Human rights violations were miniscule, thereby not affording the United States the opportunity to play the somewhat hypocritical role of moral savior. The almost homogenous population was not eager to westernize by any means, and by that measure, there was no invasion of Starbucks or McDonalds or of any chain brand that could appeal to the global market. Simply put, with a population that was a third of Washington, D.C. alone and a land area about half the size of South Carolina, the amount of return on investment for American corporations was miniscule as opposed to what could be gained, for example, from the oil rich areas of the Caspian.

The nations had indirect contact through India. There were no formal diplomatic relations, and in Bhutan's view, there was no need. It wasn't that the country had any issue with the United States; rather, it was a somewhat naïve view that diplomatic relations were borne of military alliances, and despite the fear of Red China invading and running roughshod over what had been established, it was still not enough to risk provoking China by normalizing relations with the world's other superpower. Although a great wall in the Himalayas separated the countries and gave Bhutan a sense of security, what had happened to Tibet was always fresh in their mind.

That being said, if Bhutan needed something of the Americans, it was as simple as a phone call. India and the United States were both nuclear armed and extremely close. United States companies had poured trillions of dollars into the Indian subcontinent and despite a disagreement over Israel, the constant fear of China, and to a lesser extent Pakistan, had led the two countries to forge a strong alliance. There was little doubt that if there was a threat to the security of Bhutan, India would lean on the Americans to ensure that the little nation would remain the last Buddhist enclave in the free world. As for Bhutan, they were eager to keep the image of being the happiest nation in the world. The two Americans trekking through the wilderness, hell bent on self-destruction, was an issue that the nation, and its people, did not take lightly.

Daimyo happened to be one of those people. In his role as a spiritual advisor, he had been eager to assist Travis and Esther in any manner he was capable of. That included making sure they were prepared for their respective treks through the winter wilderness, as well as counseling each of them on the spiritual view, at least in Buddhist terms, of their respective missives. It was not his job to obstruct; each was destined to walk their own path, and it was plain to the monk that he was not to interfere. However, as loyal as Daimyo was to his faith, he was almost as loyal to his nation.

Shortly after Travis had departed, Daimyo made a phone call to the governmental relations department of Bhutan. He quietly relayed what he knew, giving details of plans, times, names, and locations. The receptionist on the other end languidly took the details, not too eager to concern herself with the goings-on of two wayward Americans, despite the quiet sense of urgency coming from the other end. After gathering all of the information Daimyo had to offer, she had promised him it would be relayed to someone higher up the chain of command, and encouraged him to call back had he anything else to offer.

As tends to happen with these matters, the information was set aside for a few days, before the secretary, in a fluster, found the notes in a pile of about half a dozen others to be passed to higher ups. Giggling, she pawned them off on a supervisor who was equipped to deal with the matter.

And so it went, the memo being passed about as if it were contaminated by the plague. Everyone seemed to find a way to avoid it, on the grounds of lack of experience or a lack of station or simply because they had no idea how to face the possibility of two dead Americans on Bhutanese soil.

The memo finally landed, after a three-day journey, on the desk of an undersecretary of some sort. Unlike the ones below him, he realized the urgency of the matter. Not for the sake of the Americans; if two selfish young people from the States wanted to kill themselves, he had neither the time nor the inclination to care. People killed themselves every day. What worried him, above all else, was the perception that such an act on Bhutanese soil could have on the image of the nation as a whole. Still, absent of some manner of sensationalizing, the issue was not that important. He filed the proper paperwork and passed the thin memo on as a cable to the ambassador in India, to be forwarded to the States.

The cable runs from India to the United States were made daily. The fact that the countries shared a joint cause in the stabilization of Pakistan, as well as a general leeriness towards China, meant that constant communication was a key matter. And while India would gladly pass on anything that Bhutan wished to get in front of the Americans, there were several other causes that demanded their attention. A couple of dead kids in Bhutan were the least of their worries. The cable, detailing what was going on with Travis and Esther, was buried in a daily briefing of Bhutan, near the bottom with little or no fanfare. In fact, the embassy in India did not read the report before passing it on to the embassy in Washington.

Once landing stateside, the cable landed in the hands of Bhutan's delegate to the United Nations. As someone who was stationed to press all of Bhutan's causes before the United Nations and the world, the information therein was in no small way distressing. It was read twice, and then a light went off. The name of the American man…Travis Saint Croix. The delegate went to his desk and within a matter of minutes was online. The name rang a bell. A simple search reminded the delegate of everything he needed to know.

Despite the relatively tight knit community at San Francisco State, the story of Travis and Felix Jones had started to gain legs all its own. A trial had followed, and despite the best efforts of the district attorney, Travis had been acquitted of wrongdoing in the deaths of both Stuart Avett and Felix Jones. Amongst the minority communities of San Francisco and abroad, Travis had become a sort of cult hero. The Indian community had been one of several that Jones had slandered, despite the many contributions that Indian-Americans had made to culture and society at large, and as a result, Travis's name had been spoken with reverence in many circles.

The delegate smiled. He, unlike most others, had seen

the story behind the story. Travis's story had held scant mention of how he had lashed out at Esther, yet when the delegate realized who the second party was, the pieces fell into place. He was, however, Bhutanese to the core, and his loyalty, and his job, was to protect Bhutan's image and interests at all costs.

However, finding a sympathetic ear at either the Indian embassy or at the State Department proved difficult. India was content to play the role of the detached older sibling, guiding the little nation based on a set of ideals yet at the same time unwilling to engage for a matter that the Bhutanese were taking very seriously. Two dead Americans would do nothing but tarnish the image of the little nation. Meanwhile, the State Department was hands off. Free will, they said over and over again, and besides, with two wars and an economic crisis at hand, there were far too few people willing to spend time and resources on two crazy college kids. One person at the State Department, in a classic case of Americans passing the buck, even had the gall to express that it was the little nation's fault for allowing the pair into the country to begin with.

Hanging up the phone, the diplomat was growing increasingly frustrated. The backwards way of thinking between the two larger countries was to only address an issue when it became apparent it was a problem. Those countries had resources to overcome what would be a perceived crisis. Bhutan did not. The actions of Travis and Esther would not only negatively impact the tourism trade in Bhutan, but the story, sensationalized by the media, would lead even more to perhaps travel to the kingdom, determined to go out in their own blaze of glory. The death business was not a good one for a country so focused on happiness.

The press...that was it! Americans all loved a good sob story. It would be quite easy to bring attention to the matter, and force those in charge to respond, if there was negative press involved. Such slyness was not a practice that was common among Bhutanese politics, but drastic times called for desperate measures.

The diplomat grinned as he found the number he was looking for. Hopefully, a step such as this would bring the matter to resolution once and for all.

Toshrino Haro had been with the *Post* for almost eight years. He was not a native San Francisco native; he was born, of all places, in Portland, Maine, the son of a pair of Taiwanese immigrants who had come stateside to reap the rewards of the Chinese takeout business. At first, the family business struggled, a side effect of each of his parents missing out on the trend of Americanizing their dishes. The spicy fare was almost too much for most of the locals to handle, and for the first couple of years, Toshrino's parents feared returning to Taiwan in failure and disgrace. It was in this time—a time spent watching his parents teeter on the brink of insolvency—that Toshrino began dreaming of a profession that did not involve long hours of pandering to the locals.

After a spell, however, his mother began to get the hang of catering to the milder palates of the Americans. The fresh seafood, gathered from the natural bounty of the Maine coast, helped immensely, as did his father's procurement of a liquor license a short time later. One establishment led to a second, then a third, and before long, the Haro family owned several restaurants in a regional chain that covered nine New England states.

Tosh, as he was called, was grateful for his parent's success, and for his life in America. However, he had no desire to move into the restaurant business. He was the oldest of five children, and his siblings were content to section off little squares of the family empire. This, in itself, was a blessing, as Tosh's wish to move into another field was met with a tepid approval from his father, a warm blessing from his mother, and general indifference from his siblings. They had their own little empires to forge, and in truth, Tosh and his weird desires to write and report held no profit in their eyes.

The boy had an amazing aptitude for both language and literary arts. Taking up English came much easier for him than his siblings, and while they all excelled in their lessons, an eyeful teacher in 7th grade became aware of Tosh's skill with the written word. He was valedictorian of his senior class, excelled on both placement exams, and a combination of scholarship funds and money set aside by his parents waited to pay for any school of his choice. He applied to close to two dozen, was accepted by all of them, and to everybody's surprise, chose Sewanee.

Tosh's parents, while perplexed with their son's desire to attend college in a place with few Taiwanese students and even fewer ties to New England, were nonetheless still supportive. The truth was, while Tosh was eager to break away from the home front, he was terrified of the big cities such as New York and Los Angeles. Sewanee's facilities were world class, the class sizes were small, and the picturesque setting of south central Tennessee was something Tosh relished. His bachelor's was finished in three years, with another two devoted to his MFA in creative writing. His fiction writings were full of drama and entertainment, and alums whispered excitedly that perhaps an Asian William Faulkner was among them.

Tosh, however, shocked everyone when he applied for, and was hired as, an investigative journalist for the *New York Post*. Accolades followed for his investigative reporting, including a Pulitzer for a series of articles about the plight of intercity Hmong in Southwest Detroit. The work had been heartbreaking, depressing, and overbearing at different times. A young man had been gunned down in his presence, had even died in his arms. Ever the professional, Tosh submitted his work to his editors. Six months later, when the Pulitzer people had come knocking, Tosh was, for his own health and safety, locked down in a mental health care facility, a victim of both his own success and his own biological makeup. A friend had accepted the award, putting a mark on what should have been the highlight of a distinguished career.

A year later, with Tosh drifting with no real articles making their way to publication, the *Post* grew tired of waiting and sent Tosh packing. Another year followed, a year spent writing a novel that was lampooned by every critic. Tosh's name was now a punchline in writing circles. A young editor took a chance by granting him an interview, and after consulting a friend who was a shrink, the decision was made to bring Tosh on in a relaxed role. The doctor cautioned him that Tosh's Pulitzer days were over; however, given the right environment, he could thrive as a basic columnist.

That had been two years ago, and in that time, Tosh had settled into a peaceful little niche. His articles were mostly human interest stories, and in public, Tosh sought to cover only the positive, a niche left to him by his fellow writers all eager to seek the same sort of sensational stories that had catapulted him to superstardom. In private circles, they all whispered and laughed about their coworker, one of the greats who, just like Van Gogh, had lost his mind.

To his own credit, Tosh had started to wage his own little war against the stigma of mental health. Several of his subjects were suffering from a mental ailment of some sort, and he always made a point to point out those that had risen above their afflictions and had made a positive influence in the lives of others. In private, he mailed letter after letter, typed email after email, and made call after call to those with some dog in the fight. He rang congressmen at home. He sent letters by expedited delivery to every pharmaceutical company in America and beyond. He studied hours of lectures at campuses across the globe. In a short time, he was as much an expert in mental health as anyone. A new breakthrough? Tosh was the first to crow about its promise. A new drug? He was quick to either offer tepid support or an outright condemnation based on results, trials, and side effects. His editor let him go because, despite the words of warning, Tosh was his ultimate rehab project. If the old boy pulled off an award of any sort, he would be the hottest editor in the country.

This day found Tosh at his desk, rummaging through some reports on a new wonder drug, cordoned off in his lonely office at the end of a forgotten hallway. Tosh liked his little space. It was quite dusty, cluttered, and most importantly, in a place where he was unlikely to be accosted with small talk or some morbid overlooker. There was a single phone line in his office, one that rarely rang.

Tosh was startled by the ringing phone. He had been deep in thought, working on another piece that decried the lack of oversight on another antidepressant that had been rushed to market. He snatched the phone, only to fumble it twice as it crashed to the floor. With a gasp, Tosh lunged for it, snatching it up and wrestling it into position. "News room.... I mean news desk.... I mean, hello?" The last was asked almost as a question.

The voice on the other end laughed, and Tosh let out an audible sigh of relief. It was Kristen, the receptionist who gave directions and took general calls for the paper and three other enterprises in the building. Unbeknownst to everyone else in the building, she had been seeing Tosh on and off for several months. Their relationship had started off as a casual matter, the simple pairing of two young people that had found little success in the standard rites and rituals of dating. Drinks were had, mutual hobbies discovered, and soon the relationship had evolved into something deeper than they both wanted to admit. Thankfully, they were both flexible enough to keep things fluid. As with any relationship, there were complications. Tosh's mental state aside, Kristen had no short supply of apprehension when it came to his near zealotry of all things pertaining to mental health. On Tosh's side, things were much simpler. Kristen had a young son, and while the boy was endearing, as most children tend to be, Tosh was not sure he was an ideal role model for anyone, much less the small nucleus of a family.

Thankfully, none of these issues had become between them. For practical reasons, the relationship was kept quiet at the office, although gossip, as it usually did, made its way through the halls. They both managed to shake it off with a light laugh and a deft changing of the subject.

Chuckling, Kristen gently tsk-tsked him. "Is that any way for an award-winning writer to answer the phone?" she asked coyly. Tosh closed his eyes and grinned, imagining her green eyes dancing with mischief at the question.

"We win awards based on what we can write. It has little to do with what we say. If I wanted to have people hear me in spoken form, I would have become a TV reporter as opposed to a writer." Tosh was smiling into the phone. "And it saddens me to say that I have a face much more suited to print than to television."

Although he could not see it, he knew his response was met with a gentle rolling of the eyes. "Did you know your paper just published a completely informal, altogether silly, and in no way scientific readers' poll that showed that sixty-seven percent of women in the greater San Francisco area find self-deprecating humor to be a complete turnoff?" Her voice was light, almost teasing, and Tosh flushed slightly.

He rallied nicely, however. "Lies! Slander! I happen to know several women who appreciate that very type of humor! Besides, I seriously doubt that our paper published something like that. Tabloid fodder! Yellow journalism! It's government mind control, in place to distract us from the real issues of the day!"

Kristen laughed. "Be that as it may, mister hot shot journalist, there's someone here to see you." Her voice grew quieter as she turned from the stranger and grew serious for a moment. Each one of Tosh's guests were screened. He took no chances after what happened in Detroit. "Perhaps 5'9, 160 pounds. He's Asian, of some strain, but the features are too angular to be Hmong. I'd almost say Indian. Dark complexion, black hair, brown eyes, very well kept. He's wearing colorful, almost Oriental type robes." She raised her voice and turned back to the man, wavy red locks tossing back over her shoulder as she did so. "He says he's with the consulate's office of a place called Bhutan."

"Bhutan." Tosh repeated it, almost to himself. "What would the consulate in Bhutan want from me?" Internally, Tosh sighed. He received several requests a month for stories about the mental plight of this group or that person, and while he was eager to help, he was not always pleased with the pretense of why he was being contacted. It seemed Asians in particular sought him out because of his heritage, and while he understood the insular nature of his ancestors, it still irritated him to no end. He was an American, and had been his whole life.

"He said it was in reference to Travis Saint Croix," Kristen said lightly, and Tosh inhaled slightly. Although Stuart Avett had not been close to Tosh, he was a friend and, more importantly, a fellow newsperson. For all he complained of the closeness of his people, he was just as protective of his brothers and sisters in the media. Never had such a group faced persecution as those in the press, in his view, and like most of his ilk, he was protective of others. Although Tosh knew, if anyone knew, about the mental conditions that may have contributed to Travis acting the way he did, he was still wary.

The journalist in him won out in a matter of seconds. He had missed the first wave of Travis stories, and if there were to be a second wave, well, any reporter would love to be in the middle of the storm. He glanced in the mirror, straightened his tie, and muttered into the phone, letting Kristen know he would be right down before hanging up.

CHAPTER 21

As events unfolded on two continents, Travis was no more the wiser. He had spent the last several days making the slow, brutal trek in the general direction of Jomolhari. People in this part of the country were few and far between, and Travis was not in the mood to socialize with people as he traveled. In fact, he had only stopped to speak twice, once to a young man who claimed to be some sort of military but, in essence, was nothing more than a young deputy. The conversation was mostly spent with the young man pleading for Travis to seek medical attention for his wounded eye, and Travis politely declining and asking about provisions. The second encounter was with a monk of some stripe, and seeing as language was a barrier that neither one of them could breach, the conversation was short and fruitless.

Finally, after a number of days that Travis had lost count of, the base of the great mountain was in sight. Had he the energy, Travis would have probably wept with joy. Granted, there was still a good bit of walking to do, but all the same, he was close to a population center, or at least, a temporary one. The Buddhists of Bhutan had, for centuries, made yearly pilgrimages to the temple that was wedged into the rocks of Jomolhari. The government, seeing that these trips were not only tradition, but a source of pride to the nationals, set in place reforms to ensure that the hike and subsequent time spent were as comfortable as possible. It didn't compare to American standards of roads and travel, but when placed next to the harsh wilderness that Travis had just weathered, it was paradise. There was an army outpost in between Thangthangkha and Jangothang, and Travis approached it with a bit of apprehension. He was dangerously close to Tibet, dangerously close to the Chinese Army and the assorted tensions that went with an American being near the disputed territory, yet as he approached the post, he was greeted with nothing but smiles by the young Bhutanese privates. They were confused by his angle of approach, seeing as he had not taken the man trek path from Paro to Jomolhari. However, they were still excited to have an American in their presence.

He was fussed and worried over, coaxed inside where a blanket was wrapped over his shoulders and a mug of warm coffee was pressed in his hand. The questions were fired off in rapid succession. The privates were anxious to know who he was, where he had come from, what way he had went, where his eye was. Travis basked in the glow and did not understand a word. It went on for several minutes before a young, dark-skinned man in a lab coat chased the privates away, cracking a snide remark about how they would be too worried with the American to repel an invasion if one happened.

Once the soldiers were dispersed, however, the doctor's face hardened. Walking over to Travis, he peeled back the bandage and looked at the vacant ocular socket with a look of disdain. Travis winced as he did so, tempted to lash out. Fatigue and curiosity kept him in his seat. The doctor took out a pen and started scribbling notes on a pad before he looked at Travis and shook his head.

"You're a damned fool, you know that?" Travis jumped at the doctor's words. He was tired, hurting, and in no place to be bullied.

"And who the hell are you to call me a fool?" Travis fired back. "You think I wanted to lose my damn eye?"

The doctor shook his head, and with a wry grin, handed Travis a map of Bhutan. It was a bright, colorful affair, one made for tourists such as himself. The doctor had even taken the liberty to trace out the path that Travis had taken on his little hike. Clicking his tongue, the doctor smirked. "You saved all of three kilometers by taking the most direct route. It took you several days, I imagine. Had you done your research, you would have followed the tourist route, known as the Jomolhari Trek. The path is cut clear, and kept that way for fools like you." The doctor bit his tongue, doing everything he could to keep from howling with laughter.

Travis stared at the map, dumbfounded. Nobody enjoyed having their shortcomings pointed out to them. They liked it even less when one profound mistake was used to smack them over the head with the sheer stupidity of their actions. If he would have researched, he would be three days closer to her, he would still have his eye, he would have more supplies to work with...the mistakes piled up.

Meanwhile, the good doctor had managed to get his fit of laughter under some semblance of control, and with that, his professional demeanor returned. "My name is Dr. Dolan Selene. I am from New Delhi, India. Doctors are in short supply here in Bhutan, where, despite their penchant for happiness, the people still live in what is very much a third world state. Bhutan is developing, but with a population smaller than the city of Dallas, and a lifestyle that requires most children to carry on the family work as farmers or herders, there are very few home grown doctors here. India has always been a big brother to Bhutan, in several ways. We take care of her defense, we provide them with resources, and we press some of their affairs on the international level. In return, they give us a small buffer from the drama that is China, and Tibet. We have enough issue with Pakistan. We don't need more from the Chinese. Now, hold still while I clean and bandage this eye."

Dr. Dolan, it seemed, was not one to piddle around with the care of his patients. Grinning, he poured a shot of vodka into a small glass. "You'll need this." Before Travis could protest, he placed his palm on his forehead, bracing his head against the chair. In one swift motion, Dolan reared his arm back and tossed the contents of the glass directly into what used to be Travis's eye.

Biting down hard on his lip, Travis was forced to tense every muscle in his body, if only to keep from punching the good doctor. The booze burned worse than it did when it was put into the body the proper way. "There's no real anesthesia here in the wild, Travis, and this is the only way to ensure that the wound is sterile. Seems like a good waste of Russian vodka, I know, but it's much better than letting infection set in. Luckily, for you, it has been cold outside and the bacteria have not had a chance to set in. Hold still."

A scalpel appeared out of nowhere, and Travis clutched at the side of the chair as Dr. Dolan reached into the empty socket. Pulling the ocular muscles to the point of strain, he quickly cut them down until the jagged ends were smooth. "They'll heal easier," Dr. Dolan said dismissively as he stepped away, discarding the small pieces of waste into a wastebasket. "Trash is burned out here, lest it pile up and make a mess."

Travis was about to perk up and say something when the doctor forced his head back against the chair once more. Another round of dousing, followed by Dr. Dolan taking the sharpened edge of the scalpel and running it in a quick loop around the empty socket. Once finished, he dropped the instrument into what Travis could only assume was more vodka before using a towel to pat the wound dry. The tricky part over, his bedside manner improved, and it was with a sympathetic smile that he started rewrapping the wound, pressing a pad of gauze over the eye before wrapping it in a circular motion around Travis's head. Once completed, he plopped down in the chair across from the lad with a sigh.

"Now, Travis Saint Croix, I know who you are and why you're here. It's become a bit of a news story here in Bhutan. If something more horrid than enucleation happens to you on this trip, it will be a black eye on this country's image. That being said, this isn't the United States or Russia. Nobody is going to stop you from chasing this to whatever mad end it may come to. Along the same token, this is your last chance, Travis, to walk away and return to the comforts of whatever life you had before. There will be no rescue party. There will be no resources to hunt you down and save you from anything. Once you leave this hut, you'll be at the point of no return. People do not climb Jomolhari for two reasons. One is because local tradition holds it sacred. Violate that sacred trust, and they will leave you up there to let The Bride claim you for herself. Secondly, and far more pressing...you're getting ready to try and climb one of the tallest mountains in the world. It's been climbed, in all of its existence, six times. Only twice has it been climbed from the Bhutanese side, the last time over forty years ago. On that expedition, the Chinese shot three climbers who then fell to their deaths. It is one of the most dangerous places in the world. I know that this girl, this Esther, is up there." Dr. Dolan reached into his overcoat and pulled out a letter, one addressed to Travis in her unmistakable script. "She left this here for you. Is she really worth all of this?"

Travis snatched at the letter, staring at her writing as if it were some sort of foreign dialect, one that, despite all his trying, he could not decipher. There was the urge to rip it open and devour every word, but Dr. Dolan had asked a question, one that, in its own way, demanded an answer.

Travis was drained. Exhausted, beaten down, debased, driven into the muck, unable and unwilling to hold his emotions in check any longer; there was no stopping the torrent of tears that came forth, even if it was from one good eye.

It was almost as is his soul had been begging him to release his burdens, to cry out into the darkness that seemed to invade his being. All these years were catching up with him. They were bombarding him with memories of hurt that he had thought forgotten long ago. They started at the beginning, with the mother that he never really knew, and pressed forth through his shame and anger towards his own father. There was also regret—from years of just skating by, knowing that he was capable of more, yet never taking a chance, never putting himself out in the open for the world to see. But the burden that crushed him more than anything was Esther. His denial of her had put both Stuart Avett's and Felix Jones's blood on his head. The former filled him with remorse, and the latter had gone from a state of disgust to one of pity. Above all was the overwhelming sense that he had lost her, forever more, and no amount of sacrifice of life or limb was going to bring her back to him.

There, in the coziness of the little shack at the base of the giants of the earth, Travis Saint Croix buried his head in his hands and cried. For someone that had spent most of his existence balling up and layering almost every single emotion that he came across, the release that his tears brought was needed, and long overdue. For the first several moments, he did nothing but howl impotently into his hands, unrecognizable, inconsolable, a shattered and hollow shell of a man.

Several of the privates at the base peeked their heads in, startled by the sudden onslaught of emotions from the American. Dr. Dolan was by no means an expert on mental health, but he knew a grieving man when he saw one. Most injuries sustained in the frontier of Bhutan were those of the gruesome variety. Some were from falls from high places. Some were from encounters with animals, both wild and domesticated. Some were simply brought on by exposure to extreme elements of nature. With far too few medical supplies and only a rudimentary staff to work with, Dr. Dolan had seen far more funerals than he had ever hoped to. It was best for Travis to shed whatever spiritual and emotional burdens he had now, in the relative sanctuary of the little outpost. It was more than likely going to be his last chance to do so.

Travis's thoughts were far from lucid. In fact, his whole perception of the matter was a rush of emotions, colored by conflicting feelings that made the idea of coherence in his thoughts all but impossible. He was full of anger, rage, sorrow, and desolation, all at once. His current state was the lowest of human existence. It was all now a vicious cycle, and his tears were all he had left to escape with. He was done trying to make sense of his feelings. He had ceased to make a rationale of his actions. Although the sobbing would slowly subside, the raw edge of his emotions remained, and before Dolan was a broken, shattered man.

He finally looked up at Dolan, his voice dry and scratchy, his one remaining eye bleary and sore from crying so much, his nose red and swollen. He was beyond shame, and for the first time in days, a bit of reality set in. "It doesn't matter if I rescue her. If she does not succeed here, she will succeed somewhere else. It could be San Francisco; it could be Rome. It could be the moon for all I know. Each of us has to face death at some point, doctor. Whether we do it alone or with a loved one or even in the arms of a forsaken enemy is inconsequential. The battle is still ours and ours alone to lose. Death comes to us all, be it the infant who is born without breath or the old man who lives to see three centuries. If Esther is determined to join the rank of the dead masses, there is little I can do to stop her."

Dolan almost winced at Travis's assessment. A man normally measured in his words, he could not help but blurt out an obvious question better left unasked. "If that is the case, then why do you insist on pressing on?"

The look on Travis's face told a thousand stories, yet the overwhelming theme was that of death. "Because I have to. Despite her decisions, my action helped put her on that mountain. It's, I don't know, a calling of sorts, doc. I know she is up there, perhaps already dead, perhaps dying, maybe even at peace, and yet still needing help. I can't not help her. I love her. I always have. I have to do this, or I'm not me. I know that sounds crazy, but it's true. It took me a long time to learn what love was, and at times, I'm still unsure. But if being in love is having the will to die for someone..." Travis trailed off, turning his enucleated gaze from the doctor.

For Dolan, the whole matter was paradox, and in his line of work, paradoxes were nothing but trouble. He did the only thing he could do at the time. Reaching over, he patted Travis's knee. Frowning, he stood. "You have some reading to do, Travis. I'll leave you to it." Standing, the doctor made to walk out of the room. Almost as an afterthought, he gathered up the bottle and glass, setting them before his patient. He offered a smirk. Although it was done out of sarcasm, it held a certain mourning all its own. "Based on how your journey has gone so far, you may need this." Shaking his head, Dolan left the room, pulling the door shut as he did.

The letter lay on the table before him. It was a thousand things at once. It was a gnarled tree holding answers that Travis did not want. At the same time, it was the antidote--the one thing that could cure all that ailed him. He poured himself a shot and downed it. It burned from head to toe, but the lowered inhibitions that the booze brought gave Travis the resolve he needed. Shaking his head, Travis opened the letter and read. Despite his best intentions, something told him that this might be the last thing he read from her hand.

CHAPTER 22

Travis,

I've always been a fan of music. Not the regurgitated bubblegum pop that clogs our airwaves, nor the mile-a-minute thudding aggression that you listen to. I'm not saying that the above does not have any inherent value. They are both, however, based on a very simple premise. The former deals with the light, simple feelings of happiness. The latter, for the most part, deals with the violence, the ruthless aggression of angst that we all feel at some point or another.

Both of those sets of feelings should be tapped into time and again. They should be grown, cultivated, nurtured, and then harvested and used for whatever purposes we see fit. What most people don't realize is that they are a small subset of the gambit of human emotions. They should not be one's primary focus. The human mind is a dark, complex machine that is able to feed into primal urges, all the while helping us overcome the lesser urges of our genetic makeup.

Perhaps, one of these days, when we are beyond using the gifts of our mind to make war and conflict and tools of exploitation, we will be able to put this wonderful tool to use. Imagine the books that could be written! Imagine the art that would be produced! Imagine the diseases that would be cured, the lives saved, the benefit of unlocking the secrets of the universe. Perhaps we'll conquer space. Perhaps we shall finally find peace. Perhaps disease and famine and war will be no more.

Truth of the matter is, my love, that most of this is off in the distant future. Utopia benefits most, so the fortunate few will do everything to prevent it from happening. If the day ever comes that the unwashed masses realize that a better world can be had, if only they take it by force, then our noble race will once again grow by leaps and bounds. Until then, we'll still have war, we'll still have famine, we'll still have cancer, and we will still have minds, like mine, ravaged with afflictions that are beyond understanding. Maybe I'm being far too hopeful in hoping that these revolutions will lead to a better scientific understanding of our health, both physical and mental, but, down and again, I do afford myself the luxury of a dream.

I don't know why I am the way I am, Travis. Nobody knows. Oh sure, we have shadowing of knowledge. It could be brain chemicals. It could be environmental factors. It could be one of a million things, a handful of reasons that I'm as fucked up as I am.

It all works in unison. The world and the people in it are conflicting because it keeps things running. They chase cures and solutions that are counteracting one another because it helps serve their own selfish desires. Treaties to end war are never written to benefit the people who actually fight them. They're never written to let the losing party walk away with their dignity intact. To the victor goes the spoils. In the end, ninety percent of us get fucked.

When a man acts in such a manner, he slaughters another slice of humanity and considers it a life well spent. Men such as this are why I am here. I want no part in such self-decapitation. I have no desire to sit around and do something to harm myself in the name of helping myself. Someone else's vision of utopia is not mine. What others see as happiness, obtained through material wealth and hollow gestures, is not worth living for.

I would rather die as opposed to merely existing. It came down to a simple choice, really. Get busy becoming a shell, or get busy rounding out a story well told.

Our song is reaching its crescendo, our poem its refrain, our play its final act. It's the climax and the finale of a story that could have been avoided. All the same, I feel it needed to be told. I also feel that we were the right people to tell it. Please don't hate me for this.

While the events that ended our relationship in San Francisco are considered tragic, at least to us, they were needed. Perhaps they will save lives by bringing attention to these issues of health and illness. In the end, whatever the result of our sordid tale, I was glad that you were the one to help me tell it.

Dr. Dolan and the guards have been bribed. You're not going to be allowed to leave this post until they are sure the deed is done. My blood is enough in this matter. Yours does not need to be tainted as well.

Goodbye, Travis. Know that I always loved you.

-Esther

It was a hopeless situation. Apparently, whatever bribe Esther had paid the guards was enough to ensure that Travis would not pass. Once threats ceased to work, Travis tried bribery, and that seemed destined to do the trick until Dolan stepped in and invoked the threat of court martial on the privates. When Travis's offer was high enough to overcome even that, the doctor invoked the local monks to talk reason unto the soldiers.

Travis was, for all intents and purposes, a prisoner in the travel station. There was no escape, no negotiation, no hope of breaking out of the twelve by twelve room that had become his own personal hell. He had a decision to make. Was he to play a walk-on part in the rest of Esther's existence, destined to sit on the sideline as she departed the mortal coil? Or, would he find a way to take over as the lead again, swooping in to do what nobody else could, as he had with Felix Jones? The answer came a lot sooner than he expected.

Around midnight (Travis was no longer sure of the time. What did it matter? The only thing that mattered was getting to Esther and ending this madness!), the guards locked Travis in his room and left him alone. As physically exhausted as he was, his mind was still working a mile a minute. There was a small, primitive washroom, one with a mirror, just off his quarters. He was given access to the room so that he could see to whatever sanitary needs suited him. Walking into the room, Travis stared at a grizzled, enucleated stranger in the glass and pondered his move. Above the hole in the ground, one straddled with a seat so that one could use it as a latrine, was a window. It was a window with no bars. It was his only chance at escape. "But how?" Travis muttered to himself as he used a small bowl and a pitcher of water to wash his face.

The room was cold, and Travis thought for a moment of asking the guards to stoke the flames in the grand fireplace. That was it! A small fire would distract the guards enough for him to break the window and escape. But how was he to start a fire? A smirk came across his face as he realized that Dolan had left the vodka on the counter. Alcohol burned. But how to make a spark?

Travis spun wildly on heels as he looked for his pack. It sat, lain over on its side like a drunken child, forgotten in a corner. Digging through his bag, he grinned as he pulled out the short sword.

Setting it on the counter, Travis gathered several of the used pieces of gauze from the trash bin. He made a neat pile about three feet away from the door. Working quickly now, he doused the stack with about half of the remaining bottle. He pulled the sword and swung it against one of the adjacent legs of the steel surgical table. Sparks flew, and a few landed on his improvised tinder. A flame leapt up as cold and blue as the Bhutanese winter nights. Scooping up his pack, Travis cleared his throat and prepared for the mad dash.

"FIRE!" Travis bellowed. He watched with satisfaction as his lone remaining guard kicked open the door and stared at the blue flames in bewilderment. Quickly asking whatever god Bhutan followed for forgiveness, Travis shattered the rest of the bottle on the floor, offering an excited, maddened laugh as the flames grew fourfold.

The guard shielded his face and recoiled in horror. Travis sensed his chance. Sprinting towards the lavatory, he quickly climbed the chair and, using the hilt of the sword, shattered the glass of the window. Raking the jagged edges away, Travis crawled out the window and dropped quickly to the ground, picking up his pack as he went. Fear and desire had given him energy he knew not he had, and with a clear trail ahead of him, Travis dashed into the night.

None of the guards chased after him. The fire was put out, the mess cleaned up, and the window boarded over. Once the sentry and Dolan finished the cleanup, they joined the rest of the privates around the fire. Drinking, they discussed Travis's chances of success. The prevailing view was that it was slim to none. Raising his glass, Dolan grinned. "He's walked through hellfire and brimstone for her, lads. There may be hope for them both. And for us." Downing his drink, the good doctor returned to the guardhouse.

He would sleep through the night, and only in the morning would he inform Thimphu of what had transpired. As he glanced once more down the path, he wryly wished Travis a silent Godspeed as he pulled the guard house door shut.

CHAPTER 23

"Excuse me?" said the young flight attendant, blinking in confusion at Tosh's words. The plane had touched down a scant few moments ago, and the journalist was, once again, questioning how he had been cajoled into making this trek to Bhutan, a nation he knew little of and one of which had even less desire to visit.

It had nothing to do with the country itself. Bhutan, from what Tosh had learned, was a quaint little hamlet of just over half a million people, or about the size of Cincinnati. The problem with the country was that anything that could be experienced inside its borders could be seen elsewhere with a lot less hassle. The mountains that were in the country shared, for the most part, a border with Nepal and China. The plains and monsoon seasons were shared with India and most of Southeast Asia. Some form of Buddhism could be explored in nearby Tibet, or in any number of larger, non-landlocked nations.

It was, in a sense, what made Bhutan a treasure. They didn't beg for people to come, but when they did they were welcomed...so long as they had a ticket to return home. The happiness of the nation did not rely on pandering to either the west or the Soviet-Sino influence to the north and east. The nation was therefore able (with no small assist from Big Brother India) to exist in a state that allowed its people to truly live and focus on their own lives. Less than one percent of its GDP was spent on maintaining what was mostly a volunteer armed forces.

It was a small wonder to Tosh that the hordes to the north and the south had not swallowed up the small nation. However, the leaders of the neighboring nations seemed to have taken a turn, less intent on physically dominating each other and more keen on enslavement through financial domination.

Shaking his head, Tosh stood waiting in a short line to leave the plane. In the empty seat next to his were six in-flight liquor bottles. It seemed that this trip would bring to life more demons than just those belonging to Travis and Esther.

The beginnings of dusk broke over the opening of the cave, bleaching the Bhutanese-Tibetan border in brilliant shades of blue, purple, pink, and gold. The wind was brisk, yet refreshing, blowing lightly at Esther's robes. A few silky strands of hair blew across her face, and she could not help but absently wonder if the northern lights would be visible on this evening. Not that it mattered.

The time had come. Travis was not coming for her. She had spent enough time on the mortal coil as it was.

A certain calmness fell over her being, as if to confirm that this was it, that she was truly going to die. No more fake drugs or hours spent willing herself into perishing. No, mankind had invented weapons of war for a reason, and it was an art form that left a measured chance of success in her endeavor.

Pacing over to the boulders next to her spring, Esther bent to pick up her weapon of choice. It was, to all appearances, identical to the sword that Daimyo had given Travis in Paro. In fact, although it was a few inches shorter, it was the exact same make, forged by the same hands in the same fires of the same forge at the same time. The larger and the smaller. The dominant and the submissive. The leader and the follower. She had purchased the pair in that manner. Nothing was left to chance. It was only her hope that Travis could keep his end of the bargain after he found the last letter.

It had been pinned, several hours before, to the

entrance of the cave, held in place from the raging wind in a place she knew he would see it. It held within all the thoughts and hopes and dreams for them, as well as the successes and failures of what, in the end, had been a very meager existence. She had contributed nothing to the existence of mankind, although, in the end, it would be hard for her to know what her death would mean, and to whom.

She paced into the cave, around a slight bend, a feature that meant to hide her body from initial view for whomever discovered her. A small, vain part of her wanted her opus, her credo, her manifesto read before she was discovered, so as not to distract the reader from the meaning behind her words. As she rounded the bend, she came upon the crude twin altars she had built. Hopefully Travis would understand their meaning, and the meaning of what she had written.

She walked to the smaller one, on the right, and knelt before it, facing away. She closed her eyes, in a grief too deep even for tears. "I'm sorry, whoever is out there. I've tried too long to make myself right for whatever you had predestined for me. I've tried to overcome this hurdle you placed before me, and I've tried to be what I was meant to be to Travis. I can't do these things and I'm using this blade as my petition of escape. Whatever spirit is out there, please have mercy on my soul in death." She clenched her teeth, her face a mask of too many emotions to decipher, and inserted the sharpened blade just below her sternum, burying the blade in an upwards motion into her left lung. She forced it in to the hilt, and then, with the last of her strength, gave a final, cruel twist, to ensure the job was complete.

She slowly sank back onto the altar, blood already streaming down her chin. As she faded into the darkness of death's sweet embrace, she uttered one more curse at the universe: "Because you sure as fuck didn't have any mercy on my soul in life."

With a dramatic finality, eternal slumber rose up to

meet Esther, her end coming, in solitude, in a rock and ice encrusted tomb in the Himalayas.

CHAPTER 24

The fact that Travis had accomplished what he had to this point was nothing short of astonishing. He had fair little experience in wilderness survival, and even less in emergency trauma survival. As he cleared the final boulder to the spot on Esther's map that notated where she was located, he could not help but feel a rush of emotions. Pride on what he had accomplished, apprehension on what he would find, fear over how he would cope with his discovery. It was all a rush of adrenaline that he was ill equipped to handle. Slow, stuttering steps brought him to the lip of the cave, and with an aching heart, he saw the letter she had pinned to the side of the cave.

He knew, in that moment, that she was gone. There would be no need for a letter if she were still in the cave; rather, she had departed and moved her little treasure hunt to another locale, to another mountain, another cave, hell, to another nation or continent. The chase would be never ending, it appeared, and in a brief moment of levity, Travis realized it was no less than he deserved. Control was one thing, but when one that was blessed with the sweet gift of control decided to abuse it, it was a hollow failure for not only himself, but also the sinking pit of the masses that would use such control for anything save the betterment of all.

With a heavy heart, and trembling hands, Travis opened the final letter, dated a mere day before his arrival.

To the moon and stars in my sky, to my shepherd on our intertwined journey, to my Alpha and my Omega, my beginning and my end, my sunrise and sunset, and my eternal love Travis:

Thank you.

The mere fact that you are reading this justifies everything I ever felt for you. It makes it all right, somehow, despite the hellish way that our story will end. I've teetered on the edge for a while now, always waiting for some stupid, foolish miracle that does not exist. In truth, there is no great kingdom in the sky, there is no rebirth of a greater being for things done, no gods on the top of a mount, especially this one, and, thankfully, no lake of hell to burn in for transgressions of wrong that we may or may not have committed. There is just life, and a return to ashes, and a recycling of our organic materials that makes it all possible for someone else. It's our duty to take part in this, and yet the color of our emotions is what makes it all worthwhile.

I'm dead, Travis, just beyond where you stand now. Sadly, the paint I was given was of too bright and too violent a hue for me to handle, and once splattered onto canvas, it was not going to sustain. Its memory will live on, how vivid and bright it was, I hope, but all the same, memories fade and those who possess them step away from the life to join the artists they worshipped so.

Men and women have, since the beginning of time, bled the ground red for what they believe in. Catholics stained the grasses of Europe, Soviets made the streets rivers of blood at Stalingrad, American patriots turned the foothills of the South into bloody tombs of men that were far too young to die, and revolutionaries shook the world as their great leaders lay in state in Moscow, in Beijing, and in Hanoi. They all had causes, I'm sure, but nonetheless, dead is dead.

I've come to the conclusion that unless I do the same, people will never take the needed steps to ensure that those like me are given the attention and treatment they need to live a fulfilling life. Oh, don't get me wrong, my reasons for doing this are far more selfish than that, and I have no illusions of being any sort of martyr. However, perhaps if I am able to save one person from the literal hell that was every day of who I was, then perhaps this fight that I fought and this life I laid down was not in vain.

I spent my entire life fighting this monster, Travis. I would have a horrible day, and every part of what I was would convince me that the next day would not be darker, and it was. I was always a danger, to myself, to you, to those in my life, and to those that had no idea who I was. For a while, I thought that I had shared myself with you, and you turned you back on me when you saw how dark it was. It never wanted this. This affliction set up shop and made me its own. I tried to appease it, and it was never horrible enough, it was never dark enough, it was never the evil that the monster was truly capable of spewing forth. I blew out my own candle, Travis, in hopes that no other would be able to use this unholy light to guide their own destructive paths. Perhaps, in this, others will see that they can guide their own paths.

You have a choice, Travis, and I do not envy you for it. I have taken away from you everything you sought here, in my own final gasp of selfishness. You can go down the mountain, leave me here for time and nature to dispose of, and live the rest of your existence either hateful and broken or enlightened and introspective. I do not begrudge you this choice. If you can go on, please do so, and with my blessing. The other choice is to join me in decomposition. The reason your map was drawn in a way to deter you from taking the quicker path was so that I would have time to construct not one, but two final resting places. I rest on one altar, and if you choose, you can join me in finality by using the other. The layout is fairly simple. I leave the execution in your hands.

I never ceased loving you, and everything between us is forgiven. I hope you find peace, my love, in whatever decision you make.

Across the coil of space and time, across every dimension that was and may be, before the fate of all the broken idols and false gods that may or may not exist, goodbye, Travis. I love you.

-Esther

So, that was that.

All rational thought had vanished from Travis's body. He absently folded the note in his hands, placing it in his pack with all the rest. His play, his passion tale, the sound and the madness that had justified his entire existence these last few days, was gone. As he walked around the corner, he could not help but stare. There she lay, in all of her damnation and glory, saddled with an eternal beauty that had come at the ultimate price, being her life.

Shame filled him, for reasons that he knew all too well. Sure, part of it was the fact that he was responsible for the deathly image before him, but another, more incessant tugging of feeling revolved around the fact that, in spite of all of her blustering, she had done exactly what she said she would. To the bloody end, she had been unfailingly honest. For the first time in his life, Travis felt compelled to do the same.

The last few hours of his life were a blur. The wood, for whatever reason, was ample enough for a pyre of his own, and Travis was all too willing to build it. Next to her body, he constructed his own—lovingly, painstakingly, with every amount of care and compassion that he felt he should have shown Esther. When the pyre was complete, Travis set it alight and stood before it, his back to his love, sword in hand. Despite the fact that nobody but the Bride would hear his words, Travis was compelled to speak.

"Esther, there is no prose in the English language, or in any tongue, that describes how much I love you, but I'm going to try. As the clouds break across this beautiful Himalayan morning, and I stare out the mouth of this cave, knowing that which is the only honorable thing I have left to do, I cannot help but find myself awestruck at the breathtaking streaks of roseate, violet, and flame that make up the dawn. Yet, at the same time, I know, within my heart of hearts, that they pale in comparison to the beauty you left this earth in such a short time. I walked through hell and heaven to get here. I defiled the sacred, I assisted the sinner, I betrayed the righteous, and I forged a path that no other man would be stupid enough to forge. And I found you. I found you, despite all the heartbreak and sorrow and anger and evil I bore unto you. As you lay here, as dead as the rose after a week of winter ice storms, you have never been more alive to me." A tear rolled down his cheek, and Travis chuckled, before ramming the blade into his stomach to his spine. With his reserves waning, Travis twisted the blade, ensuring his own death. Stumbling, he fell back onto the burning pyre, smiling, shouting above the roar of the flames. "Good morning, Esther Sansui! I love you!"

EPILOGUE

The weather was altogether too perfect, given the circumstances. Perhaps in his mind's eye, Tosh had seen such an event as requiring a dreary, rainy day, overcast and blustery, as if God himself were trying to pour out the shame and misery that had led them here. And while there was enough wind to leave one's cheeks pinked, the temperature was warm enough that it was not at all unpleasant, and the sun peeking through the light, airy clouds gave a sense of lightness to the event that was altogether unfit.

After their deaths, the bodies of Travis Saint Croix and Esther Sansui presented Pno small problem to the Bhutanese authorities. The Happiest Nation On Earth could not let it be known that two young Americans had chosen their country to retreat to for the purpose of ending their lives. Thankfully, India was there with a solution. The mountain straddled the border between Tibet and Bhutan, and back in the '50s, the Chinese Army was suspected of gunning down several climbing guides, two of which had been of Indian descent. In 1979, India had obtained irrefutable evidence that, in fact, China had murdered the pair. Instead of making an international incident of the matter, the Indians had sat on it, knowing that, one day, a favor would be needed. And while a couple of dead Americans would be of little consequence to the worldview of India, it was not hard to see how such a thing would devastate Bhutan. Arms were twisted, and in the end, China offered to let Buddhist monks come in and remove the remains, to be disposed of in Tibet.

The official story would be that the pair were on the Tibetan side the entire time, including in their last moments. Tosh, being the one that had found them, knew better, and was perfectly willing to let the world know so. Chinese threats of arrest and disbarment from the funeral ceremony had convinced him otherwise, and it was with a dour outlook that he woke inside a Tibetan monastery, heart worn and exhausted from his trip and in no mood to placate a group of people that wanted to prevent him from telling the truth. It was the Hmong in Detroit that he had written about all over again. He had barely survived the last instance. He was far from sure he wanted to make it through this one.

He watched impassively as a group of monks went about the work of preparing for the ceremony. Journalistic curiosity got the best of him, and he looked around, trying to figure out where the pair was to be buried. There were no holes dug for the funeral, and for a moment, this puzzled Tosh. He kicked at the flinty earth he stood on, and then came to the realization that a traditional burial would be out of the question. Cremation came to mind, but there was nobody gathering wood or setting up a pyre. So how were they to be disposed of? It was in this confused state that Tosh noticed that one of the monks was standing next to him, wearing nothing but his ceremonial robes (which offered little in way of protection from the wind, regardless of how sunny it was) and a smile. As the monks had a habit of standing close by and saying nothing, Tosh ignored the man for several minutes, until the monk, in clear and precise English, said, "So, reporter, you are to be one of the few westerners to ever witness a sky burial."

Being as emotionally on edge as he was, Tosh nearly jumped out of his own shoes. He had not expected any of the monks to speak to him, much less address him in his own tongue. He turned to the monk, shock still apparent on his face, causing the old man to laugh. "Surprised? One of the few good things about those that rule Tibet is that they saw fit to make sure even lowly temple servants, like myself, learned a second language. Between the hundred or so monks that reside here, there are ninety-seven spoken dialects and languages. Most are dialects of the locals, although we do have speakers of Spanish, French, a Polynesian tongue, and, as you know now, English." The old man's eyes twinkled with mischief. "So, please, save your shock and awe for the ritual you are about to witness. It's not often that one will see human remains devoured by vultures, if birds as regal as this still deserve the title of vulture."

Tosh graced the old monk with a look that was mingled with disgust and curiosity. A sky burial? For Travis and Esther? Such a thing had only been recorded by modern cameras a handful of times in history, and each time was for educational purposes. It was considered a very private ceremony, one that was cloaked in secrecy, mainly to protect the last moments of the physical body. The fact that he was going to witness such a thing shook him to his very core. "But why? Why am I to have permission to witness such a thing? You know the nature of my work, right? Once I return to the States, my job requires that I report on this, and, well, this is just too much of a story not to report on." Tosh eyed the old man, suspecting a trap.

The old monk sensed as much, and placed a compassionate hand on Tosh's shoulder. "Not everyone is out to add to the pain and misery you've seen and suffered through, Tosh. Your being permitted to watch serves two purposes. First, our custom requires a member of the family to be present. That's simply not possible in this case. Travis's mother is dead of suicide twenty years, his father disowned him, and he has no siblings or close family willing or able to make the trip. Esther never knew her father, and the only family she knew, her mother, killed herself several years ago. They say suicide is not a genetic anomaly, but this is not the first time I've seen parent and child both go in the same way. Guess I should be thankful that my parents died an honorable death in their sleep." The last was said lightly, and even Tosh, he of sordid history, found he could not repress a smile.

Their bodies were brought forth, stark nude and pale. Besides her charred left arm, and the cut in her flesh from where she had disemboweled herself, Esther's flesh was a porcelain veneer, unmarked and milky white. The fact that all of her hair had been removed only seemed to add to lines that screamed of serenity, of beauty, of perfection. Tosh could not help but note, with a slight twinge of envy, as to why Travis was so maddeningly attracted to her. Tosh could not help but to think that he would have followed her to the very edge of hell itself.

If Esther's deceased body was a serene study in death, then Travis's was one that bore all the signs of the hell that he had survived in his last few days. One eye missing, several places charred and burnt from where he had tried to cremate himself, bruises on bare patches of flesh that were frozen into place...if Esther had taken herself quietly into death's warm embrace, then Travis had fought, tooth and nail, until the last bit of life left his body. Despite the fact that he had been the one to find the pair, Tosh could not help but to wince as Travis was carried by. "People should not die like this," he muttered, still very much angry at the world.

The monk nodded in agreement. "And yet, they have for ages, and will continue to do so. Some people have to face a destiny such as this, and even death has a dignity that it possesses all to itself." At that moment, the monk that had Travis's feet made a joke, and the other laughed in return as they went about their work. Tosh couldn't help but to smile at the pair. This was not the first time they had handled a dead body, and it wouldn't be the last, yet they took to their ordained task as if it was just a part of who they were.

The old man sensed a slight shift in Tosh's mood, and decided to steer the topic another direction. "I'm sure you don't need me preaching at you about the great mysteries of life and death. Why don't we focus on the ceremony for a bit?"

Tosh nodded his assent. "How does this ritual work, exactly?"

The monk nodded at the altar that the bodies had been carried to. "That altar is what English refer to as Charnel grounds. The body is taken there to be ritualistically prepared. It is flayed in such a way that the remains either decompose of their own accord, or that the birds devour them." The old man grinned wickedly at the horrified look on Tosh's face. "What, did you think that we would be able to dig a hole and toss them in? Better yet, were we to burn them? With what wood? Trust me, boy, if we had access to copious amounts of wood, we would endeavor to keep our Temple warm for those who come here to worship."

Tosh still looked appalled. "To treat the dead that way is so...so...*undignified,*" he said, still shaking his head. One of the ritualistic flayers peeled back a section of skin from Esther's heel, and Tosh could not help but wince. Meanwhile, the other grimaced and swore, concentrating heavily on removing charred, inedible sections of Travis's skin, to be crumbled up and tossed to the winds.

The old monk gave Tosh a measured glance. "Perhaps to your way of thinking it is. You come from a culture that worships one's appearance. It's a body worship fitting to the old heathen gods of the Greeks or the Romans. Ours is a faith that is concerned with the spirit, of the soul. The body is just a vessel; once death occurs, it ceases to serve a functioning purpose--that is, transport of the soul. A mere twenty centimeters below your feet is a layer of rocks and frost that not even heavy machinery can dig through. We can't leave bodies lying around, there's not a soul that wants the daily reminder of a loved one. This is how we dispose of them, and in our own simple way, give back to the earth that sustains us. It's practical as well as serene."

Tosh offered the old man a dubious glance, but he nodded, willing to at least see the sense of the matter. "How long does the process take?"

The old man grinned. "Several hours. Plenty of time for us to have a cup of tea. After all, I sense that something is troubling you, and it is part of my duties to see that such a thing is set right, if it can be. So why don't we go into my chambers and talk? The view is breathtaking, we can still oversee the ritual, and perhaps you can unburden some of what is gnawing at you, hmm?"

If someone had told Tosh that he would be in Bhutan watching two Americans return to the earth in a fashion befitting barbarians, he would have sworn them mad. Nevertheless, here he was sipping on a cup of Earl Grey, warmed considerably by a fireplace in one of the far-flung towers of the monastery. A view of what was happening could easily be ascertained from their vantage point, yet Tosh was engrossed in conversation with the old monk.

As the conversation wore on, and the birds made heavy inroads into what had been Esther and Travis, the old monk smiled. This young Tosh had as many burdens as Travis and Esther, it seemed, yet, unlike the star-crossed deceased, he was willing to unburden his load. The conversation flitted from topic to topic, and it was with no small shock that Tosh finally relented to the wave of emotions that had consumed him for ages. After a good cry, however, he was still confused.

"Why have you helped me so?" Tosh asked, unwilling to look at the monk.

"Because two suicides on our sacred land are two suicides too many. We don't need another. That's not the only reason, however, Tosh. It is my job to help, above all else, and you needed me. Despite all of their hell, Travis and Esther deserved to escape and find happiness. And so do you. Leave Tibet, go home, return to your Kristen, quit chasing stories for the benefit of others and write what makes your soul sing. We all can find happiness, if we look, Tosh." The old man grinned. "Including you."

Tosh chuckled. "I guess I owe it to myself to press on, huh?"

The old man nodded, and looked wearily out the window. "Yes, Tosh, you do. Besides...suicide is for the birds."

THE END

ACKNOWLEDGEMENTS

Writing a novel such as this, especially when most of the action takes place in a nation that I have, sadly, not yet visited, requires many leaps of faith. Although, as a research historian, I feel that my research is sound, but if I had to take some license with Bhutan, its policies, or in its perception as a nation, it was only in the pursuit of artistic endeavor. Bhutan is, by both its own decree, and the decree of others, truly the happiest nation on earth, and, as abstract as this may sound, I cannot thank the nation enough for playing host to my novel.

This novel was written in a dark period of my life, shortly after my separation from my first wife, to whom it is dedicated. Thankfully, our story, while sharing some similarities with Travis and Esther's tale, did not end in the same manner; as of this moment, I am finishing my final year at the University of Pennsylvania, and Nisa resides somewhere in Ohio, raising our wonderful children. We have our moments of strife, but, at the very least, I can thank her for inspiring this tale.

The editing process took place, or is taking place, during another period of trouble. Despite the lessons of Travis, I still have my own demons to wrestle with. Anyway, I have to thank Jade for all she has done for my career, and I can't wait to continue working together.

Special thanks to my co-authors on other projects: Nayeli, Maggie and Gus. Y'all give me the desire to drive forward. I also have to thank my children, Lydia, Nick, and Leah, as well as my best friend, Savannah.

Finally, special thanks to Melissa Jensen, my writing teacher at the University of Pennsylvania, who always demanded the best…and convinced me I was capable of it.